Single or Double?

Julia Horton-Powdrill

LLYFRAU CAMBRIA

Published in the United Kingdom in 2015 by
Cambria Books, Wales, United Kingdom

For Brian Powdrill
20 September 1935 – 13 April 2014
who said I would never complete this book!

About the Book

When twins Cass and Jo leave the bright lights of Paris and London to meet their Godmother's solicitor in a small sleepy Welsh seaside town, they don't expect their lives will change at all. Instead, they find themselves embroiled in the weird and wonderful carryings-on in Porthcwm, amidst its larger than life inhabitants. There's greedy and lascivious local estate agent Arthur Trinder, Gloria, the scantily clad, plastic surgery addicted cleaner and wicked, tourist scam inventor Bert Lloyd. Then there's the handsome, grouchy doctor, and excitable Rosa, with her miracle cowpat...

Was the arrival of the twins the catalyst for the drunken sandcastle competitions, and farm yard police raids? And is the older generation, both alive and dead, giving fate and romance a helping hand?

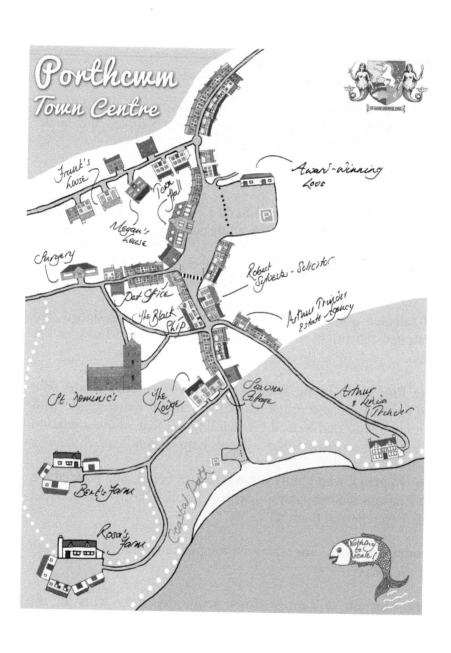

Preface

I have had amazing support from the following wonderful people who donated their time and skills to help me complete this book. I am enormously grateful to them all.

My thanks in order of appearance...

Two of my local writing pals **Sheila Leicester** and **Diana Powell** who helped and encouraged me all through the final processes.

Helen Carey, author, who advised us on Amazon, E books and publishing. Please do read her best-selling books.

My talented artist friend **Deborah Withey** who designed and illustrated the bright and brilliant cover. I love it. Look at her work .

Jean Plummer, Jayne Pollard and **Sioned Horton-Evans** who read the final manuscript. I thank them all for being gentle with their comments and Sioned for pointing out that I have a passion for exclamation marks!! See ... can't help myself.

Jean Kearney who kindly offered to proof read. She pointed out that I have a second passion - with hyphens. Oh-my-goodness!! I hope I've removed them all.

Rhodri Horton-Evans who took the publicity pics of me and my dog, Seaweed.

Amy Morgan at Carreg Construction for help with all the copying.

Trevor Collins and his team at Modern Print and Design, Pembroke Dock for providing me with wonderful publicity leaflets.

Pete Roberts - website designer at Globe Orange who created my fantastic Porthcwm website and *appeared* to remain patient with me the entire time.

Dai Powell who bravely took on the job of up-loading this whole thing onto Kindle.

Stephen Horton of SH!TV for his help with Photoshop work. Look at his show reels.

Lawrence Toms of Sheep Poo Paper (Creative Paper Wales) for some brilliant ideas.

And I should like to thank these two places…

St Brides Spa Hotel in Saundersfoot, a favourite place of mine, especially the table on the left overlooking the sea where I enjoyed writing and meeting very special people.

Jane's Teashop in Fishguard where I meet up with other writing friends to encourage each other, chatter about what we're writing, drink chocolate and gossip.

Finally, and above all, my love and thanks to my children, Lucinda, Charlotte, Rhodri and Sioned. The *next* book is for you…

CHAPTERS

Prologue

'This place needs a real shake up,' said Bea Seymour, nodding her head sadly. She was having a serious conversation with herself while she sat on the little wooden bench close to the bus stop across the street from the Post Office. A typical morning in the life of Porthcwm was unfolding before her.

'Just look at how dull this town has become. It's lost all its excitement,' she continued, directing her comment this time to her small dachshund that was leaning against her leg.

'Talking to yourself, Bea?' said a voice behind her. 'You know what that's a sign of.'

Bea turned around to see her friend Megan standing there, laughing at her.

'Actually I was just chatting to Nosey. He's such a good listener! Come and park yourself here next to me, Megan,' she said patting the seat next to her. 'I've been sitting here thinking how uninteresting it's become in Porthcwm. There was a time when things went on here. Not always good things of course, but there was often something to fight for, or against, don't you agree?'

'You're being ridiculous Bea, it's only quiet and dull because you're getting old and not able to stir things up like you used to. We're *both* getting old, come to think of it and we're moaning about boredom simply because we're not getting a slice of the action.'

'Where on earth did you pick up that saying?' asked Bea.

'Some film on the television,' said Megan. 'You see - that's it. I am reduced to watching programmes full of gibberish.'

'I miss everything that went on when the twins used to come and stay all that time ago. I only get postcards now, but they're always full of the adventures that still seem to happen to them. They're in Europe at the moment, *bumming around* as they so delicately put it in one of their cards. It's lovely to hear from them.'

'*They* used to keep the town on its toes. A breath of fresh air for this quiet place, and for me too. What scrapes those two used to get into and they always seemed to be right at the centre of all sorts of predicaments, mostly caused by themselves of course.' Bea broke into a mischievous smile. 'Those two had a strange knack for masterminding all sorts of activities which got them into trouble. They'd annoy people, and then manage to charm themselves out of a sticky situation. Well, it *nearly* always seemed to work, except with poor Simon of course, who was so shy and definitely no match for Cass and Jo. He never seemed able to stand up for himself, unfortunately.'

'No romance around these days either, Bea,' complained Megan. 'No dashing knights on white horses or damsels in distress.'

'You're right, unless you count watching odious Arthur Trinder hanging about outside his shop ogling every woman that walks past, or there,' Bea said, pointing across the street. 'At the back of the mysteriously long queue into the Post Office is Bert Lloyd. He looks suspicious even just standing there. That's what I mean; sadly this is Porthcwm at its *most* electrifying.'

'Why don't you do something about it Bea? Years ago if Porthcwm went through a quiet patch you always used to invent something, stick your nose in, make things happen.'

'Odd you should say that, Megan. Why don't you walk down to the cottage with me and have some coffee? I've had an idea or two that I should like to share with you.'

Chapter 1

'It'll be a bloody miracle if that lasts the whole journey,' exclaimed Cass when she saw her twins rust-bucket car in the car park at Bristol Airport. 'Even people in the last millennium thought it was past its best. Is it safe?'

'Sadly it's all we've got, so just keep your fingers crossed,' Jo replied.

'Maybe AB has left us some money to buy a car,' suggested Cass, 'or perhaps she's left us that ancient Box Morris of hers that we used to adore being driven around in, d'you remember? We called it Mildred and it had those useless little pointy indicator things between the windows so when she wanted to turn left one of us would have to wind the window down in a hurry and lean out to try and get it to work.'

'Don't be daft. It'll have fallen apart ages ago,' Jo responded. 'But you're right, almost anything would be better than this.'

'It certainly wouldn't have been worth anyone bothering to nick it while we were abroad so I suppose I'm not really surprised that you've still got it,' said Cass.

'I'll thank you not to complain about this heap of junk,' laughed Jo. 'Just think how much going by train would have cost us. Anyway, at least we're already half way to West Wales. It was a great idea of yours to meet up here rather than London.'

'I've already sorted somewhere to stay in Porthcwm for two nights. Just a little B&B near the top of the town, nothing special, but it'll save us having to spend loads on a hotel. My God Cass, you've got a lot of stuff for just a few days,' she added as she eyed up her twins luggage and bags.

Cass ignored Jo's observation and loaded her belongings into the car boot. She turned around and gave her twin a big hug, 'I feel really guilty that we hadn't been to see AB for ages ... years really. We've been hopeless about keeping in touch with her,' she said ruefully. 'Sending postcards just isn't the same. I wish we'd been able to get to her funeral to say goodbye. That letter from her solicitor must have been chasing us all around Europe for ages.'

'I was so pleased that you could come over from Paris, Cass ... I couldn't have done the solicitor thing on my own,' admitted Jo. She opened the passenger door and picked up some see-through triangular cartons of unappetizing-looking white bread sandwiches from the foot well and passed one to Cass. 'Before we leave let's have something to eat. It'll save us having to stop for a while,' she added. She held the door open for her twin, 'hop in,' she said. 'There's an old thermos of mine behind your seat, the coffee may be cold now but it'll be better than nothing.' They climbed into her car and began to eat an early lunch.

'Okay Cass, so how's Paris then? Tell me all about everything,' started Jo, peering inside her anaemic sandwich to try and fathom out exactly what it contained.

'Did you get to do all the things you'd planned? The Eiffel Tower? Notre Dame? Romantic walks along the Seine with someone I know you're not going to tell me about?'

'Well if you hadn't announced you were heading back to London to take that temporary job in a gallery that some old boyfriend of yours had begged you to help out with – probably because he couldn't find anyone else daft enough to do it - then you would have been there with me to find out.'

'Yes, yes, word of warning, Cass - don't trust old boyfriends. I must say I was jolly pissed off with being made redundant so soon after I started.'

'No wonder,' laughed Cass. 'But I do wish we could have done Paris together. It would have been a great way to end our travels.' And I wouldn't have had the opportunity to meet and fall for Ricco if you'd been there with me, she thought to herself.

That was the second time that Ricco had entered her thoughts in the last five minutes. And she really was trying very hard not to think about him. But when Jo had mentioned Notre Dame just now it had brought it all back again.

She had met him a couple of months earlier. She and Jo had been travelling abroad for over a year, having fun and picking up jobs as they went along. They were able to turn their hands to most things, and had between them done everything from grape picking to waitressing, chamber maiding to gardening, and bar work to dog walking.

Their final stop before returning to England and settling down to the necessary task of finding work, was going to be Paris, but right at the last minute Jo had been offered that temporary job which she felt she should accept. It turned out to be *very* temporary as it happened. Cass had initially intended to 'do' Paris quickly on her own and follow Jo home after a few days, but things somehow changed....

Cass looked out of the car window at a plane landing beyond the airport buildings. Only a few hours earlier she had been in Ricco's tiny apartment leaving an envelope behind the flowers that he had just given her to celebrate their two month anniversary. The envelope contained a cowardly little note from her explaining, in the briefest possible manner, why she was disappearing out of his life. She knew he would return to their apartment that evening with arms full of ingredients for the dinner he was planning and until then he would be blissfully unaware that she had left France and left him. God, why am I so nervous of commitment, she asked herself.

Jo's text message a few days earlier had presented the incentive she needed to make a decision she had been mulling over for a while. When Jo dropped the bombshell about AB's death it was the perfect excuse to ease her conscience in walking out on Ricco. Now he was out of her life, and although Cass really did like him, in truth she liked him a lot, she felt their relationship had become too complicated for her. She hadn't wanted to hurt him but thought that if she just 'vanished' he would get over her more quickly than if she did the grown-up-sensible thing and confront her problem *with* him, discuss it, try and find her way through it. But then she would still have left him. She knew she would.

'Cass, Cass...'

'Uh? Oh sorry Jo, I was miles away for a moment.'

'Paris, I suppose? Want to talk about anything?'

5

'Long story…' Cass tried to answer casually. 'I'll explain later.' But she knew she wouldn't of course.

Jo knew it too, 'I'm guessing there must be a man in there somewhere?'

Cass nodded, 'Mmm, but it's over. That's all there is to it.'

'You're such an infuriating person Cass; you're so cagey about everything remotely to do with romance. I just want you to be happy,' said Jo. 'Well, I want both of us to be happy actually. But now that we're both boyfriendless and jobless I suppose we'll soon start turning into a couple of old maids.'

Cass looked at her sister and smiled. In almost every way they seemed to behave and think similarly. As far as looks were concerned they were the perfect example of identical twins, a detail that they had put to extremely good use during their thirty two years of attempting to grow up. Even as individuals they would each stand out in a crowd, but together they knew that the stereo image effect of their height, long untamed hair, the colour of Oxford Marmalade and striking, if somewhat freckly, faces created a lot of attention. The fact that they were so recognisable and memorable had not always worked to their advantage of course. It got them into trouble, but out of trouble too as people would always muddle them up.

The only way they really seemed to be dissimilar was in their attitude to boyfriends. Because of Cass's commitment phobia her relationships never lasted very long although she knew she'd possibly missed out on some great boyfriends along the way. On the other hand Jo was definitely partner material but couldn't seem to find the right man however hard she looked. What a pair we are Cass thought.

'Okay then?' asked Jo. 'Let's get going.' She started up the engine and they set off on their tortuous drive to West Wales.

Cass was desperate to avoid Jo giving her the third degree as they were driving along. 'Look Jo, I'm knackered after the early start, so d'you mind if I have snooze?' she asked, stuffing her coat behind her head and closing her eyes before Jo could answer.

But it was difficult to relax. Her head was swimming with thoughts.

She worried in turn about where she was going to live and what she was going to do with her life after their visit to Porthcwm. She worried about how she could avoid any discussion concerning Paris and Ricco - Jo was bound to try and interrogate her again. More annoyingly, she worried about Ricco. Despite attempts to control her thoughts he kept creeping into her head. How would he feel when he came back to the empty apartment in the evening? What would he do when he eventually discovered the pathetic short note she'd left? Had she done the right thing after all?

In the end she tried to dismiss all thoughts of Ricco and Paris by endeavouring to fill her mind with the memories of their holidays spent in West Wales with AB.

Aunt Bea or AB, the twin's special name for her, was their Godmother. When Jo and Cass were eight years old, Frances, their mother, had been given the shocking news that she was terminally ill and their Aunt Bea was the first person that she had thought of to look after them in the school holidays during her illness. Their father Geoff had always been a high flying businessman, but being a devoted dad had never been one of his talents. When Frances eventually lost her fight for life he accepted a job offer in Australia, of all places, without giving any thought as to how he would manage with the girls from that distance. But AB was very happy to continue the arrangement of Cass and Jo coming to stay with her for the school holidays and her cosy Porthcwm cottage began to feel like home to them.

Even before the first anniversary of Frances' death Geoff had married one of his young business colleagues and astonishingly started a new family. Quite rapidly, he lost touch with the twins despite their efforts to engage his attention, something singularly difficult to do from the other side of the world. At first Cass and Jo were sad about their father ignoring them but after all, they did have each other plus their slightly eccentric Aunt Bea in Porthcwm.

After an hour or so Jo's voice broke into her thoughts, 'hey Cass, did you sleep at all? You seemed pretty restless.'

'I'm fine thanks, just catnapped I think. I was getting nostalgic about staying with AB during the hols all those years ago. I'm sure when we get to Porthcwm we'll recognise places and all sorts of weird memories will come flooding back.'

Jo shrugged, 'I'm not so sure. I thought things were bound to have changed there so I looked up Porthcwm on Google and it showed lots of pictures of the town. It all looks very smart and done up now, and it's a really popular holiday destination apparently. I don't suppose we'll recognise any of it now, or anyone that we used to know for that matter, it's all so long ago. The beaches won't have changed though, so if we get some good weather when we're there, at least we can go and have a paddle.'

Chapter 2

A hundred odd miles further along the road Porthcwm was all in a bustle. Tuesday had turned out to be one of those glorious spring days and the whole place had been buzzing with activity.

Immaculately dressed Arthur Trinder, the only estate agent in town, was standing outside his shop being pleasant and greeting everyone that passed by just in case they ever wanted to sell their houses. He needed to look just right for his public so he was dressed, as usual, in his navy blazer, light coloured trousers and shiny brown shoes. He needed everyone to like him so that they would use *his* highly personalised local knowledge to shift their property. He could pick up a lot of information standing outside like this, chatting to locals and holidaymakers as they walked past him. Mrs Trinder called it networking. Currently he was drooling and fantasising over all the money that he would earn from selling Bea Seymour's Seaview Cottage. He knew it would go like a shot.

Arthur stepped back off the kerb to survey his window display, shook his head then popped back inside the shop. He returned with a large yellow duster to wipe over his window so that every passer-by would be impressed by its interior. The spring weather had been perfect for seaside holiday makers, warm and dry, but it meant everything had a light film of powdery sand over it. He reached up high and carefully removed the Porthcwm dust from the area of window where his business slogan displayed the words '*Arthur Trinder - The Estate Agent You Can Rely On*'. He stood back again in the road to look at the outcome of his cleaning efforts. He studied his slogan too. It was fairly new and he felt that there was still scope for improvement in the wording. Arthur had thought long and hard about the words '*Rely On*' and toyed with the idea of replacing them with '*Trust*', but even he thought that might be going a little too far.

Showily, he passed the duster over the glass so that onlookers would see he was not uncomfortable doing menial tasks. He could have asked his receptionist, Rhonwen, to do it but he liked to be seen doing it himself. There, he thought, now all my properties can be seen clearly.

Rhonwen had worked for him for about five years. He first took her on when she was a slim, attractive 20-year-old. He taught her everything she knew about the Estate Agency business, and about being a receptionist of the highest excellence. He had plans of teaching her *other* things too, and even now he gave a little shudder of excitement just thinking about how he had managed to hire the most striking administrator south of the Preseli Hills. But somehow she had turned into a fat lump of a thing. It seemed to Arthur that it had occurred almost overnight, as if she had gone home after work one afternoon and reappeared the next morning looking like a huge pudding. Of course it hadn't actually happened that way, but because he had taken his eye off the ball (Rhonwen) so to speak, and had another target (Janey) in his sights for a while, it did seem to have happened when he wasn't looking.

It was his fault really. He'd thought that he would work on Rhonwen gradually, let her settle into her job and find her way about the business - after all that was why he had engaged her. Well, mostly anyway. The rest of his seduction plan was supposed to fall into place smoothly after he'd gained her confidence. In the meantime, and during this period of self-enforced restraint, he had discovered Janey working part time behind the bar at the Black Ship.

The random hours of Janey's job had proved to be very rewarding and fulfilling for Arthur who would fit her in during house valuation appointments. When she moved on to a better, full time job at one of the hotels a little further up the coast, he had visions of vacant-bedroom-fun but the relationship all rather fizzled out when the hotel owner discovered her prodigious talents on the customer side of the bar and decided to ensure *he* should benefit from them as well.

So when Arthur's body tingling memory of Janey had all faded away and he decided it was time to groom his gorgeous Rhonwen, he couldn't comprehend how she had found the time to morph into a pumpkin. Pumpkins didn't turn him on. Arthur liked slim women in figure-hugging clothes. Pumpkins in figure hugging clothes didn't do it for him at all. However, her office skills were second to none and she was courteous, pleasant and efficient, but if push came to shove with a difficult customer she could become quite tough, and could deal with almost anything. She was a near perfect receptionist.

He continued to live in the hope that she would slim down again and he could carry on with his lustful plan. After all, she was talking a lot at the moment about losing weight and trying to decide which diet to embark on. However, yesterday while he watched her stuff a huge cream cake down her throat at the rate of knots he realised that she was obviously either still undecided or was reconsidering the whole slimming idea. Consequently Arthur felt free to set his sights in yet another direction until Rhonwen made her mind up.

Hearing voices, he glanced up to see two women scurrying towards him.

'Good afternoon, ladies,' he offered jovially as they approached him. An odd couple to be so closely engrossed, he thought, and wondered what they could be talking about. The small skinny, weasely looking one, Blodwyn Harris, was the Postmistress. What was she doing away from her post, he wondered. He laughed inwardly at his unintentional pun. But it was her companion, Gloria Prothero, who he was really interested in. He knew she was oblivious to the fact that she was about to become the latest object of his attention. He didn't see the point in hanging about for ages, especially since Rhonwen wasn't going to become trim and desirable for quite a while whichever slimming programme she decided to follow. Maybe she would just remain large. So he had convinced himself there was no point in wasting valuable time.

Gloria was considered rather a *goer* locally and his heart missed a little beat. He'd always rather fancied her. He had fantasised about her ever since her bosoms had brushed up against his back in the Post Office when he was queuing to send off a parcel.

He had often wondered about that incident. Surely you knew how much space you had when you carried bosoms around with you permanently. Rather like driving a car, you knew what gap you could get through because you were familiar with its width. Maybe she had wanted to encourage him and had done it deliberately. A shiver of excitement ran through his whole body, including those areas that were seeing very little action these days. His thoughts lingered on that moment rather too long. He looked at the two ladies continuing down the street and was about to call after them again when he heard Douglas Sidebotham's booming voice behind him.

'Arthur, my friend, what are you doing loitering on the steps of your workplace? Eyeing up the local totty going past, I'll warrant. I saw you watching the two lovely ladies just now. You'll have to be careful or your Mrs Trinder will catch you at it. Let me guess which one you were thinking about?'

'Don't be ridiculous, Douglas,' Arthur said, colouring right down below his crisp white shirt collar. 'So what are you up to, apart from spying on me?'

'Actually, can't stop. . .' Douglas replied as he rushed off in pursuit of the ladies. Lucky devil being widowed, thought Arthur enviously as he watched boring tweed jacketed Douglas Sidebotham follow Blodwyn and Gloria down the street. How could any woman in her right mind be interested this dull retired salesman from London?

Then Arthur thought of his wife, Linda, and told himself how fortunate he should consider himself really, though he was not entirely sure why.

Arthur and Linda Trinder (how he hated hearing those rhyming names together – why couldn't she have used Susan, her middle name after they were married, he wondered) hadn't lived in Porthcwm all their lives. They had moved there about 25 years earlier. Mrs Trinder had been an enthusiastic teacher in a small Herefordshire village school, but when she realised that several rural schools were under consideration for closure by the County Council Arthur had suggested that Linda applied for a teaching job in distant Porthcwm.

They had originally visited the area on holiday so knew what the small town was like. Arthur, already an ambitious junior estate agent, realized that it was an opportunity for Linda (but more particularly for himself). Linda was not hugely keen on leaving the comparative sophistication of a tiny English village for an end-of-the-track-town in farthest West Wales, but Arthur persuaded her, and after all, in those days this was one of the cheapest places to buy property. No-one wanted to live there, not even the locals who were more intent on chasing up to the bright lights of London, or more strangely, Carmarthen, a mere hour along the road.

Initially they had found it tough going with Arthur's business, but they managed to survive on Linda's income. Slowly things improved and they now had a very enviable lifestyle. They had gradually moved upwards on their own property ladder until reaching their dream house where they would be able to live happily ever after. It perched high on the cliffs, just outside Porthcwm, set back enough not to be scary, but close enough so as to give the feeling, when standing in the sitting room, that they were on board a cruise ship.

They had been on a cruise once. Linda had always wanted to have that sort of holiday and Arthur had eventually given in to her. Only the once of course, as he hated being away from his business in case he missed out on any property opportunities. He felt smugly contented now that every time she looked out of the window she would feel as if she was on a cruise. A *permanent* holiday, in fact. He was convinced that Linda would be grateful for evermore, even if she didn't show him in any special or personal way.

Surprisingly, Linda seemed to blossom in this quiet town, and she was fortunate to take over as Headmistress of the Primary School when ancient Miss Myfanwy Vaughan-Davies popped her clogs at the blackboard in the middle of a nature study lesson, the white chalk that she still insisted on using clasped tightly in her bony old fingers.

Chalk and blackboards were no longer part of daily school life after Miss Vaughan-Davies' passing, and 'progress' in Porthcwm continued on all fronts. The town improved and prospered, and house prices began to rise. Linda became more of an asset to Arthur and increasingly more useful. Although somewhat frumpy and mousy, both to the eye and to the ear, she was a popular, friendly woman and was trusted in the community. She belonged to all manner of local groups, consequently seeming to know everybody one way or another. That was good for Arthur's estate agency business, of course. He encouraged her to socialise with her friends in the WI, the Historical Society and the ladies choir and to extol the advantages of living in Porthcwm area to the parents of prospective pupils.

He picked up lots of clients that way. And when their families grew too large for their current home and needed to take a step up the property ladder he was there again with his invaluable advice and smooth attention.

His thoughts were interrupted suddenly. 'Oh yes! Good morning Mrs Hughes, yes, it is a lovely day. Yes, busy, busy, *busy* as usual, just having a breath of fresh coastal air.' He smiled at her and wished privately to himself two things; that he *was* busy and that Megan Hughes would sell her house. She was too old to be rattling around alone in that charming property and should be in an old people's home somewhere. Still, the time will come. Hopefully fairly soon, he thought greedily.

Arthur, who was ready to take money from anyone, was finding things a little tough at the moment. People seemed to be hanging on to their houses and not moving, so there were very few of quality on the market. That's why he was looking forward to selling Miss Seymour's property.

In fact Seaview Cottage was becoming an obsession of his. He had already designed a little brochure on his computer. He knew he wouldn't have to do much. It would be money for old rope. The only problem for Arthur was that no-one had even approached him about selling the property yet. He shuddered grumpily. Maybe he was counting his chickens...

He was getting seriously concerned that whoever was dealing with Miss Seymour's estate might intend using one of those superior sounding agencies, with their posh triple barrelled names and expensive glossy brochures. No, surely that wouldn't happen with Seaview Cottage, surely they, whoever *they* were, would come to him? With all his local knowledge and contacts he was bound to get it.

Linda hadn't picked anything up on the grapevine either. Was that good or bad? And the fount of all knowledge, Blodwyn the Postmistress, knew nothing either. Arthur would complain about

14

her on a daily basis. He hated the sneaky manner in which she uncovered interesting gossip from her customers whilst she was finding stamps or dealing with parcels and pensions, but he couldn't help marvelling at her skill. She successfully extracted the most secret facts from those who wouldn't normally have responded to the thumbscrew. Blodwyn really had a gift. In the past he'd found her discoveries most useful and could usually rely on her to let him have information on most of the goings on in Porthcwm.

He promised himself to ask her again if there was any news about Miss Seymour's cottage. He just *had* to know what was going on. He couldn't get his mind off it.

He turned swiftly on his shiny polished brogues and went back inside, just as Jo and Cass drove past his shop.

Chapter 3

'Phew! Finally made it…' said Jo, as she slowed down outside a stone building with a flight of steps up to the entrance. 'Good old solicitor, his directions were perfect. I'm just going to go on down the street and turn the car around. We can park it back up there in that car park we passed.' Tired as they were they had decided to go straight to the solicitor's office instead of looking for their B&B.

The receptionist led them through to a room which appeared unassuming and rather Dickensian. It smelled of books and files and faintly musty paper and Mr Robert Sylvester, who looked as old as the hills, was waiting to greet them.

'Welcome my dears, welcome, please come in. Now do sit down here next to my desk. I shall quickly run through the details of your Aunt's bequest to you. I know you will be tired from the journey down.' He pulled out a chair for each of them.

They both watched him as he moved around to his side of the desk. He was slightly stooped at the shoulders but was still a tall man; his pinstripe suit which hung on his thin body had seen better days a long time ago. He had wispy grey hair still with a fleck of ginger remaining around his temples and a handsome lived-in face that was charming and instantly likeable. He had an agreeable demeanour and conveyed an air of old-fashioned honour and trust that made them feel immediately at ease with him.

'Thank you both for coming as soon as you could,' he continued. 'It was difficult to locate you and I am sorry that we couldn't manage to contact you any earlier. It is such a shame that you were unable to be here for Miss Seymour's funeral. She did mention to me that you would be hard to track down when we had one of our last little chats about her will, but you'll be glad to know that she had a wonderful send off and all her friends were present to celebrate her life. And it was, of course, a *very* full life.'

'It is ages since we spent time with Aunt Bea,' said Cass, 'but we did used to have the most marvellous adventures when we were here with her. We've been unforgivably hopeless at keeping in touch the last few years.'

'Yes' Mr Sylvester said. 'We all remember you both very clearly; everybody knew when you were down here staying with your aunt.'

Jo caught Cass's eye.

Mr Sylvester moved the papers around on his desk and cleared his throat. 'Miss Seymour's will is very straightforward really. But prior to carrying out her wishes I shall endeavour to fill you in on a little of your aunt's situation prior to her passing. Firstly there was a small bequest to Rosa to help her a little on the farm.'

'Rosa?' they both asked.

'Ah! Yes...Rosa Bellini. She and her husband Benito have a small farm further down the lane from your Aunt's cottage. For the last few years she cleaned for your aunt and undertook all sorts of chores for her. Rosa helped her sort out all her personal things there and what she was paid went towards running the farm. She is an incredibly hard worker and turns her hand to anything. She makes ice cream in a very small way and sells it locally. I am embarrassed to admit that my favourite is her delicious Gorse Flower flavour. She picks it from the bushes that grow all the way down the track past your Godmother's cottage.' Mr Sylvester's eyes misted a little and he seemed to be transported to another place briefly.

He suddenly shook himself back into the present moment, 'I shouldn't say this of course, but as I am acting for your Aunt's estate I think it's permissible for me to mention that Rosa is a somewhat highly strung Italian woman, not unhinged you understand, just very passionate and over-enthusiastic. She is as honest as the day is long and your aunt was very fond of her. I think Miss Seymour liked people with spirit and passion.' He winked at the twins rather knowingly and took them totally by surprise by slipping out of his solicitorial manner. But it was momentary and he quickly resumed his previous slow and measured way.

'Ahem, yes... so she remembered Rosa in her will. She was particularly caring in Miss Seymour's last few months although your aunt did hate being fussed over. Nothing was too much trouble for

Rosa to help out with and she even promised your aunt that she would have her cats when she passed away. She tells me that they love it on her farm apart from being chased occasionally by her neighbours dreadful dog. Her neighbour is called Bert Lloyd and he is notorious around here for one thing and another. I don't think there are many people in Porthcwm who have not had problems with him in some way. I'm sure my dears that *your* time will come.'

'Well, it may not of course, unless the Lloyds move very fast,' laughed Jo.

'Oh?' he said.

'We'll be going home fairly quickly when we have found out what you need to tell us…I'm sorry that sounded all wrong…Cass has to get back to France and I have to get back to…'

'But I told you, I'm *not* going back.' Cass shot Jo a look.

'My dear ladies, I don't think you realise that your aunt's bequest could change your lives. She has left you her property.'

Jo and Cass were speechless.

'I can tell you are both surprised,' Mr Sylvester said, breaking their silence.

'Utterly,' said Jo. 'We thought we might each be getting a piece of her furniture perhaps, or a personal memento. In fact we were wondering whether we would get anything else into the car as Cass has so much clobber with her.'

'So isn't there anyone else to inherit anything?' asked Cass.

'Well…no. But she said when you moved down here you would sort …'

'What? I don't understand… move down here?' interrupted Cass.

'Yes my dear.'

'Well of course it's all a bit sudden and naturally a wonderful surprise,' said Cass, 'but my immediate thought is that selling the cottage would help us both out, to be honest, right at this moment. We both have plans, so we could do with the money to fund us.'

'Actually I agree,' said Jo. 'It couldn't have come at a better time for us to be completely honest, Mr Sylvester. Pity really, as we've always loved visiting Porthcwm. I realise we haven't had any time to discuss it, but personally *I* couldn't imagine living here. I know it's a beautiful place but we couldn't actually *be* here permanently.'

'I rather thought you might keep that property and use it as a holiday let to earn some extra money for you both.'

'That's the problem Mr Sylvester; we don't have *any* money to begin with. So we would have no option but to sell it.'

Mr Sylvester looked at the twins and then at his pile of paperwork.

'Do I assume then that you will be selling the house as well?' he asked.

'Yes,' said Cass. 'As we just said, we'll be selling it.'

'My dears, I think that we are talking at cross purposes here. Perhaps I should have started at the beginning?'

'You've certainly lost me,' said Jo, and looked at her sister who nodded in agreement.

'I understand that you used to come and stay in Seaview Cottage with your Aunt during the school holidays when you were younger, because your father lived so far away?'

They both nodded.

'And it was always the cottage you stayed in when you were here?'

They both nodded.

'Am I to understand then, that you knew nothing about your Aunt's house next door?' They both stared at him.

'What house?' they said together.

'I did think that it would be most unlikely that you were aware of the Lodge. Certainly I know of no one here that has any knowledge of Miss Seymour owning it either. Your aunt was very secretive about some things, even with those closest to her...' Mr

Sylvester seemed to drift off into a brief private dream again. '…Well, if you picture Seaview Cottage up that little drive you may remember that it was attached to a much larger house on the left, rather Georgian looking but a bit decrepit. They were separated by a wall and hedge, and it has its own drive, so to all intents and purposes they are totally independent of each other.

'Your Aunt used to let the house out and live in the little cottage. She didn't need any more space than that as it was only her and the dog and the two cats. She still had one spare bedroom, of course, which you used when you came to stay. The Lodge gave her an income. The people who rented it for the last 25 years have both gone into a home now - so sensible of them and good timing for you under the circumstances. Miss Seymour hadn't re-let it because it needed some attention and improvements before she could instruct me to advertise for new tenants. And then she suddenly died.' He looked sad.

'Are you saying, Mr Sylvester, that we have inherited a house as well?'

'Indeed ladies, you have inherited a house and a cottage *and* a small amount of money. Both properties have nice, but slightly overgrown gardens, some useful sheds and also a garage each…which rather reminds me, the garage at Seaview Cottage contains your godmother's beloved car, which of course is left to you as well.'

Jo laughed and said, 'I hope it's not Mildred, that old Box Morris she used to speed us round in?'

'Yes my dear, it most certainly is,' replied Mr Sylvester and smiled at them. 'Miss Seymour said you would enjoy being in that again, though driving it yourselves now of course.'

Jo and Cass looked at each other 'But surely…'

'I know what you are going to say and yes, it still works very well. It has been looked after carefully all these years and Benito, Rosa's husband takes it out for a run every so often. It has a current MOT and tax in readiness for you using it. Your aunt assumed each of you would have been keen to pass your driving test at the first opportunity, so would both be able to make use of it'

'We'd have to get insurance,' said Jo.

'Oh that will not be necessary. It has been insured in both your names for about 10 months already, using the address at the cottage. Miss Seymour saw to it herself. She said that if you were as spirited now as you were all those years ago you would be bound to want to cause a stir by driving around in it.'

'This is like a bizarre dream...' Cass muttered to Jo.

'Now, back to the Lodge. Your aunt never lived in it, but it *is* a splendid place.'

'How did she come to have the house as well, and why didn't she ever tell us?'

'When her parents passed away they left her their house at the top of the town. It was a nice enough place but Miss Seymour sold it to buy the Lodge next door to her little cottage. It came available at just the right time and she felt as they were attached it made sense. She never told anyone because she said it made her look too well off, and she never lived in it as she felt she and the cottage suited each other perfectly. It was kept as a sort of pension for her should she have needed it, and to do some good with, which is why she has left it to you two.'

'But why us? Surely there were relatives as well?' asked Cass.

'Ah!' Mr Sylvester's eyes dropped. 'Well, she had a big sadness in her life but she told me that when you two came to live here you would sort all kinds of things out.'

'What kind of things, Mr Sylvester?'

'Yes, well, I think that's about it for the moment, my dears,' Mr Sylvester said abruptly, ignoring Cass's query, 'as I can see you now have much more to consider. I think this might be a good time to conclude this meeting so that you can go away and chat about what you want to do.'

'Here are the keys for both properties,' he said. 'Do go along and have a peep. Then after that if you still intend to sell everything you could make an appointment with Mr Trinder, if he is your preferred estate agent. His shop is in the main street a little further down from the Post Office and on the other side.'

'Yes I'm sure we'd be quite happy for Mr Trinder to deal with it if that's who you'd recommend,' said Jo looking at Cass. 'We may as well get it all sorted as soon as possible.'

Just as they were leaving the office Cass turned suddenly and said to Mr Sylvester, 'you said there was a dog?'

'Oh dear, I should have mentioned him to you properly. Your aunt realised that she was beginning to see you less and less, as you got older and began to travel and work in different places so she decided she needed some permanent company and she got Nosey. He's pretty elderly himself now of course but very energetic still. As your Aunt was expecting you to move down here as you had, in her words, 'things to sort out,' he gave them another strange look, 'she was assuming that you would take the dog back to the cottage with you. He's a dear little chap. He's in kennels at the moment and apparently hating every second of it.'

'It's a pity, but it simply won't work, not in any way. Isn't there someone else who could take him on and give him a home? We have no idea where we'll be yet and it would be hopeless in London. Perhaps you could ask around for us Mr Sylvester? We'll cover all the kennel bills and any other costs of course.'

Jo and Cass walked a short distance down the hill away from the solicitor's office in silence.

'It's not often we're stuck for words,' Jo suddenly said.' But bloody hell, I don't know where to start. This could set us up, Cass, you know, business wise. We could do all sorts of things with whatever we get from these properties. We could buy a flat in London to share, or one each, unless you want to go back abroad again and find another handsome man.'

'Jo, you're impossible, just because you're craving a steady boring relationship doesn't mean I have to search for a guy to stick to for eternity as well.'

'No I didn't mean that, but your men don't last long.'

Cass shrugged, 'Okay, I admit it. I can't bear the idea of commitment, it frightens me. Let's just agree to disagree about men shall we and if that's about the only thing we beg to differ on, then thank goodness. It would after all, be terminally boring to be completely the same.'

'Shall we look at the Lodge first and save Seaview 'til last?' asked Jo, looking at the bunch of keys Mr Sylvester had given them and selecting a large old brass key with a crumpled brown luggage label tied to it saying concisely 'Lodge' in faded handwriting.

They walked down the street and turned right into the lane, passing the first gate with its sign saying Seaview Cottage, and turned through the gates of the Lodge. They stood on the gravel drive and looked at the house.

'It's lovely, but I just have no memory of it at all,' said Cass, looking around her. 'This garden is so private. It'll be fantastic when someone buys the place and cuts the grass and tidies it all up.'

Jo unlocked the door and they went into a large entrance hall. 'It's amazing, so big and old,' she said. 'No wonder AB didn't live here, she'd have rattled around.'

They wandered slowly through the house. It had some lovely old furniture in it, but the carpets were frayed and worn and the curtains were faded from the sun. It had an air of sadness about it, beauty too, but mostly sadness.

Beyond the entrance hall was a corridor, its floor covered in old dark red linoleum, blackened and curled at the edges like thin burnt toast. There was a door at the end which opened into a huge, old fashioned kitchen. The ceilings were high and the floors laid with flagstones burnished by constant use. The scullery and larder each had a door leading off from the back of the kitchen and the windows looked out onto a shady cobbled yard where small stone storage sheds were built up against a wall. This was obviously the cooler side of the house.

Leading up from the main hall was an imposing staircase, sweeping around generously at the top onto a wide corridor. The twins walked along it opening every door and exploring each room in turn. A door at the far end opened onto a small landing where a simple narrow staircase led up to the top floor and down to the kitchen areas. They went up the stairs and found the small, simple rooms which had obviously been for maids and staff in the years

24

when the kitchen would have been running at full throttle for a resident family. The whole house would have been humming along, gleaming and busy.

Back downstairs, the old living rooms were glorious, large and airy, all with their original cornices, plaster work and fireplaces.

'It's stunning,' said Jo, 'we should get a really good price for it. Though, not as good as if it was brought up to date. It might need lots of expensive work done so we mustn't get too carried away. I'm sure this Arthur Trinder will get us the best possible price. Shall we go and rediscover the cottage now.'

'I remember the first time we came here,' said Jo, stopping outside the doorway into Seaview Cottage, 'it was with Mummy, when she found out she was ill. I can still see her now, standing just here and hugging AB, both of them crying, and then she asked us to go and play in the garden while they discussed something.'

'It looks so small now,' said Cass. 'Didn't it seem enormous when we were children?'

The cottage did appear to have shrunk, but was otherwise mostly unaltered as far as they could remember. They went straight upstairs and looked at its two bedrooms. Their aunt's room looked just the same. There were lots of books along one wall. She had loved books. A neat mahogany dressing table with one large central mirror and one more on either side stood near the window. It had a heavy glass top on it to protect the wood and on that sat an old hairbrush with a monogrammed silver back and a matching hand mirror. There were three cut glass pots with silver lids too and a couple of old bottles of perfume. A pretty carved box lay with its lid bursting open and twirls of old ribbon poking out over the top. A faded handwritten poem and a few old photos with dog-eared corners were stuck around the side of the central mirror.

'Look,' said Jo, 'that's a beautiful one of AB in that group picture. How old do you think she is there, early twenties maybe? Maybe younger? She looks so full of life and wickedly attractive don't you think? And I think that's Mr Sylvester standing in the back row with those other people. He was a handsome man wasn't he? And here - look - one of us is in this picture, is it me? I can't tell, and that awful boy who AB seemed to dredge up all the time for us to play with.'

'Yes, definitely you in that picture,' said Cass. 'I remember you particularly disliked him and made his life misery. He lived somewhere here in Porthcwm though didn't he? I don't remember him being on holiday like us.'

'Yes, I think he was the doctor's grandson. Why couldn't AB have found us some nice girls to play with instead?'

'Simple Simon!' said Cass suddenly. 'I remembered his name. I think she must have felt sorry for him because he didn't have any brothers or sisters.'

'Well done you. I never thought about that. Yes, poor thing, we were awful to him weren't we?' said Jo 'particularly me. It took him a long time to realize that there were two of us. But it was such fun. Do you remember that when he eventually cottoned on to the fact that there were two of us we made him think that there were two more by changing clothes and disappearing in different directions?'

'It was so obvious really, but I suppose at that age it's easier to confuse someone. I wonder why we picked on him. Do you think we've scarred him for life?'

'Don't be ridiculous, I shouldn't think he even remembers it now. He was the only person who lived near AB that seemed to be our sort of age, or was he just the only one who would put up with us? I really can't remember. His father was the butcher I think. Anyway AB was always asking him around to play. D'you think she knew how beastly we were to him?'

They began to laugh at the memories of what they used to get up to.

'Remember that time we sneaked off to the beach before AB woke up in the morning and how we managed to return before she missed us, then driving her mad by begging to go the beach, because she didn't know we had already been?'

'Or the time we cadged a lift back with the milkman with buckets of pretty glistening pebbles off the shore,' said Jo. When AB had asked us where the piles of now dull looking stones had come from we told her that they'd been left on the doorstep by Simple Simon.'

They leant on AB's bedroom windowsill and looked out across the small garden.

'You see,' said Cass. 'It's not a surprise that we wouldn't have remembered the house next door let alone think that AB owned it.'

'Well, who would think about anything at all like that when they were the age we were when we stayed here? All we wanted to do was mess about on the beach and explore.'

'And be a pain to that boy,' added Cass

'For goodness sake – we must've been pretty horrible. There was that older couple too, maybe about twentyish. We plagued them as well. AB had a sort of rhyming name for them.' Jo tried to remember 'What was it? We followed them around everywhere because they acted so secretively. How irritating we must have been. Can you remember when we followed them down to the bay once as if we were detectives following criminals, and hid behind that upturned old boat and watched them for ages?'

'God, yes and we even ate those sandwiches that AB made for us despite the sand in them,' laughed Cass.

'That was your fault, you were the one that decided to try and tunnel under the boat to get closer and listen to what they were saying. It was so uncomfortable; I can still feel the sand now. We hadn't brought towels with us, and the sand got everywhere. I suppose we thought we were in a Famous Five adventure.'

'Except there were only two of us,' Cass added. 'But we *were* as good as five people, weren't we?'

'I wouldn't count on that after what Mr Sylvester said. He seemed to be quite certain that we weren't as sleuth like and effectively secretive as we obviously thought we were,' said Jo. 'Now I come to think about it AB was amazingly trusting and very lenient. As long as she knew roughly where we were she wasn't too concerned. And we didn't bother her much; after all we didn't get in the way or under her feet because we were out all the time.'

'Well, that's why we have matured into two incredibly chilled and independent adults,' laughed Cass. 'I think she did us a great favour being so laid back. Don't you remember Dad mentioning once early on, how he was anxious that we were allowed to roam about too much? As if he had ever really been concerned about our welfare down here.'

'Yes, he said AB had turned us into free-range twins.'

'I wonder why she never married,' said Cass thoughtfully. 'She'd have made a great Mum.'

Chapter 4

'Let's go and have a drink in the pub,' said Jo. 'We'll have plenty of time to come back and see the place again, plus we'll have to get on with deciding what to do with all AB's personal things and how we go about clearing all the rooms out.'

They walked back up the lane and into the street. The Black Ship stood slightly away from the road and had a few pretty tables with umbrellas outside. Inside it was busy and friendly and once they ordered their drinks they retired into a quiet corner where they could talk privately about the properties, the money, and how they thought they would spend it.

'I still haven't taken it all in,' said Jo. 'I was getting quite excited about the thought of maybe getting a small legacy, you know, enough for a little car perhaps, but this is incredible, I just can't get my head round it at all.'

'How much do you think the houses would be worth, Jo?'

'No idea. We shouldn't get obsessed with money.'

'It's difficult not to be though,' said Cass. 'When I had no money I longed to have some so that I could start my own business. Now we have this amazing windfall coming to us I can't think exactly what I'd like to do. I mean the timing is perfect, and for you too. This could set us both up; more foreign travel, some investments, buying a flat, car, or what? As you've only been renting a flat then maybe you should use some of whatever we get to buy your own place, just for security's sake. I could do the same too for that matter and I could let it out if I ever wanted to go abroad again.'

'At least we'd each have somewhere to call our own. Perhaps when Arthur Trinder gives us some idea about values we'll find it clearer. We may as well just call in and make an appointment with him as we go past.' suggested Jo.

As they finished their drinks their conversation briefly returned to their holidays in the cottage and their fondness for their Aunt, and they giggled as they remembered even more pranks that they played on unsuspecting people in Porthcwm. When they left the pub they decided to go in search of some of the locations of their most successful spying missions. They walked slowly through the town to see what places they remembered. They picked out various landmarks where they had hidden on some occasion or other, and decided that Porthcwm hadn't really altered much after all. It was still smallish with no immediately apparent new developments, but had obviously become a very popular tourist hotspot because of the local beaches and coastal scenery. The shops had changed with the times though and appeared to be a mix of smart clothes and stylish accessories, trendy seaside furnishings and the obligatory souvenir, ice-cream and candyfloss, bucket, spade, and shrimping net corner shops. But it was colourful and busy and everyone seemed friendly.

'You know it doesn't really seem to have changed apart from being a bit more commercially orientated now, after all it's years since we were here, and everything looked different from a kid's eye view anyway,' said Cass.

As they followed Mr Sylvester's directions to Arthur Trinder's Estate Agency they saw the Post Office on the corner opposite. 'Oh,' said Cass. 'I can remember us hiding in there from someone, it was perfect with all those counters and shelves. I wonder why there is such a long queue trailing out onto the street?'

'C'mon Cass,' her sister said and pulled her towards the Estate Agent's door.

They introduced themselves to the rather substantial but pretty young woman at the reception desk and enquired whether they could make an appointment for three o'clock the following afternoon.

'Hello, I'm Rhonwen,' the young woman said with a big smile. 'I'm certain that time will be okay but I'll just go and check with Mr Trinder.'

'Thanks,' said the twins together as they watched Rhonwen, whose large bulk seemed to be wedged in behind a desk designed for a much smaller person, struggle to stand up, disappear into the office beyond and return a couple of moments later with Arthur Trinder hot on her heels.

'Ladies, ladies, how lovely to see you. You must be Miss Seymour's nieces. Thank you for making an appointment to see me. Tomorrow afternoon at three will be perfect. Have you been to see the old place?' The twins both nodded. 'Marvellous, marvellous. I think we should get a generous price for Seaview Cottage. Yes, yes, do look at my other properties,' he said as he noticed them looking at the sales particulars on the walls. 'Nothing as nice as yours, of course.' he added. 'We are in short supply of special properties so I'm sure we'll get an offer almost immediately.' He rubbed his hands together like Uriah Heep did in such a disturbing way in David Copperfield. Both the twins shuddered a little.

'We met up with Mr Sylvester,' said Cass, 'and it appears that our aunt owned the house next door too, the one called the Lodge.'

The twins got enormous pleasure from seeing Arthur's eyes pop open in greedy astonishment, and watched with delight as he stood still, trying to look cool and as if the possibilities were scarcely of any interest to him at all.

'Do you think you *might* want to sell the Lodge as well?' he enquired as casually as he was able.

'Yes,' the twins said.

'My goodness ladies, what a turn up for the books...uh, for you,' they could see Arthur's eyes light up at the prospect of yet another sale. 'I'm astounded to learn that Miss Seymour owned the Lodge, everyone has always thought it might belong to old Sylvester himself as he dealt with the tenants and everything else to do with it. He must've been working for Miss Seymour all that time.'

'Well, we're astounded too and now the mystery has been solved for everyone,' said Jo. 'It just shows how successfully some secrets can be kept.'

'Marvellous, marvellous. I have people on my books even now who would jump at the chance of getting their foot in down here to start a guesthouse. The Lodge would offer a rare opportunity, yes, a *rare* opportunity. Ladies, would you mind if I went along to see it so that I can formulate some ideas on value for the open market before we meet? I'll keep the B&B idea in mind as I look around. I did go into the cottage a few years back but I should appreciate a fresh look at that too.'

'Yes, that seems like an excellent idea.' Jo rootled around in her bag for the bunch of keys that Mr Sylvester had given them earlier and passed them over to Arthur. 'You may as well have these now and we'll look forward to hearing what you think tomorrow.'

The twins walked to the door that Arthur was holding open for them 'Yes, yes of course ladies…'

They saw him suddenly get distracted by a woman in a short skirt and white high-heeled boots walking past on the opposite pavement.

'Gloria, Gloria,' he called across to her. 'Might I beg a moment of your valuable time…'

The twins took the opportunity of this distraction to slip past him and escape up the road.

'He's seriously weird, Jo.'

'Look we only have to meet up with him a few more times and then hopefully most of the other sale stuff can be done by phone,' said Jo. 'I bet he's creepy on the phone too though. And did you see the way he ogled that woman with the short skirt even though he was getting excited about raking in a high percentage for selling *two* properties.'

'I guess house sales and short skirts both excite him,' said Cass. 'But he doesn't know what to do when they occur at the same time.'

'Cass, I've been thinking in the night…' said Jo the moment she knew her twin was awake next morning.

'Mmm…I've been awake half the night thinking about the whole thing,' said Cass.

'Ok, in a nutshell,' said Jo. 'This is how *I* see it. Neither of us has a home and neither of us has a job.'

'So?'

'Well, we both love it here and have loads of happy memories, so we're not strangers to this place. Creepy Arthur says that the Lodge would do as a B&B, why let someone *else* come in and change it and use it as a guest house. Why are we planning to go and start a business or try and find a job or a home somewhere else when we could just stay here? It's perfect isn't it?' Jo paused for breath.

'Oh... D'you know, I actually disagree,' said Cass. 'I still think it would be good to sell them both. After all, do we *really* want to wait on guests hand and foot and clean up after them? I know it's gorgeous here but nothing goes on in a place like this and we'd get bored witless very quickly wouldn't we?'

Jo remained silent.

'Well...wouldn't we?' demanded Cass again. Her twin's apparent change of mind surprised her. It wasn't often they were completely at odds over things.

'I think you're wrong. It could work really well,' said Jo 'we've done a lot of travelling, tried our hands at all sorts of jobs successfully. Surely all that experience would be of enormous benefit in the B&B business. You must see that?'

'I just feel that we have a great opportunity to make some money. We should sell and move on,' argued Cass.

'Well if *you* want to sell, then I have no choice.' Jo said dejectedly, 'I can't force you to agree with me.'

When they were half way through their cooked English Breakfast, (why English thought Jo – this was Wales), the stroppy, gum-chewing, teenage waitress that had been serving lukewarm congealed breakfasts to the guests in a couldn't care less manner sidled up to their table to tell them that Mr Trinder 'wants one of you on the phone'.

'I'll go,' giggled Jo, '...don't think I can eat any more of this stuff. You plough on if you want to.'

A few minutes later she was back and was thankful that the remainder of their breakfast had been removed.

'Well?' asked Cass.

'Ok, this is how it is.' Jo wrung her hands like Arthur did, 'Arthur is *really, really* looking forward to seeing us this afternoon to discuss the sale, but wanted *very much* to give us the value that he thinks the houses are worth, so that we can enjoy thinking about it in the meantime.'

'And...? Come on Jo, what does he think?' Cass said, getting excited.

'He thinks the cottage is worth about £250,000 and the house about £340,000.'

'That sounds a little on the low side, don't you think?' said Cass after a moment's more serious consideration. 'I feel rather disappointed. I know there's work to do on the big house, but I thought it might be worth a bit more, after all he keeps telling us that properties of that quality are thin on the ground here.'

'Yes,' said Jo, as they started to walk upstairs to their bedroom. 'But after all, a few days ago we thought we might perhaps inherit a piece of furniture which was exciting enough, then we find we've been left a cottage and then suddenly we have two properties. And now we are beginning to sound greedy.'

'I know Jo,' said Cass quickly. 'However I still think selling them *is* the right thing do. We need to move on. We can't get stuck down here at the end of the world when we could be off starting a new life, a new business or going travelling again. There's nothing for us here. We'd find it boring. It wouldn't seem as exciting as it did when we were kids. But I agree that we must get the best price for the properties.'

Jo looked disappointed. She somehow thought that Cass might have come back around to her way of thinking. 'I'm convinced that we'd be mad to miss the opportunity of staying here,' she said, having one final shot at trying to change her sister's decision.

It obviously wasn't going to work. She sat on the edge of her bed and suddenly felt quite tearful. She knew how stubborn Cass could be when she'd made up her mind.

The twins arrived a little early at Arthur's office. They were offered a seat by Rhonwen and given cups of coffee. After they had finished their drink and Arthur had still not appeared they went back outside and spent some time looking at prices of other properties advertised in the window.

'Do you know?' said Jo suddenly, 'if you look at the prices of these other properties, including the bungalows and terraced ones, it does make ours look rather on the cheap side, don't you agree?'

'I was just thinking that myself. He surely wouldn't be trying to pull a fast one. Why would he? After all the more he sells the properties for, the more he stands to make on commission.'

'Yes, it's odd. Shall we let him go through with his spiel before we challenge him about the values?' suggested Jo.

Cass nodded in agreement. They went back inside and asked if Arthur was now available to see them. They could see the look of unease on Rhonwen's face as she disappeared out of sight through the door behind her.

'I don't think he should be long now,' she smiled apologetically when she came back. 'I'm really sorry but his previous appointment is still in with him.'

Jo was getting impatient. 'Yes, but our appointment was for three o'clock,' she muttered to Cass. 'He should be finished with them. It's well past three now. You would think he'd be smarmily beside himself to get us in there as fast as possible, bearing in mind he's going to be selling two properties for a lovely bit of commission.'

'I'll go and ask him again,' offered Rhonwen, who had overheard what Jo had said. She had no sooner struggled to stand up than the door to Mr Trinder's office opened and the creepy estate agent, looking slightly flushed, made an appearance.

'Hello ladies,' he offered somewhat breathlessly. 'I'm sorry to have kept you waiting, why don't you come in?'

They followed him through to his office where his last appointment was still sitting. Jo and Cass remained standing up waiting for the seat to be vacated.

'Ladies, may I introduce Trisha Phipps. Mrs Phipps, these are the lucky ladies who have the Lodge and adjacent Seaview Cottage to sell,' he blustered.

The twins said hello and stood aside for her to leave the office but she just stayed put. They looked at Arthur who shuffled from one foot to the other seemingly unable to get his words out.

'Oh perhaps I'd better explain?' he managed to say at last.

'Please do.' the twins chorused.

'I have taken the liberty of telling Mrs Phipps about the impending sale of the Lodge. She has been looking for ages for just the right property to buy to run as an up-market Bed and Breakfast establishment. Goodness knows this town needs one, don't you agree ladies?'

'Absolutely,' they answered, now in twin response mode.

Jo thought that this brassy super tanned woman looked very much used to getting her own way and was amazed how very comfortable she appeared to be in a meeting that she had obviously hijacked.

'Now ladies, Mrs Phipps is very interested in buying the Lodge and is willing to offer you almost the asking price so that she can realise her dream of setting up a much needed business here.'

'Arthur, we *can* call you Arthur can't we?' said Jo. 'May we sit down first please?'

'Oh! Of course, of course, dear ladies, how rude of me to neglect you.' He opened his office door, 'Rhonwen, uh … Miss Travers,' he called. 'Please might I have two more chairs for the lovely ladies?'

The twins watched as Rhonwen found it impossible to get through the doorway with both chairs at once. They waited whilst she took two journeys to get everyone in the office seated.

'Mr Trinder,' began Jo. '*Why* would you not put the properties on the open market as you originally suggested to us, and *why* do you think we would accept a price for the Lodge which is even below the rather disappointing valuation that you gave us this morning?'

'My dear ladies, I thought this would be a good arrangement for you both.'

'But why would you knowingly undersell the property and not make yourself the correct amount of commission?' pressed Jo.

'Look *girls*,' Trisha Phipps said patronisingly, getting to her feet and suddenly finding her voice. 'I've been looking for a property suitable for my needs for ages. Arthur here has been keeping his eye out for me so that I don't miss out on any opportunity that comes along. He said you'd be keen to unload this property quickly so that you could move on after your dear aunt's death. He said you were distraught and wanted to sell as fast as possible so that you could get back to the bright lights of the city.'

'Did he?' the twins retorted, both staring disbelievingly at Arthur.

'We had presumed, Arthur, obviously foolishly, that you would have tried to get us the highest possible price for the properties.' Jo said sharply.

'For God's sake!' Trisha Phipps erupted. 'Look, I'll pay you the asking price then, for immediate possession. I can't say fairer than that can I?'

'I don't think so,' said Jo. 'We haven't even had a proper meeting with Arthur to discuss it all. We have no idea what the asking price would be for either of the properties yet. When we arrived here for our meeting today we were kept waiting and then find you in here, uninvited, trying to organise a speedy purchase of the Lodge with Arthur.'

They could see an angry red flush beginning to show through the fake tanned skin on Trisha Phipps' cheeks. Arthur was blustering and tutting and obviously about to make some excuse.

'Ok,' said Cass, standing up. 'That's enough. Here's the deal. It's definitely a NO. In fact we are not selling at all. We are keeping both the properties. This ridiculous meeting has been useful in one way as it's confirmed our thoughts on what we intend to do here in Porthcwm.'

Jo shot Cass a look of surprise and smiled at her twin, amazed at her change of heart about keeping the properties. She stood up too and they both turned towards the door.

'Is that it? Is that *it*? You won't even discuss it? You won't let me make you an even better offer?' Trisha Phipps shrieked, also getting to her feet and moving towards them.

'Correct,' said Cass.

'So what are *you* going to with the Lodge? Why on earth would *you* want to keep it?' she stood very close to them, spitting out the words into their faces.

'Why,' said Cass, 'open it as a B & B of course.'

Chapter 5

Jo poured out two large glasses of wine to toast AB and celebrate their first official evening in the cottage. All the legal formalities had been dealt with and they had moved the contents of Jo's flat down to Porthcwm and this was their very first day in their new home.

When Cass and Jo had told Mr Sylvester the news that they were planning to stay in Porthcwm, they could tell that in his own reserved way the old solicitor was beside himself with pleasure.

'Miss Seymour knew you would make that decision after thinking everything through,' he said and gave them a knowing nod and a nearly smile and shook each twin firmly by the hand. 'I'm so, so very pleased. Welcome to Porthcwm. I'm certain you will do as your aunt wished and bring some of her spirit back into the place. Plus of course put a few things straight...'

They had spent the afternoon making a space in the cottage for their own belongings and shifted one or two things around to suit themselves. AB had been a very house-proud woman and everything seemed to be tidily kept in its place. It was lucky for them that there wasn't much sorting to do as they wanted to get on with getting the Lodge up to scratch as fast as possible.

The only area of their Aunt's cottage which was less organised than anywhere else was the middle drawer of her oak dresser. It was jam-packed full of photographs. Some were neatly arranged on dark grey card pages in fabric bound albums and held in place with little black corners. Some of the remainder were grouped together in various bags and boxes but most of them were loose and stuffed haphazardly into the drawer. Jo and Cass couldn't make out whether they were collected together for a reason or just shoved together randomly.

Despite the urgency to get on with everything else they were fascinated by this enormous collection of pictures. So after their wine and celebration supper they sat down to have a look at some of them. There were some really old ones of AB and friends dressed up to the nines for parties and lots of posed group pictures. They came across some of themselves too, dressed in little bathing costumes, climbing rocks, swimming in the sea and picnicking.

There were even some of Jo and Cass taken in the town and a couple where they looked as if they were hiding from something. 'Very odd, these,' Jo said. 'Why do you think anyone would bother to take these photos?'

They laid some out on the table, 'You know, Jo, we had fantastic holidays down here, didn't we? I don't suppose for one minute we realised how lucky and privileged we were. We just did what we wanted and didn't have to bother about anyone else,' said Cass.

'We always seemed to be eating too,' said Jo. 'Look at these photos of us here, we're eating something in all of them.'

Jo picked up another pile of pictures and looked at them more closely, turning each one over before she passed them on to Cass. 'AB has written on the back of most of the ones in this bag which is helpful. Maybe she was starting to go through them before she died. We seem to be in most of this lot. Look at this one. There's little Simple Simon, I'd forgotten what he looked like. He looks quite frightened in that picture.'

'Well that might have something to do with you,' said Cass. 'I mean, look at that huge crab you're holding.'

'Hey! I don't suppose you were much better either. Look at these then. D'you recognise anyone there?'

'That's that couple whose names I was trying to remember. Look AB has written the names on the back with two exclamation marks. *Bev and Rev!!* Most odd. She always did seem to be very amused by them, but not unkindly. Do you remember that huge telling off she gave us once after we'd been tailing them sleuth like around town and she'd been shopping and happened to catch sight of us creeping behind the grocer's delivery van? I think that was the only time we saw her angry, you know. She was usually the most remarkably good natured person.'

40

Jo broke off from looking at the photos and glanced along the mantelpiece at the personal bits and pieces belonging to their godmother. It was the sort of collection that grows organically; postcards, little ornaments, a pale posy of dried flowers leaning up against her old silent clock, photographs, odd scribbled quotations on discoloured paper and a misshapen half burned candle in a brass candlestick, a drip of wax clinging to the edge as though it could still fall at any moment, and bizarrely, a red rubber ball. It appeared to be a once happy, now rather sad, faded collection of sentimental memories.

'This mantelpiece is full of AB's favourite objects,' Jo said. 'It's rather beautiful and poignant at the same time. It's a display of little parts of her life that bring a lump to my throat. Some of these must have been here for years.'

'Except this one...' Cass took a photo off the mantelpiece and passed it to Jo.

Jo looked at the picture. It must have been taken fairly recently. AB was sitting near the fireplace in the big comfy armchair where Jo herself had been curled up earlier. There was a rug over her knees and lying beside her was a dog with its nose resting on a red ball. AB looked small and timeworn.

Jo looked at the back and suddenly started laughing, 'I think I know why,' she said. 'Have a look, see what she says too.'

'AB looks very frail. I wonder why that particular photo was put there right in front of some much more interesting things.'

'Yes Cass, but look at the back...'

Cass turned it over and looked at the back as Jo had done and then laughed too. In spidery writing their godmother had written *"To Josephine & Cassandra - meet Nosey, my faithful friend to the end."* 'See, there's the red rubber ball that's on the mantelpiece on her lap. It's all a big hint isn't it?'

They looked at each other and laughed, each reading the others mind.

Next morning the twins were outside Mr Sylvester's office bright and early. He gave a broad knowing smile when he saw them.

'I expect you have come for this my dears.' He held out a piece of paper with an address on it.

Jo took it. 'How did you guess?'

'Well, I didn't think it would take you very long to make a decision about Nosey. Are you off to fetch him now?'

'Yes, we are taking AB's Mildred out to give her a run.'

'Oh that lovely motor vehicle. If that car could speak it would tell you such stories…'

He turned to his receptionist, 'Mrs Tyler, would you be so kind as to carry the basket and so on down to the car for them, you know where it's stored.' He looked at the twins, 'You will enjoy having the dog; he's as bright as a button despite his age. Good bye for now.'

Mrs Tyler came out of a side door of the office with a lovely old wicker dog basket and a brightly coloured blanket. They put the basket into the back of the Morris and the blanket on the back seat. As Mrs Tyler handed over the blanket she said, 'Your Aunt knitted this herself. She used to make them for a charity and called them Dorcas blankets. Everyone used to give her leftover balls of wool and she just knitted up random coloured squares. When she'd made sufficient she would sew them together into patchwork blankets and send them off to the charity. She must have made this one especially for Nosey though, lucky fellow.'

The kennels were only about five miles from Porthcwm and the twins found the place easily. As soon as Cass had parked the car a tall, skinny man appeared from the direction of a large outbuilding which had small enclosures running along the front of it. 'I'm glad you've come, I was beginning to think you had decided against having him. Nosey is as miserable as sin here. Some dogs take to kennels and some don't. He doesn't. He hates being restricted, much happier mooching around on the beach making a nuisance of himself and looking starvingly at visitors' picnics. My name's Ron, by the way.'

'Oh did Mr Sylvester ring you to say we were on our way?'

'No, but your Aunt told me that you would come sometime.'

The twins smiled at each other. They were beginning to get used to everyone seeming to know what they were going to do before they did.

Ron laughed as if he read their minds, 'Your aunt *was* an extraordinary woman. Anyway you'd better meet Nosey.'

He walked back towards the building from which he had first appeared and returned with a wire-haired dachshund trotting along behind him on a lead. Nosey was beside himself with joy. He bounced up to Jo and Cass as if he had known them all his life. He wagged his tail and licked their hands.

Ron passed the red leather lead over to Jo. 'I hope you have great fun with him.'

Soon they were back at the cottage sitting down with mugs of tea, watching Nosey who was fast asleep. He looked as if he had never been away from the place. He was settled on the armchair on his blanket having completely ignored his basket that they had put under the old pine table in the kitchen.

'This has all been a bit of a stitch-up hasn't it really?' smiled Jo.

'You're right, everyone seemed to know that we'd give in and have Nosey.'

The doorbell suddenly rang and the twins jumped out of their skins. Nosey perked up his ears and dashed to the door wagging his tail frantically. The door opened a little and a voice called 'Helloooo… anyone about?'

Jo opened the door wider to find an elderly man with wispy white hair and a lovely kind face standing there smiling. He was wearing a crumpled linen suit and had a yellowing white dog collar at a crooked angle around his neck.

He introduced himself as the local vicar, Tomos Thomas. The twins invited him into the sitting room and brought through tea and some indulgent cakes that Cass had bought as an unnecessary part of their supplies for the cottage.

He explained that he had been a close friend of Miss Seymour who apparently used to be one of the Church Guides for visitors. 'I wanted to welcome you officially to Porthcwm. You won't remember me of course, but I do remember you both when you used to stay with your aunt. How *could* any of us forget? I remember Miss Seymour bringing you along to a few services too when you first started coming down here,' Tomos Thomas laughed heartily. 'She only tried it a few times though.'

Cass and Jo grinned at one another.

'I'd forgotten about going to church,' said Jo. 'I didn't realise that AB was so involved. It's odd really, considering she was a non-believer, I would have thought that was the last thing she would think of doing.'

'Well your aunt was a wonderful woman and she hated most conventional things on principle. She would often join in on something just to make a point, even more so if there was possibility of irritating one or two of the pompous, difficult members of this community. I never let her know that I realised what she was up to, partly because she achieved a lot of good results that way, but also I rather admired her ruthlessness. She was a spirited and singularly strong-willed person and Porthcwm was a better place for her living here. I believe that you two have inherited much of her essence.

'I used to be impressed, if not a little concerned at times, about the….*adventures* shall I call them, that you two, aided and abetted by Miss Seymour, got up to when you were staying down here.' his eyes held a wicked twinkle. 'I shall look forward to seeing you settle in here and become successors to your aunt's individual ways. It will make my retirement much less boring to see what you get up to.'

Over the pot of tea and cakes he filled them in on all sorts of groups and societies that they could join, and lobbied heavily on behalf of the bell ringers and choir, who the twins discovered, needed some 'young blood' to keep going. He also gave them the names of 'useful people' who would help them get their business started including the local tourism group, and Phil Fixit the handyman-builder whom he had christened many years previously. He warned them about Blodwyn Harries at the Post Office who was the 'nosiest woman on God's earth', and the local estate agent, surprise, surprise who would sell anything that wasn't nailed down.

He attempted to lure them into his flock too, but realising he wasn't getting anywhere told them instead about the bright young vicar who was replacing him on his imminent retirement, 'Such a nice chap,' he explained. 'We are so pleased he's been able to return here to us at St Dominic's. Huw Evans or Evans Above as the rather cheeky members of the youth group commonly refer to him. The nickname seems to have stuck and I've heard one or two older members of the congregation call him that too recently. At least it seems to indicate that he will be a popular incumbent even before he starts. I've been secretly hoping that Huw would inspire you to get involved with one or two things. After all, you'll probably realise when you meet him that you rather *owe* it to him.'

Cass and Jo exchanged glances.

'Lovely wife too. They will inject a spark of fun and enthusiasm into the congregation. It's sadly in need of it now, I'm afraid.'

He took his leave after reminding the twins again about the shortage of bell ringers and choir members, and threw in the WI for good measure whilst bidding them farewell on the doorstep. 'I enjoyed your cakes very much. May I call again?'

'We'd love to see you again and I promise to make you lots of cakes myself next time if you tell us more about our aunt,' said Cass.

When the door closed Jo said, 'You can't make cakes Cass, you never do kitchen stuff.'

'Well there's going to be a new me, I've decided.'

'Yeah! And the proverbial pig just flew over the garden.'

When the doorbell rang again, Nosey who appeared to be in a deep slumber, shot off his chair, barking as ferociously as he could manage and hurtled towards the front door. He sniffed noisily along the bottom of it picking up a scent that was wafting underneath. He curled his lips back, snarling with some serious menace. Jo held onto him as Cass opened the door and peeped around. It was a shock to her, but probably not a complete surprise, to find Arthur Trinder standing on their doorstep, grovelling and wringing his hands as usual.

'Ladies, a very, very good day to you both. When I heard you had moved in I thought I should visit you to wish you good luck with your new venture and perhaps offer my apologies for any misunderstanding that might have occurred at our last meeting. How *are* you getting on in your magnificent new home? It will be such a lot of hard work for you...' He took a step towards the hallway as though he had been invited in, but the twins stood still and he couldn't pass. 'Ah well! I wondered whether I could offer you any advice or help now that you have decided to stay in Porthcwm. I'm sure there are many things you may need assistance with here.

'Have you decided yet whether you are going to live in the cottage, or are you going to move into part of the Lodge?' He gestured towards the house next door. 'I was just thinking, because I do have people on my books who would like to rent instead of buy,' he took another step towards the hall but the twins remained in his path. 'I would be able to find you the perfect tenants for either property. I would check them myself thoroughly of course, to make sure they are suitable for wonderful homes such as these. And they *are* wonderful properties aren't they, ladies? You obviously saw the potential in them straight away. I assumed you would be selling them and going back to city living but I was wrong and can understand that I might have misjudged the situation a trifle. Of course should you decide to sell one of them for any reason then I should be only too glad to assist in finding you the right purchaser.'

'Like you tried last week for your friend Fi...uh -Trisha Phipps, you mean?' Jo looked at her sister and then at Arthur Tinder. 'Goodbye Mr Trinder.'

He looked as though he was about to say something but thought better of it. He began to walk away, then hesitated. 'Well I shall see you soon ladies, I'm certain,' he called out with a smarmy little smile on his face. He turned away again and strode along the drive towards his car which was parked outside the gate, possibly in case he needed a rapid getaway.

'The cheek of him. You know, I nearly called her Fishnchips,' said Jo as Arthur beat a hasty retreat. 'And she's just as greasy as he is. I'm sure we haven't seen the last of that grovelling little man or his mate Fishnchips. They're both so thick-skinned I bet one of them'll be back again pleading with us to sell the house, but it's too late now, they're totally stuck with us.'

Chapter 6

'What a day it's been so far,' muttered Cass. 'I don't feel as if I've actually achieved anything.'

Realising that Jo wasn't even around and that she was talking to herself she decided to ring the Phil Fixit chap to see if he could come and give the house a good look over. His jolly sounding wife answered and said that he was busy, 'working up the coast somewhere' but Mrs Fixit promised to get him to call in and see them 'early evening'.

Phil Fixit rang the doorbell at 6 o'clock exactly. When they all had a mug of tea in front of them the twins began to explain how they came to be in Porthcwm and what they were thinking of doing with the house.

'I'm sure it won't surprise you to discover that most of the town knows all the whys and wherefores of you being here already,' Phil Fixit said, laughing, 'though I suspect as usual there will be a great number of embellishments and inaccuracies. My mother remembers you both staying here years ago too. She said she recalls you getting locked in the church tower during a service once and how you had to climb to the top and shout out to old Tomos Thomas as he was walking home round the back of the church. Of course he was the younger Tomos Thomas then.'

'Oh God, I'm sure we'd both forgotten that, I certainly had, I'm surprised that he didn't mention that when he was here earlier,' Jo said.

'Yes, I'd forgotten too,' agreed Cass. 'Was that when he brought us back to AB's and told her he was impressed that we had, at last, managed to spend some meaningful time in the church?'

'Mm, not sure, but I *can* remember him bringing us back here on more occasions than that, though I can't recall why...'

'Never mind that now, anyway,' said Cass, then turning back to Phil Fixit said, 'let's go round to the Lodge and chat about what we'd like you to do, if that's okay?'

They downed the last of their tea and walked off in the direction of the Lodge explaining on the way some of their thoughts and plans. Phil Fixit listened intently. He very quickly made sense out of the ideas that the twins gabbled through together. After an hour or so looking around the building with Jo and Cass, he left, promising to return the following week with some costs and plans.

'Here I am again,' he announced when Jo answered the door in her nightie at 7.30am seven days later.

'God, you're early Mr Fixit. Come in. Do you always start this early?'

'Yes I do, Miss, and my name isn't Fixit, it's just what they call me. It's actually Jones, but there are too many of *them* around already. Just plain Phil will do thank you.'

'In that case Phil, we don't want you to call us Miss, it makes us sound like two spinsters, which I suppose is what we actually are, but for us it's just plain Jo and Cass, okay?'

'Okay Miss.'

When Cass finally made an appearance, Phil Fixit carefully took them through what he thought needed doing in order of importance and produced a long list of projected costs for the Lodge.

'You're lucky with most of it, quite honestly. It looks worse than it actually is. The important thing is that there doesn't appear to be any problem with the roof and there's no apparent damp. Most of it will be cosmetic, tarting the Old Girl up really, and you can make that as expensive or cheap as you choose. May I suggest that you go for a middle price range for paints and so on? She's a lovely house and deserves some pampering but we can do a good job without spending obscene amounts, don't you think?'

Before Phil Fixit went, he gave the twins the job of spending some time with the Old Girl, as he continued to call the house, deciding what colours they wanted, plus any other details that they

50

needed him to take care of. 'All that sort of stuff takes longer than you think,' he promised.

'Goodness, he seems a bit of a find doesn't he?' said Cass as Phil Fixit drove away in his van.

'Yes, how brilliant was the old vicar suggesting we use him. Perhaps we should join his flock after all,' said Jo. 'We'd better spend some of today going through our ideas again and deciding what we need to do first and then we could go out for some fresh air with Nosey. It's tough isn't it, living here in such a fabulous place?'

On the way back from their walk they decided to make time to call in at the church and see if they could see Tomos Thomas and thank him for recommending Phil Fixit. St Dominic's was a chocolate-box church, attractive and well cared for. It was below the street which wound downwards towards its great porch. The grounds and graveyard were beautifully manicured and an avenue of ancient limes that showed a history of being pollarded marched through the church grounds from one end to the other. At each end there was a pair of large and beautiful iron gates which were kept permanently locked to stop all except those on foot from using the churchyard as a rat run through the town. The gates were only opened when a wedding car delivered a bride or a hearse was due to come through to drop off its passenger.

'It's so peaceful and pretty,' said Jo. 'I can barely remember it though you know – can you?'

'No, I actually *do* remember it,' said Cass. 'AB brought us down here on a few occasions, but we just fidgeted too much and were annoying during the service.'

'But we didn't come often though surely?' asked Jo.

'I do remember we were made to come down here once to apologise to the vicar. He mentioned something about it when he called in – we'll have to ask him.' suggested Cass.

'It was probably the last time AB risked taking us,' said Jo, 'although I do recall us actually suggesting we attended church once.

AB was completely thrown by the idea but she indulged us in the hope that we were starting to be well behaved and sociable.'

'Fat chance,' said Cass. 'Didn't we have some ulterior plan involving shadowing someone who went to church quite a lot? We thought it was important as spies to keep an eye on them and see what they were up to. When AB found out she wasn't at all pleased with us which was peculiar as she'd always appeared to rather encourage adventures...'

'Only thing is, the *more* I remember,' said Jo interrupting Cass, 'the more I feel uncomfortable about what we used to get up to.'

Jo tied Nosey up outside and followed Cass into the church. They looked around but there was no sign of Tomos Thomas, and it was eerily quiet in there. When they asked the Verger, who had suddenly appeared from nowhere, he told them that Tomos Thomas expected at any moment and invited them to sit for a while in one of the pews to wait for him.

After roughly twenty minutes when they were beginning to get a bit restless and wondering whether to leave, they heard footsteps behind them. Turning round, Cass could see a figure in the shadows at the back of the church walking around the pillars behind them. But it wasn't Tomos Thomas. She tugged at Jo's sleeve, 'Quick, kneel down and pray hard to be made instantly invisible.'

'What are...?'

'Just do it and shut up.'

They knelt down quickly and Cass hastily pulled her hood up over her head. The footsteps were accompanied by a swishing sound which came gradually closer and closer. With one final swish and a light draught of air, the footsteps came to a stop next to Cass who was at the end of the pew nearest the aisle. She turned her head to the side and peeped down to her left. All she could see was a black dress and clumpy black shoes sticking out from beneath the folds. Fighting her instinct to stay still, but feeling ludicrously stupid in this position she pulled back her hood and slowly looked up, 'Oh hello,' she whispered hoarsely to the man who was wearing a dog collar and looking down at her. Jo, who hadn't moved a muscle until she heard her twin's voice, looked up too now and also managed a muffled greeting whilst trying to appear as if nothing at all was out of the ordinary.

'Well, well. The two ginger sleuths have come back to visit the scene of their crimes.' declared the figure in black.

The twins slowly scrabbled up to a sitting position on the pew again and stared at the man.

'Your aunt said you would return. She felt you would need to. So welcome back to Porthcwm. I'm really sorry that it is her death that has brought you back. She will be sadly missed. I was very fond of her and she was a true friend.

'I'm Huw Evans,' he continued, 'known locally I believe, as 'Evans Above'. I am shortly taking over from Tomos Thomas. Now, I know your aunt had her own nickname for me, a rhyming one…' He sat down in the pew in front of the twins and turned around to talk to them.

Cass started laughing and looked at Jo, 'Come on Jo, haven't you twigged yet? It's 'Bev'n Rev' or at least the Rev part.'

'Oh my God – goodness I mean.' Jo managed at last. 'But why didn't AB just call you Huw?'

'Weird sense of humour and whacky ideas – like you two, I guess.' replied Huw. 'We didn't mind as we knew she was fond of us. She was very supportive of us too as Bev's father was a chapel goer and thought his daughter had lost her marbles getting involved with a C of E priest. Miss Seymour used to let us meet up in her cottage and didn't let on to anyone.'

'So that's why we saw you quite often,' said Jo.

'Yes and she loved her little jokes and her little secrets, I'm sure I won't be the first person who has said that to you. And I'm sure she was as mischievous as you two were when she was your age. That's why she loved having you around; it made her feel young again.'

'So, what about Bev?'

'Well Bev, Beverly, my girlfriend, who you both shamelessly stalked along with me as if you were on a vital secret mission, affording us no romantic privacy ever, is now my wife. We have two children too. Teenagers.'

'I'm pleased for you both. And we're sorry; we must've been such a pain when you were courting. We were looking for Tomos Thomas, actually,' explained Cass, 'but it is really nice to see you again.'

'When I saw you both there in the kneeling position I assumed for the briefest moment that Tomos had managed to convert you both when he visited you the other week.' teased Huw.

'He did try very hard,' admitted Jo. 'In fact extremely hard. He was very helpful in other departments though and suggested people that we'd find useful with all our plans for the Lodge.'

'It was a surprise to find out Miss Seymour owned the Lodge,' admitted Huw. 'She was exceedingly good at keeping her own secrets as well as other people's.'

'Rev, could you point us in the direction of AB's grave please, we should like to go and talk to her?'

'Of course. You can't miss it. There are always a few flowers left there. I don't know by whom, no one has been seen leaving them. She had one of the last plots in the churchyard. She chose it many years ago. Although it was highly irregular she persuaded Tomos Thomas to reserve it for her. It's the nearest one to the gateway up into the town. She thought that it would be the perfect spot for her to be buried so that she could keep her eye on everyone who slipped into the churchyard, for whatever reason.'

Later in the day when they were unpacking a couple of boxes of their books to add to their aunt's collection, there was a knock on the door. Jo and Cass both went to answer it only to be beaten by Nosey who was jumping around enthusiastically. As Jo opened the door he shot outside to make a fuss of their latest visitor. There fussing Nosey in return was a small, round, dark-haired woman beaming from ear to ear.

'Ah! I see you have the Nosey back at last. Hello. I am Rosa.'

'Hello Rosa,' said the twins.

'I am Rosa.'

'Yes?'

'I am cleaner, no?'

'Cleaner?' repeated the twins together.

'Cleaner, yes.'

'This is a silly conversation. Why don't you come in Rosa?'

They went into the kitchen, Rosa leading the way, seemingly quite in charge and at home.

'I am Rosa...' she started off again.

'Okay Rosa, hello, I'm Jo and this is Cass. We have heard lots about you...all good of course,' she added quickly.

'I have heard of you also,' Rosa responded.

'Obviously, true to form, none of it good?' Cass laughed.

Rosa didn't reply.

The twins caught each other's eye, 'So what can we do for you Rosa?'

'Is more what I do for you.'

'Okay - fire away.'

'I come to clean, no? I work here for your Aunt a long time, cleaning her cottage and then towards the end I nurse her and sort things...her eyes welled up. My husband, sometime he help her in the garden, keep it tidy, no? And he help with her old car. 'We both very fond of her...'

Rosa picked up the two plates off the table that had held the twins' lunch and took them to the scullery as if it were second nature and rather late in the day to have them hanging about.

Taking the opportunity, Cass whispered, 'What the bloody hell is she going on about, I'm quite lost?'

Rosa returned to the kitchen, 'So when I start?'

'Start?' the twins said together.

'Good, I come Monday.'

Chapter 7

Monday morning arrived bright and clear, and Rosa breezed into Seaview Cottage along with the welcome sunshine. She turned up at nine o'clock precisely in her battered old farm truck with a tea towel covered basket over her arm. She walked straight into the cottage deftly avoiding Nosey who danced excitedly around her ankles threatening to trip her up, and plonked the basket down on the kitchen table.

'I bring ice cream. This is chocolate one,' she said, pulling out a plastic box from underneath the red and white striped tea towel. She went over to the cupboard beside the back door and pulled out two bowls, and then to the top drawer in the dresser, returning to the table with two spoons and an ice cream scoop as well.

'There, I serve it, no?'

'So this is the ice cream you make and sell, Rosa?' asked Jo, 'We've seen it advertised, and they use it in the pub too don't they?'

Rosa served it all out and passed them each a bowl and spoon.

'It's so decadent having this for breakfast,' drooled Cass. 'What a great way to start the morning? It's so much nicer than that awful stuff we bought in Porthcwm the other day.'

'Oh, you mean what that Blodwyn Harris sells in the post office? Says it is full of goodness and natural ingredients and made locally. It is *none* of those,' her voice rose passionately 'is full of rubbish, *rubbish*. When you start have guests you give them ice cream from my cows, no?'

'Well,' said Cass. 'I'm not certain that we could give it to people for breakfast, Rosa, wonderful as it is.'

'Dinner, I mean you give it for dinner, no?'

'No sadly. We're not going to do dinners for guests. They can always go to the pub or one of those little restaurants that we haven't explored yet,' said Jo scraping the last spoonful of cold chocolate heaven from her bowl. 'But if we did ever decide to change our minds we would definitely have your ice cream on the menu.' she added hastily.

'Will you bring some more flavours in for *us* to try though?' Cass said, smiling at Rosa who seemed to accept that as the promise of a regular order. She picked up the empty bowls and put them in the sink, 'Your aunt like my lemon one best, I bring that next.'

And so the week continued. Rosa came in most days to help around the place and always with a different flavour ice cream hidden under a tea towel in her basket. Eventually Jo had to say something, 'Rosa we love your ice cream but can you only bring us a new flavour once a week otherwise we shall be so grossly overweight by the time we open this place to guests.'

'Why you think I am this shape?' said Rosa patting her stomach and laughing at her own honesty.

The twins quickly made all manner of suitable complimentary noises about the ice cream so that Rosa wouldn't get into an indignant huff and storm around the place in a grump. She had done just that a couple of days earlier when Cass had mentioned how they liked the look of the farmhouse that was down the same track as Rosa and Benito. It had taken them ages to get Rosa back into her normal cheerful self but only after she had spent a long time telling them in excitable Italian-English about her horrible neighbours, the Lloyds.

The twins had Rosa working in the Lodge too now and not just in the cottage. She did all sorts of jobs to keep the decorating and dressing of the house moving along. She got annoyed with Phil Fixit when he caused the inevitable dust problems every so often but on the whole things were going forward at a pace and everything and everyone was working towards the day when it would be acceptable to open the door to guests.

Phil was progressing well in the tarting-up process of the Old Girl and already the downstairs area appeared lighter and brighter and fresher. It was amazing what a difference just some cosmetic paintwork made. Phil was still astounded that the place was so problem free. However, the bathrooms were pretty old fashioned, and although they would be perfectly usable in a family situation, the twins knew they had to get them up to the standard that holiday makers now expected everywhere they stayed. After all, their plan was to have a friendly, comfortable house that people would enjoy visiting without going down the route of the whole 'boutique' hotel thing.

'We need more bathrooms Phil,' Jo said over tea one morning. 'Two just aren't enough, despite the fact one of them is large enough to hold a party in.'

Phil nodded in agreement, 'I've been thinking along the same lines. The Old Girl isn't listed so we could make some alterations...and before you say anything I know that you want to have everything in keeping as much as possible because you love the place. I can see how you feel about her, and I agree. We must do everything sensitively. So I suggest that if you're happy to have just four letting rooms instead of five then we can easily manage to have a bathroom for each without too much expense and disruption.'

Within two days he had called in a plumber mate of his to help him install the bathrooms and it was all falling into place. He had suggested halving the large bathroom which had obviously been a bedroom in its distant past. That would make two ensuite bathrooms for the bedrooms on either side once a partition had been erected and two new doorways put in. The other smaller bathroom only needed its existing doorway blocked up and a new one knocked through into the next door bedroom. The existing fifth bedroom would be made into the final bathroom. It was a smaller bedroom than the others and had probably once been a dressing room as there was still an outline of an old blocked up doorway into the adjacent room.

Cass and Jo decided that the two rooms in the attic would just have a facelift of light coloured paint to freshen them up and obliterate the old dark green paint that had obviously been there for years. They would have one of these rooms each and the dated bathroom in the attic would stay as it was as it was perfectly usable just for them. It meant that there could always be at least one of them sleeping in the Lodge in case of any emergency.

The house renovation was all running smoothly and without hitch. Phil worked quickly and with as little disruption and mess as possible. They got on really well with him. Mrs Fixit had called in one day to see how he was progressing and over a cup of tea in the Lodge kitchen the twins heard some more stories of their antics during their holiday stays with AB. It was going well with Rosa too. She tidied around the cottage after them and fussed about generally in the Lodge. A hard worker, she had so many other commitments that it was amazing she was so punctual and reliable. The twins counted on Rosa and Phil and felt fortunate in their choice of paid helpers - not that they had been given much choice in the matter because it all appeared to have been pre-arranged.

What little free time they had was spent searching antique shops or going to sales to pick up pieces of furniture which would fit comfortably into the setting of the Lodge. They always took Mildred, and Nosey accompanied them everywhere. So many people they met already knew him; he had obviously been quite a celebrity. The appearance of the twins at shops and auctions always caused a stir. They were an attractive pair, lively and friendly and they were beginning to feel that they had lived in that area all their lives. People were so welcoming to them, especially the older residents who always mentioned AB and some prank from which she had had to rescue them.

They were beginning to get the feeling that they really had been quite an irritation to most people when they stayed in Porthcwm all those years ago, getting into trouble and being mischievous. Obviously what *they* had thought was a bit of childhood fun, appeared to have left a deep mark in some people's memories. It also struck the girls that people seemed to hold very fond memories of AB herself but were curious about her ownership of the Lodge and why it had been such a secret. AB really did seem to be a bit of a mystery.

Anyway, whatever was in anyone else's minds, Jo & Cass were very happy with their lot in Porthcwm and were looking forward to welcoming their first guests. June had arrived and the weather forecast was looking good. Although they had missed the customary rush of earlier bank-holiday tourists they were pleased that they had done everything properly in their redecoration and revamping of the Lodge. They felt that once they completed the final bedroom they and the Old Girl would be just about prepared enough to receive visitors.

They had been working together to get all their leaflets and advertising sorted, taken beautiful photographs of the Lodge and the surrounding area then Tweeted and Facebooked regularly to keep anyone and everyone up to date with their progress. They had even put up a little ad in the window of the Post Office, although they were not certain whether there was any point, as Blodwyn Harris thought she knew everything and was quite convinced she was qualified to give out information, such as number of bedrooms (correct information), or how much it cost to stay there (incorrect information). The twins had hoped that their ad with its accompanying photo might catch the attention of any spur of the moment holidaymakers, so maybe it was a good idea after all, and at the very least Blodwyn could study the accurate details instead of picking it up from jungle drums.

On Rosa's advice Jo and Cass decided they should become members of the local tourism group. She had given them a leaflet advertising the next meeting telling them it would be worth making an effort to attend because they would meet some of the other accommodation providers and could network with people who were already involved in the tourist industry.

So here they were, sitting with two dozen other people in the hall at the library. Far from talking about how they could attract more people to the area as a united group, Porthcwm's tourism members seemed to be on a path to self-destruction, with heated exchanges and fist waving over what appeared to be minor issues right from the first item on the agenda. From the colour and type of flowers in someone's window boxes, to the obviously ongoing saga of why their chairman's house appeared once again on the cover - already in print of course - of the current accommodation brochure, the debates ploughed on from one petty niggle to the next.

Determined to stick it out to the bitter end, Jo and Cass stayed behind to have the obligatory cup of instant coffee. It gave them the opportunity to have a good look at who was present and the first that grabbed their attention was Fishnchips who was in deep, and obviously private, conversation with the chairman.

'There'll be something sneaky going on there, I bet,' said Jo.

'A *baptism by fire*, or whatever other appropriate saying would describe your first meeting,' said a voice behind them, halting any further discussion. 'My name is Megan Hughes, welcome to the Grizzly Group.'

The twins laughed and each shook hands with Megan whom they liked immediately. She was small and attractive with a clear young-sounding voice which belied her age which the twins guessed was probably around 75.

'Your name seems to ring a bell,' said Jo. 'Did you know our Aunt perhaps?'

'Indeed I did, and we were great friends. I have been meaning to call around and introduce myself but never quite made it, obviously. I met Bea at this group in fact, and we hit it off instantly. She used to make these meetings most entertaining. She wouldn't suffer fools, and there were, as there are now, a great many. She spoke as she found and she worked tirelessly to keep tourism round here humming along. Of course it wasn't such a well-known holiday destination then and we had no computers or social networking to help us keep this town on the map.'

'We've learned a lot this evening,' said Jo, 'but mostly about the people here.'

'Yes, it's quite fascinating how they can get so worked up over something as simple as the colour of flowers in someone else's window boxes. They still waste so much time moaning and arguing about trivial things instead of getting on with the business of the meeting. Strangely the most outspoken ones aren't even directly involved in the tourist industry at all. I think they come along just to nose about and complain. They should be trying to get onto the town council if that's their forte instead of terrorizing us here.'

'We've been trying to work out who some of the people are Megan and you're just the person to fill us in.'

'Why don't we sit down at that table in the corner,' Megan suggested, 'then you can point the individuals out to me.' They made their way through the chatting groups and rearranged some chairs so that they had a better view of what was going on.

'Fire away then…' encouraged Megan.

'Well there's that rather scruffy chap over there that everyone seems to give a wide berth to, he hardly seems the sort of person that you'd want to stay with in a B&B.'

'Aaah…that is the infamous Bert Lloyd from Porthcwm Farm further down the track past your cottage,' said Megan.

As they drank the disgusting cool coffee Megan told them about the Lloyds. Apparently the farm wasn't actually called Porthcwm Farm but the Lloyds thought it would make it sound more important if it had the same name as the town. 'He's tried everything to do with tourism, mostly rip-offs, and usually illegal in some way, flouted the planning laws and ignored anything official that was required of him,' she said.

The tales about them seemed endless. Megan admitted that it had been a bit quiet on the Lloyd front for a while, but she was certain that some new swindle would come to light soon. 'There's usually some scam bubbling away under the surface with that man.'

'So this is the neighbour from hell that Rosa got all worked up about the other day when we asked her about Porthcwm Farm,' said Cass.

'Well maybe it *wouldn't* be a good idea to ask her anything about them again. She doesn't make much sense when she gets overexcited as you may have discovered, so you don't want to be responsible for one of her outbursts.'

'The next person we wanted to find out about is Fishnchips and why she's here.' asked Cass. Jo quickly dug her in the ribs and said, 'Sorry, she might be a friend of yours…I mean Trisha Phipps.'

Megan laughed, 'What an excellent name, I wish I'd thought of that myself. And no, she's not a friend of mine, though she's attempted to be. She was trying to buy my house or rather that odious Arthur Trinder was, on her behalf. She wants to get into running a B&B but it's probably too small really for what she wants. It didn't stop them harassing me regularly though and it became thoroughly tiresome. I supposed they just hoped they'd wear me down. They stopped for a while but now they're starting again and I'm simply not going to sell to her, or anyone else for that matter. And anyway I rather like running a small B&B and having one or two guests in every so often. I just have people back who've been before. It entertains me and I know them all very well now, so I shall keep going for a little while longer.'

'I think you had a break from Arthur and Fishnchips for a while because she was after the Lodge. They'd hatched a plot to get their hands on it for a low price, then we decided to stay here and do accommodation ourselves,' said Jo. 'They hadn't considered that we might not sell up so they were furious. Arthur's already called in to try again and to 'offer his services' but we sent him packing with a flea in his ear.'

'I'm glad to hear it. Now, if you two need any help to do with B&B things then do let me know and if you feel like extending an invitation for me to see the changes that you have made at the Lodge I'm sure I'd accept. I went there once to a coffee morning when it was rented out to old Mr and Mrs Perkins. They'd been living there for years and years and loved it, but they never found out who the owner was. Apparently all the transactions were carried out by old Sylvester. I never imagined for one moment that Bea owned it and she certainly never even referred to it in any way. I only found out about it by the local tom-tom when you two discovered you had inherited it along with the cottage. Then of course it was all round the neighbourhood. She was a secretive old bird, your Aunt Bea!'

'And who is that lady over there talking to Fishnchips now?'

'Linda Trinder, the loathsome Arthur's wife. Everyone feels sorry for her. She is incredibly long-suffering and patient with him. I can't understand why - he's a womaniser, a liar and an altogether thorough cheat. She manages being his very better half extremely well and never complains. Linda is the headmistress of Porthcwm School, wouldn't say boo to a goose, let alone Arthur, but seems to cope very well with all the children and their overindulgent parents.

I'd call her ploddy, boring and quiet, but good natured and kind too. Good heavens, I am sounding like a sour old biddy. Probably because I am.

'As you get older and slow down you begin to see things happening around you and stories unwinding in front of you,' she continued, 'and no-one seems to notice that you're noticing - it's wonderfully liberating really. Bea was like that most of her life though, she knew how to watch people and observe what was going on around her. She had many secrets herself of course.

'Well, I'm beginning to ramble on too much. It has been lovely to meet you, Jo and Cass, particularly after hearing so much about you from Bea. She told me you would come back and sort things out, and here you are. Don't forget to ask me around to look at your Lodge sometime though. I could come the day after tomorrow at three as it happens. I'll tell you a bit more about the Lloyds then.'

'Perfect,' said Jo. 'See you then.' Megan smiled, and the twins watched her potter off across the room and go home.

'What an interesting evening. I've quite enjoyed it in a rather peculiar sort of way,' said Cass.

'Yes,' agreed Jo. 'We've discovered loads of info, but absolutely nothing about tourism.'

Chapter 8

Two days later, Jo and Cass decided to walk down the track towards Rosa and Benito's farm and try to have a good look at the Lloyds farm next door. They wanted to do it whilst Rosa was occupied in the Lodge and before Megan called round that afternoon.

They turned out of their gate to the right. 'You know Cass; the view from the cottage bedrooms must have been almost as splendid as the one from the Lodge before the trees grew so tall. It seems odd that AB let the view disappear, it must've been glorious. The walls and hedges would've been enough to keep the tourists and the world out, if that's what she wanted.'

'It's as if she didn't want to see anything else outside her garden,' said Cass. 'Maybe we could open the view up again, if we're allowed to remove one or two trees? I'll try and find out from the Council.'

The Lodge and Seaview Cottage were the first buildings at the town end of the track but the tarmac continued on past them for about a hundred yards before turning unceremoniously into a basic rough roadway with grass down the middle. It was sunny and warm and the view in front of them was spectacular. Although it was a public footpath they knew that this track didn't lead right to the coast so they had never explored it as children for that reason. They came to a point in the track where it divided into two. The footpath sign pointing in the direction of Rosa and Benito's obviously took walkers through their farmyard and out across some fields returning to the road somewhere above the town. The other went right-handed towards the Lloyds farm. There was no footpath sign on that one but they decided to follow it anyway.

The track that ran between high gorse topped banks became increasingly more pot holed as they neared the farmyard. They could see that the farmhouse was a low building, local in its design and obviously from the random-school-of-architecture. Long overdue for some TLC, it commanded a near perfect location, with the all-important view of the sea, but was several fields back from the actual coast itself. There were two large and ugly modern barns next to the house. They looked more secure and well maintained than the farmhouse itself with their large shiny well-fitting padlocked doors.

It was obvious that they never got rid of a single piece of machinery. Or anything else for that matter. The rusty heaps of unusable old iron stood next to gleaming specimens of the most modern machinery. It was a strange sight. 'It's an odd place,' said Jo. 'Could be charming in the right hands but everything looks cheap and tacky and unloved, doesn't it?'

At that moment a door at the side of the house opened and the man they had seen at the tourism meeting came into view.

'Shit,' said Cass. 'Just wave at him and smile.'

'Good morning Mr. Lloyd,' they yelled in unison as he walked towards them, rolling a cigarette between nicotine stained fingers.

'Oh it's you two, I saw you last night.' He had lit his cigarette and was dragging laboriously on it. It seemed to stay stuck to his bottom lip as if by magic and danced around as he spoke. 'Come for a nose around have you? Just like your aunt used to. I told her to bugger off too. This is private property. The footpath goes up past the Eyeties place along there.' He waved his hand to the right.

'Well, it was nice to meet you too, Mr Lloyd, c'mon Cass, let's go back to the Lodge.'

'Yes, you push off back to your little castle, and don't come snooping round here again.'

The twins turned and walked away up the lane. 'What a nasty piece of work he is,' declared Jo.

Before long, they were back home and as busy as ever. Jo was in the kitchen engrossed in her new interest of bread making and attempting to improve on the previous result. Phil Fixit was completing the decoration of the last bedroom. They would soon have another two ensuite bedrooms ready for guests. It was all falling into place. Cass and Rosa were upstairs hanging some curtains on the landing. Cass paused mid curtain hanging and looked outside. The large windows offered one of her favourite views from the house. Rosa had shown her that if she stood tight into the right hand side of the bay window she could just see the Bellini's pretty farmhouse and the sea beyond it. It looked idyllic, a beautiful corner of peace and quiet during the manic holiday season. Even the Lloyd's farm looked attractive at a distance, but sadly, since they'd had the pleasure of meeting Mr Lloyd face to face earlier and seeing the tip that was his property they could understand Rosa's problems.

On the dot of three Megan turned up at the Lodge. Although it had been quite a while since he had seen her, Nosey recognised her and immediately rushed around dementedly. Cass eventually managed to calm him down and he pottered off to lie quietly in his bed.

'I swear he will just keel over with excitement one day, he's far too boisterous at times for his age.' Jo said apologetically.

'Well, I say jolly good for him,' said Megan. 'I'm beginning to think we should all grow old rather more disgracefully than we do. Your aunt just about got it right. Those of us who knew her well always recognised what she was up to, but those that didn't remained completely in the dark and thought she just had a screw loose.'

'It's so strange that no-one knew that this house belonged to her,' said Jo. 'You would have thought that she would have told someone, wouldn't you. What a remarkable secret to keep all those years.'

'Old Mr Sylvester knew of course because of all the legal details, we could ask him I guess,' said Cass. 'I don't know why we didn't try and find out when we had the opportunity.'

'We were too excited Cass. I expect he was quite relieved we didn't.'

'My dears, I should imagine it will go to the grave with him, but maybe we *shall* find out eventually, and then all will fall into place. Now perhaps you would be kind enough to show me around her secret house. I can hardly wait.'

They walked round the rooms slowly, at Megan's pace, stopping to chat to Rosa and Phil Fixit and about beds and cupboards and lots of B&B type things. She asked what they were going to put in the bedrooms or bathrooms as little extras for the guests and made one or two helpful suggestions about how to make their Welsh Breakfast a meal to remember.

'A marvellous breakfast with locally sourced ingredients is so important. We have such a wealth of local food producers here, and you can collect laver from the beach yourselves if you can find time.'

'Laver?' asked Cass.

'Yes, my dear... lovely seaweed that the Welsh particularly enjoy at breakfast, I'll show you how to cook it sometime. Anyway I'm sure you'll find what you want without resorting to those appalling supermarkets. I shall give you a list of where I buy things and at least that will start you off until you discover your own special places.'

'Thanks Megan, that'll be a great help, now come and have some tea in the cottage and tell us more about the Lloyds.'

They walked across to the cottage with Nosey dancing around them again in the vain hope he was off for a walk. They didn't want Rosa to hear them talking about her neighbour and join in the discussion in her heated Italian way and it meant that Megan had an opportunity to see the cottage again. They sat in the little kitchen, and after Nosey had sloped off into the sitting room to curl up on his armchair they tucked in to their tea and some of Jo's home-made biscuits.

'We met Bert Lloyd this morning Megan, he was every bit as unpleasant as you had promised us. We thought we'd go on a bit of a snoop after what you had said about him. We just wanted to sneak a look at his farm and he caught us out.'

'What bad timing,' laughed Megan. 'Well at least now you've seen him in action.'

Megan needed no excuse to embark once more on the catalogue of Lloyd scams. She explained how almost everybody was under the misconception that they had lived at the farm since time began. It was a tale started by Grandfather Lloyd himself in the nineteen thirties and had since become local myth. Their chief aim it appeared was to get as many visitors through their gates under whatever pretext they could so that they could relieve them of their money.

'I expect you noticed the farm implements lying around?' she said. 'You could hardly miss them really, all rusty and ugly? Well, a few years ago Bert decided that they'd make some money by turning themselves into a Farm Museum. He hauled out their shabby, wrecked machinery from its graveyard resting place in amongst the nettles and brambles and gave it a cursory clean. Then he sprayed it with unsuitable paint and installed it in the Museum - one of those two big modern barns that you'll have seen at the side of the house. They put some signs displaying dubious information and distinctly strange spelling above the ploughs and harrows and so on, and Bert got his wife to sell refreshments from their 'Café' - a shack type structure which they had built inside the barn.

'Of course, Bert being Bert, the cakes were from the Cash and Carry and the sandwiches from some other place but they were advertised as home-made. Carys Lloyd is a nice enough woman really but incredibly simple and totally under Bert's thumb. She just had the food spread out on a few trays in her Café-shack, most unhygienic. One shudders to even imagine.

'At the top of this lane right up here outside this cottage and *actually* leaning on your Aunt's wall Bert put an impressively huge and scruffy old metal tractor door with the glass still intact, hand painted with the words "Welcome to the Farm Museum" and an arrow pointing down the track. Try as she may Bea couldn't get Bert to take it away. It irritated her enormously because he was so rude and unresponsive about any of her concerns. Of course the local council were slow off the mark to even come and see what was going on, so in the end she dealt with it in her own inimitable way. She crept out one night and painted 'Closed' in huge white letters across it.

'Bert went mad about it and came round to see her, banging on the cottage door, all shouting and red in the face. Anyway the council suddenly woke up and took notice of your aunt and other locals and the complaints from visitors who said they had been fleeced. But the scam had been up and running for most of the holiday season, and no further action, or even investigation, was undertaken. Bea said it was because one of the councillors was related to Bert's wife and another 'owed him a favour' whatever that meant. So the museum was closed down, but not before the Lloyds had made a quite a killing on entry charges. Most people said they were lucky not to have made a killing in another way what with the dangerous old implements and dangerous old sandwiches.'

'Bert told us we were as bad as our aunt. I expect he thought we were following in her footsteps, no wonder he was so nasty,' said Cass.

'Ah! But the Museum swindle wasn't the end of Bert's creative rip-offs,' continued Megan, now in full anti-Lloyd flow. 'They'd barely had that closed down before they started another. Not daunted by the lack of support for their creative projects they then partitioned off the same barn into units which they advertised as 'craft workshops'. This time the council got to hear of it early on through Bea's vigilance and they moved in quickly and shut them down before it actually got underway, and before there was any public access. Bert never forgave your aunt for preventing them from getting that idea up and running.

'They've also had an illegal camp site and had a quick stab at being a caravan park, and I heard talk of them wanting to do bunkhouse accommodation in the old barn around the back of the house, so I suppose that's still to come.'

'Goodness, they're busy,' declared Cass. 'We'll have to keep our eye on them like AB did.'

'I'm convinced they're up to something again, said Megan. 'They've tried most things but I'm certain that they'll come up with more swindles before I pop my clogs. Still, as I said the other day, when you get older you have time to notice what's going on. It's really *most* rewarding. Well, I must be off and let you two get on with all your good work.' She heaved herself to her feet and stretched, 'I get quite stiff now from sitting too long.'

They twins began to walk up the path with Megan. Nosey rushed around excitedly in the vain hope that they might be about to play a game. Then in an instant it happened... Megan stepped back from admiring some flowers in the long border beside the path just as Nosey shot around behind her. She didn't see him and tripped, her body pirouetting rather elegantly before landing in the very clump of blooms she had just been looking at. The twins rushed forward apologising for their crazy dog and helped Megan slowly to her feet. Jo grabbed one of the wooden garden seats nearby and they lowered Megan into it slowly. She was rubbing her left knee but saying that it was totally her fault for leaning too far forward to look at plants, 'I just can't resist beautiful plants and I can actually remember your aunt planting those. My goodness, how it's grown into a wonderful display, now. Well - until I squashed it flat.'

The twins could see that she was obviously in some pain and was trying to cover it by continuing with her jolly chatter. Then Rosa and Phil Fixit appeared from next door and ran across the lawn to them. 'Rosa happened to see Megan fall,' said Phil as he reached them.

Nosey was now sitting calmly at Megan's feet and she was stroking his head. Her other hand remained on her knee. 'I think you two should take Megan along to Dr Rees and have her knee checked over,' Phil suggested. 'You can't be too careful. I'll bring Mildred around,' he said, running off into the cottage to fetch the keys.

Between the four of them they managed to prise Megan carefully from her seat and half lift, half push her into front passenger seat of the Morris. She was still protesting loudly that she was fine and that it was all her fault, but agreed that it would be a good idea to have her knee checked out so offered no opposition to their plan to take her to Dr Rees' surgery.

Cass took the keys from Phil and got into the driver's seat once Jo had clambered into the back of the car. She drove very slowly through the town to the modern surgery which had been built about five years ago. The twins had been to the surgery only once before, just to get their names put on Dr Rees' list when they had decided to stay in Porthcwm. It was a far cry from the original old surgery that they remembered visiting as children. AB had taken them there when Jo had cut her knee open quite badly during one of their surveillance operations involving Bev & Rev and the rocks on the beach.

Cass parked as close to the door as possible and ran inside to see if she could find anyone. It wasn't surgery time but the lady behind the reception desk said she would see if the doctor was available to see Megan quickly and disappeared off down the corridor. 'That's fine,' she said to Megan when she reappeared. 'Dr Rees can see you now. Let me go and fetch a wheelchair to get you into the surgery.'

Megan, Jo and Cass all sat in a row on the waiting room chairs. The twins were apprehensive about any lasting damage that Nosey might have caused to their new friend, but the patient herself seemed quite relaxed and was deeply engrossed in a magazine she had managed to reach on the little table beside her.

A few moments later the receptionist returned with a wheelchair which they succeeded to get Megan into despite her protestations and they pushed her along the corridor until they reached a door that said 'Dr Rees' painted on a wooden sign. The girls manoeuvred Megan through the doorway and into the consultation room. They swung the chair around beside the doctor's desk and sat in two chairs behind her.

Dr Rees turned around from washing his hands and looked across at the twins. 'Good morning,' he said brusquely. Jo and Cass both caught their breath and then looked at each other and back at the doctor. There in front of them was 'Little Simple Simon', one of their main victims from all that time ago.

He caught their reaction but made no comment. He turned instead to his patient who was smiling at him and encouraged her to give an account of how her accident had happened. Then he began to examine her knee, gently pressing, prodding and moving his hand around it to see where any tenderness lay. Megan flinched rather half-heartedly a couple of times but didn't seem to be in too much pain.

'I think, Mrs Hughes that you've been extremely fortunate not to have damaged yourself more than your twisted knee. I'm going to give you some pain killers and when you get home I want you to rest with your leg up. I don't want you speeding round the place like

I know you normally do and I realise it's all part of your plan to grow old outrageously, but I insist that you take things very gently for the next few days.' He turned to his computer and ran off a prescription which he passed to Jo, 'I assume you will be able to get Mrs Hughes back to her home and settle her in without any *other* mishaps?'

Jo and Cass felt, and probably looked, as uncomfortable as he was obviously intending, but they nodded and wheeled Megan out of the surgery at the speed of light. They squeezed her back into the car as gently and as rapidly as possible and after calling at the chemists to collect the pain killers they set off following Megan's directions to get to her house.

'So what did you think of our lovely Dr Rees then?' Megan enquired. She was greeted initially by silence, and then Jo muttered something from behind the steering wheel.

'I didn't catch what you said, my dear?'

'I said *okay*, he was okay.'

'He's *very* popular here,' said Megan. 'The women love going to see him rather than old Dr Richards. It's a local joke that most of them don't have anything wrong with them at all when they make an appointment at the surgery. Handsome, wouldn't you say?'

There was silence again from the twins, a rare occurrence that Megan picked up on. 'He's obviously made an impression on you both. Now we just need to go down this next turn to the left and I'm that white house up the drive there. Yes, that's the one. It's so kind of you to take such care of me. I've taken up so much of your time today when you could have been doing more productive things.'

The twins helped Megan out of the car and supported her as she managed to limp to the front door. She handed Jo her key and steadied herself against the door frame whilst the door was unlocked. 'The sitting room is the second door on the left. I think I shall make that my sickbay headquarters. If you wouldn't mind just passing that old picnic rug from the chair out in the hall, I think I'll just lie on the settee with that over me and read my new library book.'

Jo had found the kitchen and made a cup of tea which she put on a low table next to Megan. 'If there isn't anything else that we can do Megan, we'll be off now. Just ring us if you need us to nip round and help.'

'Thank you so much, both of you, for being so understanding after I made such a fool of myself and a mess of your lovely plant. The pain does seem to be easing a little now, but if I need to visit that lovely Dr Rees again perhaps you might be able to take me?'

'We'll be happy to help in any way we can, but would probably get Phil Fixit to take you in his van as there is so much more space for you to get in and out,' said Jo quickly, knowing that it would be the last place that either of them would want to go.

They said their goodbyes and went out to the car. 'That was quick thinking on your part, Jo. At least it would mean we don't have to see Simple Simon again. Bloody hell, I nearly died when he turned round and gave us that kind of withering look that said *not so simple now then am I?*' said Cass. 'I couldn't wait to get out of there.'

'God yes,' replied Jo. 'but Megan was right, he's turned out to be okay looking though, hasn't he?'

Chapter 9

The following morning Jo gave Megan a call to see how she was feeling but there was no reply. 'No answer,' she shouted to Cass. 'I'll try again later. Maybe she's resting or didn't want to rush to the phone. I've left a message anyway so that she can always ring back. On second thoughts, what d'you think if I take Mildred when I go shopping and call in afterwards just to check on her?'

'Good idea,' replied Cass, coming down the cottage stairs. 'I still feel sort of responsible for her fall because of Nosey, but I shan't come with you though if that's okay? I need to catch up on some of the time we lost yesterday. I'll be over in the Lodge for about an hour if you need to call me, then I think as we're nearly ready to have guests I may spend some time revising those press releases I started last month and get them ready to send off.

'It'll be nice and tranquil with Rosa having her day off and Phil doing quiet jobs. Can you take Nosey with you, and let him have a quick run somewhere then at least he'll think he's had a bit of a walk and save us some more time later?'

Jo grabbed her basket and went around the back of the cottage to fetch the car. She allowed Nosey to jump into the passenger seat and once he had settled down they set off out of the drive and left up the hill. She parked in the car park near the centre of the town and dashed across into the Post Office to collect the local newspaper and buy a few flowers from their dubious selection to take to Megan's. Blodwyn Harris was on duty and making it her business to gossip to each customer in turn.

Jo attached herself to the queue and watched other new customers join the line behind her as they came in. Eventually they trailed back almost to the door. She was beginning to wonder whether there would be a queue right down the road soon if Blodwyn didn't stop trying to bleed information from the customer who'd got stuck at the counter for ages. As she was contemplating this possibility she noticed through the window a little blue car pull up and park on the double yellow lines on the other side of the street and couldn't believe her eyes when she saw Megan climb out of the driver's side and go up the steps to Mr Sylvester's office. She most certainly wasn't hobbling anymore and appeared to be showing no ill effects after her accident the previous day. On one hand she was relieved and on the other she thought it rather odd.

Jo was wishing that Blodwyn would get on and serve all her customers, so she could attempt to catch Megan before she drove off again. With relief she saw the queue eventually begin to move forward and at last she reached the counter and the prying postmistress. She prayed that she wasn't going to get stuck there for too long but Blodwyn seemed anxious to get to grips with the lady standing behind Jo so she was dealt with at amazing speed. She picked up her change then headed past the tailback of customers and out of the Post Office door but was disappointed to see that Megan's car was no longer there. When she walked back to the car park and dumped the newspaper and flowers in Mildred she was surprised to see the blue car parked near the public toilet block. She must be in the loo she thought and walked down towards the unattractive rectangular building which housed the Public Conveniences that had been officially given the Best Loos in the County Award. She stood in between a smart black 4x4 and an old white van and waited for Megan to emerge. Suddenly from behind her a voice said 'Up to the old tricks then?'

She swung around and there was Simon. She didn't know what to say. So she said nothing. That would be the best bet she thought.

'Old habits die hard don't they?' he snapped. 'Who are you following these days?'

'Noooo-one at all.' Jo retorted.

'Then why are you standing in the car park next to my vehicle and hovering round near the toilets?'

'Oh, it's yours is it? Well I really don't see that I need to tell you why I'm here. There's nothing *wrong* with me standing here.' Jo paused and then thought perhaps she should tell him about seeing Megan. 'But if you must know, I was waiting to catch Megan because she seemed...'

78

At this point Megan appeared and began to walk towards her car. She didn't appear to be in any discomfort at all, but the moment she caught sight of Jo and Simon she began to hobble. She waved and gave them a big smile.

'So how is my patient today?' enquired Simon who didn't seem to have noticed her walking perfectly soundly a few seconds earlier. 'You are naughty being out so soon after your fall. I suppose you drove yourself into town too?'

'There was a little business that I *had* to attend to and I couldn't do it on the phone! It's lovely to see you both. I know you will think I'm very strange but I do rather enjoy making use of the loos here. I've no idea who is responsible, but someone goes to a great deal of trouble to make them look as pleasant as possible. Do you know,' she turned to Simon 'there are even little vases of wild flowers in each cubicle. Now if you'll excuse me I must get back to my settee and rug.'

'I was just coming up to see you,' said Jo, 'then I caught sight of you from the Post Office.'

'Oh, I'm fine my dear, much better for seeing you both, but thank you for thinking of me. Maybe we could have tea together in the next couple of days at my house? I'll give you and Cass a ring. Bye now.' Off she limped to her car.

'Well there you are. You can see that I was telling the truth,' said Jo, relieved that she hadn't managed to tell Simon about Megan. In reality she was probably worrying about nothing. 'I've got to get back now.'

Jo and Simon waved at Megan as she drove past them grinning. 'Me too,' he said, jumping into his car and driving out of the carpark quickly.

Jo climbed into the Morris and sat for a moment, thinking. She knew that she hadn't been mistaken about Megan's leg looking perfectly fine. It was very curious.

'What are the flowers for?' asked Cass, as Jo brought her shopping into the cottage kitchen.

'I thought I'd take some to Megan and risked buying them in the Post Office as they looked almost fresh for once, and then whilst I was waiting to be served by that prying Post Mistress I saw Megan outside.' Jo went on to tell Cass all about Megan and bumping into Simon and how he'd spoken to her. 'I was so taken aback that I forgot to get the flowers out of the boot for her. I'll put them in a jug on the windowsill for us to enjoy instead.'

'So are you *certain* that Megan looked fine when she got out of her car? And then was hobbling when she saw you and Simon?'

'Yes absolutely certain, but I just don't understand why. She said we must go to tea next week so maybe we'll find out then.'

'Very odd. Well, I must get on and finish tweaking this press release whilst it's still fresh in my mind and then we'll have some lunch.'

When Cass had finished her work on the computer and Jo had been round to the Lodge to check on Phil they settled down to a quick lunch of their favourite homemade butternut squash soup.

'I forgot to give Nosey his walk after seeing Simon and Megan,' apologised Jo. 'How about us getting some air and having a short walk after we've finished eating?'

Having cleared the table they clipped Nosey's lead onto his collar and walked down the road to the coast path. Jo and Cass had decided to revisit a little cove above which they had once set up a secret camp. It was in a sandy hollow which they were convinced no-one else had found. Gradually they were rediscovering old haunts of theirs along the coast, and this was one they had been looking forward to seeing again.

Nosey was so excited as they started along the path above the cliffs. The twins always marvelled at how he seemed to respect the fact that there was a deathly drop down to the sea and managed to steer clear of the cliff top despite his manic charging about.

They hadn't gone far when they met Douglas Sidebotham and paused to talk to him for a while before moving on.

'Isn't it odd how some men seem unable to relax? Douglas never looks or dresses any differently,' said Cass. 'He always seems to be in his tweed jacket and brogues even to go walking on a warm day.'

'I suppose that is how he feels most comfortable. I couldn't imagine him in a brightly coloured anorak.'

Then they passed one or two walking couples dressed much more appropriately and exchanged the time of day with them before rounding the corner close to where they had camped all those years ago above the cove.

'It's quite exciting really, coming back here, it even smells the same. All the times we hid here when we didn't want to be found and AB never discovered us. Look, there's the little dip in the ground that we found so inviting originally and made us want to explore.'

They walked around the corner and through a narrow gap in the gorse. They were confronted by a picnic area with two wooden tables that looked as if they had been there for years. The timber had weathered to a silvery grey and they were both leaning away from the sea slightly, like so many of the surrounding windswept trees. A woman was sitting at one of the tables deep in thought, her eyes fixed on the distant horizon.

'Oh it's all changed. It's not a secret anymore,' said Cass disappointedly. The woman glanced up as if she has been woken suddenly out of a dream. 'I'm sorry,' offered Cass. 'We've disturbed your peace.'

'Oh that's all right. I ought to be going anyway.'

'We saw you at the tourism meeting recently. Megan Hughes was telling us who everybody was. You're Mrs Trinder, Arthur's wife.'

'Yes, but do call me Linda. I know who you are of course, I think the whole of Porthcwm does by now! Lots of people seem to have long memories when it suits them!'

'We used to call this our secret place when we came to stay with Aunt Bea,' said Jo. 'We thought no-one else knew about it and

AB never came and found us here. It was like being in a different world and there were no tables here then, just a hollow in the ground that you couldn't see from the path.'

'It is lovely isn't it? Megan told me once that it had been one of your Aunt's favourite places to come and read quietly, because it's so sheltered.'

'So she knew about it all the time. How funny, she must have been pleased that we loved the same place that she did, and didn't want to spoil our secret hideaway.'

'I must be off now,' said Linda. 'I sneak off here occasionally too, on the weekend or in school holidays. But I hadn't discovered it until the council put these two tables here, so I never had it as a secret hideaway like you did. I'm very envious.'

Linda stood up and gathered her bag and sweater. 'How is Megan by the way? I heard she'd taken a tumble.'

'I think she's on the mend now, thanks. We're going to call her again this evening and check up to see how she's feeling. She seems so independent though really.'

'I think she has become that way. I'm glad you're looking after her. It's been lovely meeting you properly, I'm sure we'll see each other soon. Bye.' Linda climbed out of the dip and disappeared from view.

'Fancy AB knowing all the time about this spot and never letting on. This place is full of secrets and we thought ours were the only ones.'

'We ought to get going too,' agreed Cass. 'Come on Nosey, your fun's over for today.'

When they got back Jo went off to the kitchen to continue with her bread making. She had left some dough to rise whilst they were out. It was a new recipe, which looked promising. All her other attempts were still pretty unsuccessful.

Suddenly there was a crashing sound from the direction of the front door, followed by the familiar squeaking of the kitchen door but at an unusually fast speed. It closed with a bang. Jo spun round mid-knead, her rhythm thrown completely. Rosa was standing behind her, bright red in the face, out of breath and barely able to speak. 'It'sa my Queen she has sheet something special. Come look, you must see it.' She could hardly get the words out. Not easily understood at the best of times, she surpassed herself by being hysterical and jumping up and down maniacally.

'Isa Alizabeth!' she shrieked.

'God, has she died?' asked Jo.

'No, but is God who has spoken to her. He has made her sheet in the shape of the Blessed Virgin Mary and Child! Is a miracle, no?'

Cass suddenly rushed into the room. 'What on earth is going on? I could hear a terrific din from the top of the stairs.'

'For goodness sake get her to sit down somewhere,' said Jo. 'I can't understand her either. She's so excited, it's impossible to follow what she is talking about! Look, drink this.' She handed Rosa a glass of water. 'Okay Rosa, now tell us s-l-o-w-l-y what on earth is going on.'

'Is a miracle!' confirmed Rosa.

'Yes, yes, we've got that bit, but you need to tell us *exactly* what is it that's a miracle?'

Phil Fixit ran into the kitchen just as Rosa was about to open her mouth to continue. 'I can hear you all yelling from upstairs, what's wrong?'

'Rosa seems to have experienced a miracle and was about to explain. Okay Rosa, now everyone in the house is here, please try to explain exactly what has happened.'

'Well, is obvious, no?' said Rosa, suddenly bursting into frenzied life once again. 'I go to check my cows at early morning and there it is in the grass. A miracle sent by God.'

'WHAT?' the other three screamed.

'My favourite and very special cow called Alizabeth after your proud Queen of Britain has done a sheet in the shape of the Blessed Virgin Mary and Child. Is God showing us a miracle, no?'

Everyone started talking at once in a muddle of words that included God, Queen Elizabeth, miracle and cowpat. Phil Fixit raised his arms in the air and told everyone to shut up. He turned to the twins and said calmly, 'Would you mind if I said something?'

'Not at all, please, go for it; if you can make sense of this then we can all get on,' said Jo gratefully.

'Thanks. Well, I think that one of Rosa's cows has had a shit in the shape of the Virgin Mary and Jesus, and she is assuming it's a miracle.'

Everyone looked at Rosa.

She beamed proudly from ear to ear. 'Yes, is true. You look now with me?' she demanded and leapt to her feet. 'I have my truck.'

'But Rosa we must get on here, couldn't we come later?' asked Jo as Rosa headed for the door.

'I don't think we have any option,' said Cass 'We'll never get those rooms finished or anything else done today if we don't go with her now.'

'Yes then, let's go. Will you come too please Phil? We can all do with your calming influence. Perhaps we could both come with you and then Rosa won't have the opportunity to get us all killed on the way - her driving is rubbish at the best of times. You grab the camera, Cass as I'm sure we'll need it. We'll follow you Rosa, although are you going to be okay to drive?' but Rosa was already on the way to her truck.

They followed Rosa who sped right-handed out of the gate and down the lane. The bumpy bit probably hadn't had any work done on it for years, but Rosa still drove with the same speed and determination and was oblivious to the change in road surface. She was obviously desperate to return to the scene of her miracle. Phil Fixit's van bumped at a more sedate pace along the track that headed towards two farms, the Lloyd's and the Bellini's.

Just after Rosa passed the turn in the track to the Lloyd's farm and before she reached her own, she stopped her truck suddenly, jumped out and opened a gate, waving impatiently for them to follow her into the field. They drew up next to her truck, got out and walked after her towards a circle of electric fence which they assumed was there to protect the miracle dollop.

'Don't touch the fence,' warned Rosa 'you will be shocked.'

'No kidding, I'm shocked enough as it is to be standing in the middle of a field about to look at a pile of poo, when I should be at home baking bread.' declared Jo.

'See, look, is how I described, no? There Baby Jesus and there Madonna? You see of course?'

'Well Rosa, with some imagination it *is* possible to see what you mean,' said Jo, 'Can you take some pics Cass?'

Cass nodded, and walked around the electrified area snapping from all angles.

'You send us some through please to put on our improved website? Is miracle and a sign you 'ave to agree, no?'

'What do you think it's a sign *for*, Rosa?' enquired Cass, as she clicked away.

'Is from God telling us what to do, no? I tell you tomorrow when we have decided exactly how we use his advice.'

'Well, it's certainly interesting,' said Phil, still slightly in awe of the whole situation. 'What are you going to do with it now?'

'I move my cows already to make safe the holy picture. But I have much work to do now, to care for it and preserve it, so I tell you tomorrow.' Rosa continued to look rapturously at the glistening cowpat.

'I guess there's no point in trying to get her to come back in to work is there?' Cass whispered to Jo. 'She wouldn't concentrate anyway.'

'We'll manage. It shouldn't be too busy today.' agreed Jo.

'We're off now, Rosa; we'll see you tomorrow then?' Cass called across to her, but she was deep in thought and didn't hear.

Phil, Jo and Cass hopped into the van and drove back to the Lodge.

'I don't think she'll be back to work for days,' Jo said 'she's totally off her mad Italian trolley.'

Chapter 10

Early next morning, Cass telephoned Rosa to check what her plans were. The twins had decided that they didn't want to just wait around to see whether she turned up or not. It was just as well, because she was, as they had guessed, totally wrapped up in the miracle dollop. She still sounded very excited about it but had regained sufficient composure to have returned to moderately understandable English. She told Cass that they had been busy discussing all sorts of ideas on what they could 'do' with it and invited the twins down to the farm to tell them the result of their deliberations.

As it sounded likely that Rosa *was* going to be busy doing something else – though they couldn't imagine what on earth anyone could do with a pile of poo – Jo and Cass did need to find out exactly what was going on. They arranged to meet her in the gateway of the field they had parked in the previous day. Rosa was already there when they arrived, holding a bunch of keys. The gate was now secured with two large padlocked chains, one on either end so that no one could gain entry by lifting it off its hinges.

'Gosh Rosa, you have become very security conscious all of a sudden.' teased Jo.

'Yes, well I do not think you understand how important this is to us. Someone might sabotage the miracle sheet.'

'So what have you done to the holy pile since yesterday then?' asked Cass.

'I show you,' Rosa said, unlocking the gate and padlocking it again after they had gone through.

The twins couldn't believe their eyes. 'Have you both been working all night Rosa?' asked Cass, 'it's amazing. What a change.'

'Talking and planning and working. There is much to do, no? Just earlier we finish the shrine. It will shelter and protect it good.' Rosa said, waving her arms in the direction of a not inconsiderably sized building that looked remarkably like a Swiss chalet.

A path had been mowed down towards the shrine and the area originally surrounded by the electric fence the previous day was now much larger.

There, a tired and dusty-looking Benito was busying himself loading wood and equipment onto the trailer hitched up behind his antiquated tractor. 'Good morning,' he called, and they waved back to him. There were some floodlights, now switched off, standing to the side of the shrine, and an old generator already loaded onto the trailer. He must have been working outside throughout the night.

The area around the miracle cowpat had been mowed too, and according to Rosa the blades of grass closest to the pile of poo had been trimmed carefully by herself using a pair of scissors so as 'not to interfere with the view of the Holy Picture'.

'See,' Rosa said, pointing in the direction of her miracle. 'Is getting clearer as it dries a little, no?'

'Yes,' they agreed, watching the flies gather in some sort of holy reverence on the pile of shit.

'So how is your Queen Elizabeth today then?' asked Cass. 'Does she realise what she's done d'you think?'

'She is very happy and so is Eddie.'

'Eddie?' the twins asked in unison.

'The Duke of Edinburgh, of course. He is smiling too. I have put them together in a field over there and he is looking after her.'

'Won't the miracle dollop eventually dry out and curl up?' asked Jo.

'It will of course, but for now I spray with a mist of water to stop it drying too much, and the shrine will keep the worst rain and sun off it for the time being. If you look now when you get home you will see we have a new website. It is telling how we look after this wonderful miracle and what we are going to do with it.'

'Rosa, you do move fast,' exclaimed Cass. 'I can't believe you have done so much.'

'We talk to Benito's cousin in Italy. He has been up all night doing things with our website and we have a new name for the business because it is a miracle we want to share with everybody.'

'But what are you actually going to 'do' with it?' asked Cass.

'You look at the website,' Rosa repeated. 'You will see how God gives us a new direction. I hope to be very busy.'

Cass and Jo still hadn't actually discovered whether Rosa was going to continue to work for them, but if they had understood her final comment before they left the field to walk back up the lane, she was expecting to be totally engrossed with her new project.

'Give it a day,' Jo said optimistically, 'and then see whether she makes any decisions herself. She'll probably have recovered by tomorrow and we'll all be back to normal, whatever normal is. If not, then we'll have to look for a new cleaner. It'll be a real pain to start looking around for someone else who suits us as well as Rosa does.'

Cass went off to their makeshift office and logged on to find Rosa's new website.

'My goodness Jo, come and look at this,' she shouted through to her.

The best photographs that Cass had taken and sent through to Rosa the previous evening were up there for everyone to see and the changes to the Bellini's original ice cream site left the twins almost speechless. Jo and Cass looked in amazement at the professional website and shrieked with laughter when they saw the new name of her business; 'Holy Cow Ice Cream' and the strap line *'Heaven Sent!'*

'Bloody brilliant actually,' said Cass. 'I really like it, you know. They've certainly got a useful cousin as far as websites are concerned. It's so brilliant. Perhaps we could get them to upgrade ours sometime?'

Rosa's employment decision was taken out of their hands when she rang up the next morning and announced very excitedly that she was going to really push her ice cream now it had a new name and God was on board with the whole enterprise.

'It sounds as if the Almighty has been made a Director of Holy Cow,' said Jo.

'There we are then,' Cass said. 'No surprises I guess, but we must look around for someone else to come and give us a hand as soon as possible.'

'Maybe if we put an ad in the post office we might get a quick response. Everyone in that huge queue that Blodwyn causes has plenty of time to read all the ads stuck up there.'

'Ok, we'll do it now,' suggested Cass. 'I'm on my way up there anyway. You put something on a card while I write the shopping list.

Cass looked at what Jo had written as she walked up the hill. The card asked for an adaptable, friendly person with initiative to help in a fledgling Bed & Breakfast business and offered a little above the minimum wage. They knew they would have to keep their fingers crossed. Finding a person who would fit in with them perfectly for what would possibly be considered a pittance was a tall order.

Cass could see Blodwyn Harris pottering around the shop part of the Post Office when she arrived. Blodwyn perked up a little when she saw who had come in, possibly in the hope of finding out some tiny, useful piece of gossip. Noticing that she was the only customer in the place Cass felt slightly disconcerted and wondered whether she would be trapped and interrogated until someone else came through the door. Blodwyn looked at the card Cass passed to her in her usual inquisitive manner before handing over two mean little bits of Blu-Tack for Cass to stick the ad in her chosen position on the door. She squeezed it in at eye level so that it could be seen from outside the shop when the door was closed as well, and put it between a grubby card advertising a child's buggy and one advertising a position as farm hand at less than the minimum wage. The name on both was Lloyd. In fact, when she looked closely,

Cass realised that over half the adverts stuck up in the post office had the same telephone number and the name Lloyd on them.

'Gosh the Lloyds have masses of ads here,' she said to Blodwyn

'They always have something for sale. Am I right to believe that their neighbour, Rosa is no longer working for you now then?' she asked, looking at the card on the door. That was sudden wasn't it? But she does tend to chatter on a fair bit and get diverted.'

'Oh we haven't parted with her out of choice. She just wants to concentrate on her ice cream business. What do I owe you?'

'Nothing thank you, it's a free service.' replied Blodwyn.

Cass suddenly caught sight of creepy Arthur Trinder striding up the street heading for the post office with a handful of envelopes and decided to make a speedy exit so that she didn't have to speak to him.

'I'm sure you'll find someone soon...' Blodwyn called after her as she escaped onto the street and turned left to avoid coming face to face with Arthur.

She ran one or two little errands at the greengrocers and the chemists before heading off back home. The Lodge seemed unusually quiet and even Nosey failed to greet her straightaway. 'Jo?' she called into the house.

'Cooey...' came the reply from the kitchen. When did her sister ever use the word 'cooey', she thought, as she carried her shopping through.

She was surprised to see Jo putting the kettle on the hob and the woman who wore the shortest skirt in Porthcwm sitting at the kitchen table.

'Cass, this is Gloria Prothero, she has called around in response to our advert. Gloria this is my sister, Cass.'

They said hello to each other and as Cass walked past Jo to set down her shopping basket she gave her twin a look that could only be interpreted as *what the hell...?*

Jo just raised her eyebrows and smiled sweetly.

Gloria actually seemed very pleasant and somewhat overqualified for the job as general dogsbody at the Lodge but seemed to grasp what they wanted her to do quickly and without question. In no time at all it was all sorted and Gloria agreed to start the next morning.

'Did that really happen just now?' asked Cass after Gloria had gone. 'I'd only just put the ad up in the post office, belted down to the grocers and chemists and come straight back and there you are, interviewing someone already.'

'I wasn't really interviewing her. She just rang the doorbell and said she'd seen the advert and could I explain what was needed. She seems okay though, and worth a trial. She obviously needs to earn something but didn't even query the amount we're paying, which rather surprised me.'

'There's not much about in the way of jobs. I only noticed one other advert from the Lloyds who are looking for a farm hand and they are offering even less pay than we are.'

'Well I guess she wouldn't have gone for that,' said Jo 'She'll probably be fine.'

'I still can't understand how she got down here before me. Someone must've told her about the job.' puzzled Cass.

'Phil Fixit's eyes are going to pop out of his head if she has to bend over anywhere near him, and how is she going to clean properly?' asked Cass. 'She'll surely topple over as she's so well endowed and those heels look precarious. I so hope we haven't made a mistake in taking her on so readily. She's the complete opposite to Rosa. Perhaps we should have waited to see if anyone else applied.'

'It's too late now. She'll dress completely differently for work anyway so let's just see how it goes.'

When Cass came downstairs on Gloria's first day Jo had already started to show her where everything was in the kitchen and scullery. Jo caught the meaning of her twin's raised eyebrow message and looked at Gloria's outfit. Her working gear was just the same as her everyday attire. Cass stared at the functionless overload of zips stitched all over her black microscopic mini. Her heels had straps that wound their way up around her calves and her very skimpy lime green top accentuated the unnaturally shaped results of much plastic surgery.

They had both been entirely wrong in imagining their new cleaner would dress more appropriately than the vision they were looking at now.

'Hi Cass,' said Gloria. 'I brought this with me for you to see.' and she passed the local paper to her. There was Rosa, Queen Elizabeth and the predictable poo picture which the local weekly had come out with. The reporter had gone to town on the miracle bit and Gloria said the paper was flying off the shelves in the post office.

'It's such an exciting thing to have happening here,' she said, 'and everyone knows Rosa. There's never usually anything really interesting to read in the local rag, although that's not a surprise in a dreary place like this.'

They left Gloria to her own devices when Phil Fixit arrived. As they helped him move one of the old carpets out into his van Cass told him about Gloria answering their advert in record time. 'I expect Blodwyn Harris gave her a call about it. She knows that Gloria was looking for some part time work as she's saving up for some more surgery. Or maybe Rosa could have let her know but I'm guessing she wouldn't have even thought about that, considering the state of excitement she's in.'

'*More* surgery for Gloria?' asked Cass. 'How much has she had done already? Apart from a boob job, that is?'

'Well it's true you can't miss her copious assets but no-one is quite certain now how much of the original Gloria is still there. She's rather well known in Porthcwm for her, what shall I say...generosity? It's said that that's how she accumulates money to put towards the next plastic surgery fix. Local rumour, which you are welcome to disregard, has it that your Arthur Trinder is currently showing great interest in her.'

'He's not *our* Arthur Trinder.' shuddered Jo.

A few hours later after the twins had ignored the telephone's persistent ringing on several occasions Jo found an answerphone message that had been left by Rosa.

'Cass, Cass, Rosa's left a message to say that she's got two reporters coming down to do an interview, one for a national newspaper and one for the BBC. They each wanted somewhere to stay so she said we would be able to put them up. She said it'll give us some publicity too. It sounds as if they'll arrive early this evening. They're obviously not together so that'll mean a double room each.'

'That's it? The mad miracle woman that she is, isn't giving us much choice is she? Thank goodness we happen to have two rooms that are reasonably prepared. Let's go and check them now and then we'll be halfway ready if either of them rolls up early.'

They quickly finished the rooms, Jo putting posies of garden flowers on the windowsills, and fluffy towels and locally made soaps in the bathrooms, and Cass flying round the sitting room with dusters and the vacuum cleaner in case the visitors wanted to use it.

They were just about to grab a quick glass of wine when the doorbell rang and a pretty blonde woman poked her head around the front door. Jo ran through from the kitchen and welcomed their first guest who was crouching down, engrossed in making a fuss of Nosey. Looking up she introduced herself as Marsha from the BBC.

Jo gathered up Marsha's bags and carried them upstairs to her room explaining on the way that they were only just starting up so weren't too organised yet and that Rosa hadn't given them much warning. Fortunately she wasn't bothered at all. 'It looks charming, please don't worry. You should see some of the places we get to stay. My cameraman is turning up a little later tomorrow morning but I decided to get a bit of background info and have a sneaky few hours at the seaside on my own before he arrives.'

A little later, after Marsha had gone down to look at the beach, and the twins had actually managed to snatch a few moments to pour themselves a glass of wine, Sandy, the journalist turned up. She was very talkative and loved the rooms and the Lodge itself. She sat at the big scrubbed pine table in the kitchen drinking wine and chatting to the twins as if they were old friends. She had such a great natural way with her that they talked about everything. She would certainly be the right person to get the most out of Rosa's story the next day.

The piece that Marsha did on Rosa and Benito and their Holy Cow Ice Cream was short and appropriately sweet. It appeared the following evening at the end of the news as one of those feel-good, whacky features aired to cheer everyone up after all the grim or stuffy news items. The twins sat with a drink and some cheese biscuits that Cass had succeeded in baking in between phone enquiries, and watched with anticipation. There were some lovely shots of Queen Elizabeth with a view of the sea as a backdrop and a close-up of the miracle pile of poo that really did seem to show the outline of the Virgin Mary and Baby Jesus. Marsha stood outside Benito's shrine surrounded by pots of geraniums and lavender and interviewed Rosa who recounted in an uncharacteristically calm manner the tale of her amazing miracle discovery.

'I guess we have to be pretty grateful to Rosa and Queen Elizabeth for our premature launch into the world of the B&B,' said Cass.

They couldn't believe their luck. Wonderfully mad Rosa was sharing her good fortune and they loved her for it. They clinked their glasses together in her honour and settled down replay the recording they had just made of Marsha's feature.

Chapter 11

The following Saturday everyone in Porthcwm was taken by surprise with the newspaper article. When Jo raced up into the town as early as she thought decent to buy the weekend papers, she was confronted by a picture in the shop window of Benito holding Queen Elizabeth on one side of the cowpat shrine, and Rosa eating a huge ice cream on the other. The newsagent had pulled out a copy of the colour supplement and displayed it, propped up against two packets of dog biscuits. It was at just the right angle for passers-by to be able to read the headline "A Story that's *not* Bull****"

Jo bought two copies and sped back down to the cottage. 'Cass, Cass…' she yelled as she burst through the door narrowly avoiding Nosey who thought as usual it was a signal for the beginning of a game. When Cass came rushing through to see what the commotion was about they retreated into the kitchen each taking a copy of the colour supplement and excitedly read random bits out loud.

Sandy had recounted Rosa's story just as she would have told it herself. It was so intriguing. It was the tale of hard-working Rosa and Benito, their devotion to the Catholic Church and how they had started making ice cream in Porthcwm because they saw an opening locally for it.

Inside there were more photos of Benito and Rosa and Queen Elizabeth. There were some very clear close-up pictures of the miracle poo and a drawing of it just in case there were readers who couldn't see the outline of the Mother and Child clearly.

But most thrilling of all for the twins, was paragraph at the bottom of the page describing where Sandy had been staying and a small but beautiful photograph of the Lodge.

Almost an hour later the phone rang, 'Hello - the Lodge…' answered Jo and gestured to Cass to get her some paper and a pen. She continued to talk on the phone as she scribbled information down on the back of the Church Newsletter, the only writing surface available that Cass could lay her hands on.

'Who was that?' asked Cass, when Jo had hung up.

'Well it's a booking from a lady in Cheshire who wants to come and stay in three weeks' time. She saw the article and thought the Lodge looks wonderful so has booked the 'best' double room.'

'We'd better decide which one's the best room.' laughed Cass 'I'll go and find the diary; it should really be kept near the phone. We're so disorganised about being ready for taking bookings.'

Whilst she was out of the room the phone rang again. By the time Cass had returned to the kitchen Jo had details from another couple who wanted to book in. It rang again and again. Each time they answered it there was someone who had seen the article and wanted to come and stay in Porthcwm.

By the end of the day, the girls were almost going mad with the sound of the phone. But they were excited with the impact that one small mention of the house and accompanying picture could make. Most of the callers were intrigued by the miracle story and asked all sorts of questions about it. They wanted to find out whether the twins knew Rosa well, and would they be able to meet her, but the most popular question of all was whether they would have the opportunity to try the ice cream.

'Seems crazy but maybe we should actually get some in after all and offer it to them for breakfast,' suggested Jo.

Sunday came, along with another flurry of phone calls from prospective guests, and one from Rosa saying she, like them, had been frantically busy on the phone as well. She'd also had a lot of interest from newspapers and a couple of enquiries from Italy. She had set up interviews for the Monday with three more journalists, one of whom wanted to stay at the Lodge in a single room. She had also been taking orders for the ice cream which meant she was busy producing as much as she could. Rosa had made Benito camp next to the shrine the last two nights as there had already been a stream of people wanting to see it and they had discovered curious people taking photos in the fields on several occasions She explained how they were going to charge people to view it and how all the money taken would go to a Catholic Charity.

Holy Cow Ice Cream was getting continuous publicity. There was barely a newspaper that hadn't mentioned it by now and magazines were also jumping on the bandwagon each with their own individual take on the situation.

Rosa actually managed to find the time in her new busier schedule to call in as she passed the gate a couple of weeks later. She was in a whirl as usual and barely had time to stop so there was no opportunity for the girls to find out how everything was going apart from one or two cursory questions. Rosa had made copies of all the articles about her and the miracle poo for Jo and Cass's scrapbook and thrust a folder containing them and a new ice cream sample into their hands. 'Soon we have more time to speak, no?' she said and was gone.

They opened the folder and began going through all the photocopies. It was extraordinary how every magazine and paper seemed to want to be in on the act.

The *County Magazine* had a big spread about it. Rarely did they get such an odd but intriguing story as this to fill their glossy pages. They were very supportive of local good luck stories and they obviously recognised that this one had the possibility of running and running for quite some time.

The *Farmers Weekly* commented on the state of the economy generally for farmers in the area and how diversification was always going to be the way forward now and wasn't this a shining example of how to make the most of an opportunity.

Waitrose magazine did a piece on how to use Holy Cow Ice Cream in some recipes. Bizarrely the nearest Waitrose store was at least fifty miles away. The local *Tourist Association Newsletter* had obviously come out early so that the committee appeared to be in the know from the very start. They saw the chance to tell their members how they were involved with the tourism opportunities for the area right from the beginning. Of course this was far from the truth as they very rarely did anything for Porthcwm except hold the sort of meeting Jo and Cass had witnessed when everybody bitched about everyone else's tourism businesses.

Practical Woodworker had a description and plan for a DIY shrine in case any readers wanted to build a shrine to the memory of their cat or dog in their garden and *Craft Weekly* had a pattern of how to replicate the miracle poo in 3D collage using old newspapers and flour and water paste. The overriding colour scheme was brown and green apart from a little bluebottle-blue on the three starring flies. Uncannily realistic...

Even *Horse and Hound* did a surprising piece on Holy Cow bearing in mind there was no direct link that anyone could see. They talked about how an occurrence like this on a larger scale could cause the exclusion of hunting access across farmland, but not a soul had a clue what they were talking about really as the local hunt never ventured near the countryside around Porthcwm.

The Catholic Church Times was alarmed about the implications of 'this kind of pseudo-miracle'. They were concerned that if people saw these fairly rare happenings as money making, there may be a deluge of 'minor miracles' or even 'fake miracles' appearing all over Great Britain. Sites of miracles could become places of pilgrimage or places of worship, and the Church was very worried about the possible mass hysteria which could take over if a miracle was considered genuine.

They offered the example of Vincenzo Di Costanzo who went on trial in northern Italy in 2008 for faking blood on a statue of the Virgin Mary after his own DNA was matched to the blood. Authorities of the Catholic Church it was said, were always very careful in their approach and treatment of this sort of religious event, and generally set very high barriers for their acceptance. But nowhere, they said, had they come across any instances of a miracle in the form of cow dung.

'I'm going to start a scrap book with all sorts of local goings-on for the guests to look through,' said Jo with delight.

'I shouldn't think there'll be anything more of interest in this dozy town after this, so it'll probably be a pretty slim offering.'

The next day Jo was feeling organised and efficient and therefore rather complacent. She had set out early on her errands, had already left Mildred in the car park and was making her way into the main street. Her first port of call was the Farmers Market to buy some sausages and wonderful home cured bacon in readiness for breakfast the following day. She decided to pick up some eggs and some local cheese with nettles in it too and so far she was making good time. But she was anxious not to get waylaid. There was usually someone who asked her to give them the next piece of news on the Holy Cow Ice Cream, or talk about her aunt, or recall memories of them staying years ago, but today she managed to avoid everybody. She only had to go to the greengrocers on the way back and then at least her shopping chores were completed.

She had even put some bread to rise and prepared some fruit compote before she'd gone up into Porthcwm. The guests who had been staying the previous night had wanted a really early start so she was able to get up into the town earlier than normal. It was sunny and warm and she was feeling pleased that she was getting on without any hindrances.

'Bugger it, I thought it was too good to be true,' she muttered under her breath as she caught sight of Arthur Trinder crossing the road to head her off. She looked away and pretended that she hadn't seen him, but it didn't work.

'My dear lady...' he never could tell which twin was which, so resorted to his usual vague greeting. Jo tried to ignore him but he kept going, 'How *are* you this beautiful Porthcwm day?'

'Fine thanks.' answered Jo curtly, giving in but trying to keep walking and not get into conversation with him. Somehow he managed to swing round in front of her on the pavement and stop her in her tracks.

'And how *is* the business going? I expect you have had lots of bookings since Rosa received all that publicity? Very strange goings-on if you ask me, and quite ludicrous. As if a miracle would take place in Porthcwm. All fabricated by that unhinged Italian woman no doubt; well it certainly worked for her, very clever piece of hype. Yes, yes and good for you too, of course, and propitious under the circumstances.'

'What circumstances would they be then, Mr Trinder?'

'Well, you've been extremely fortunate to get a good start in your business without much promotion of your own. You've done very nicely out of the miracle ... much better than anyone else.'

'Rosa is a friend and we help each other', Jo snapped back at him 'and we've passed on any bookings we can't take to other B&B owners like Megan Hughes. I must get on with my shopping now if you'll excuse me?' And off she went at the rate of knots, leaving Arthur Trinder staring after her and cursing the name of Megan Hughes who was *still* coping with taking a few guests instead of being shut up in an old people's home.

Jo sped down to the greengrocers annoyed that Arthur had succeeded in stopping her to air his jealous moans. How on earth could *he* know how many visitors they'd had and what they were up to at the Lodge? With her chores all complete the only other thing she wanted to do was check up on Megan and give her some of the eggs she had bought, before getting back to the Lodge.

The local bus pulled away from the side of the kerb just as she rounded the corner of the road leading back up to the car park. She was still niggled about the Arthur incident and without looking where she was going she cannoned into someone coming in the opposite direction.

'I'm so sorry,' she said. 'I was miles away.' She looked up into the face of a very attractive man.

He looked shaken, almost as if he was confronted with something impossible to contemplate.

Then his demeanour changed. His look of surprise changed into a look of delight. He smiled broadly at her, 'My goodness, it *is* you, how wonderful, I cannot believe it...that you are here. I never imagined I would ever see you again. You did not tell me where you had gone but here you are...I did not think of finding you when I come to England...' he said with a beautiful accent, obviously excited at seeing Jo. But she hadn't a clue what he was going on about.

He was carrying a suitcase and had a rucksack on his back so had obviously just got off the bus.

'Look I'm sorry, it's not England. You're in Wales and I don't know you. I apologise for walking into you...'

'Come on, that doesn't matter now, I might not have seen you otherwise. Please don't pretend you don't know me. Nothing matters anymore...' He put his suitcase down on the pavement and stepped towards her with his arms outstretched. 'It's such a coincidence though is it not? Who would have thought we would meet each other here?' he asked, moving up very close to her.

Jo had had enough. What had started out to be a day of organised calm was turning into a nightmare. First Arthur Trinder and now this handsome weirdo coming on to her in the middle of the street, so she dodged around him quickly and ran up the short incline towards Mildred in the car park. She unlocked the door, shoved her shopping unceremoniously across onto the passenger seat and leapt inside as fast as possible. She could see the stranger following her into the car park. She prayed that the engine would start straight away for once and wished there was someone else around that she could call out to if she needed help, but there was no-one about. Typical. And today she hadn't brought Nosey with her either, not that he would be much of a deterrent to someone intent on doing her some harm, but he might at least have just been his normal awkward self and got in the way.

Astonishingly, the engine burst into life instantly and she shot forward, swerving to avoid the man who was almost at her door. She left the car park through the entry gate and prayed that she hadn't been seen doing that illegal manoeuvre. She shivered when she glanced up at her mirror and saw the stranger still staring after her with his arms outstretched. She took a few slow, deep breaths from the safety of the Morris and turned left at the next junction towards Megan's road.

'This is a lovely surprise my dear, how kind of you to call in,' said Megan, obviously glad of a visitor. She took the eggs from Jo who was hoping that they were all intact after being flung across Mildred's back seat, and put them on her kitchen table. 'Now sit down and I'll make you a cup of tea. You look as if you could do with it. What have you been up to?'

'I've just had a ridiculous morning. It started out alright but then I got waylaid by that dreadful creepy Arthur who never knows which of us is which...'

'Ah, my dear, I expect you do nothing to help him out of his dilemma of course, what fun. It must be quite like the old days and the trick playing? I'm sorry, do go on...'

'Well he was just sniffing around to see how much business we were getting off the back of Rosa's miracle. I'm sure he and Fishnchips would still like to buy the Lodge...or your house in fact. They just seem hell-bent on getting a suitable place for her to have as a guest house.'

'Yes, he's a thorough bad lot, he's been on the phone to me this morning would you believe?'

'Then that must be since I saw him. I'm afraid I did mention that we'd sent you some of our B&B surplus. I made it sound like we'd passed on loads of people to you instead of just that really nice sounding couple from Surrey. I'm so sorry. It must have fired up his envious and greedy streak again.'

'Not to worry. Then what?' enquired Megan putting a cup of tea in front of Jo. 'It can't just be Trinder.'

'You're so clever at seeing through me Megan,' said Jo. 'I wasn't going to say anything but just as I was making my rapid escape from Arthur I bumped, actually physically bumped, into this odd guy who pretended he knew me. It was a brilliant chat-up line really but it didn't work with me. He wouldn't leave it alone and even followed me up into the car park. I couldn't get away fast enough. The brilliant old Morris started first time for once and I just drove off quickly.'

'What did he look like, this chap?'

'Actually, quite normal. Good looking too. A slight accent of some sort, Italian perhaps. He was probably harmless but it didn't half unnerve me though. Anyway, I've recovered now so I'd better get back and catch up with some stuff at home. Cass and I want to try and get down to the beach this afternoon if we have time. Thanks very much for the cuppa. See you soon.'

Megan tried to pay for the eggs but with no luck, so she stood at the door to wave goodbye to Jo, wondering about these two lovely young women and what the future held for them. They would be fine, she was absolutely certain, but probably needed a little more help...

Chapter 12

Back at the cottage Jo unpacked her shopping. Cass was putting the bread in the oven. 'I hope you don't mind but I thought I might as well get on with your baking, I didn't realise you'd be so long.'

'No, that's fine. I wasn't going to be long at all, though I knew that Megan would probably want me to have a coffee and a quick chat as usual. Actually, I was grateful for a cuppa by the time I got to her place though; I'd had a shit morning. I knew as soon as I saw Awful Arthur intent on talking to me it was going to go pear-shaped.'

'What did he want?'

'Just a snoop into the business here really. He talked about our guest numbers and how we had obviously been fortunate enough to have piggybacked on Rosa's publicity, so why he bothered to ask how the business was going in the first place, God only knows. Then I knocked headlong into this guy who'd just got off the bus with a case and rucksack and he chatted me up in a way-too-familiar manner. He even followed me when I ran up into the car park. I felt quite panicky so I drove Mildred out through the 'No Exit'. It just unnerved me.'

Cass started to laugh, 'I'm sorry, it just sounds so funny Jo, you must admit. Perhaps he genuinely fancied you. Anyway, he's probably here on holiday so you'll only have to hide for a couple of weeks.'

'Oh ha-ha, Cass, very amusing. But it was weird though, as he did seem to think we'd met somewhere,' said Jo, wandering out of the kitchen and into the sitting room. 'He was rather handsome actually and had a slight Italian accent.' she added over her shoulder.

Cass froze... Ricco? It couldn't possibly be Ricco...could it? How would he know where to find her? Jo still didn't know any details about her boyfriend in Paris so wouldn't have made up the Italian accent just to wind her up. She told herself to get a grip, why on earth would it be him? There are masses of foreigners around. Well… maybe not actually *masses*.

'You okay Cass?' asked Jo coming back into the room and noticing her sister's anxiety.

Cass was saved from replying by the phone ringing.

'Good morning,' said the recognisable creepy voice. 'Or is it good afternoon?'

Jo, who had answered the phone, mouthed A-R-T-H-U-R to Cass. 'I hope my call finds both you ladies well?'

'Same as when I saw you earlier.' Jo replied curtly.

'I have a nephew who needs somewhere to stay for tonight. We'll actually be away otherwise he would have come to us. His employers said they'd put him up for a night whilst he is working in Porthcwm. Then he'll come and stay a few nights with us. Linda will be glad of the company as I shall be …well…um, busy. He's a nice enough young man, a bit on the shy side, can't decide what to do with his life really, you know the sort, twenty seven years old and still drifting about unchallenged, trying to *find* himself.' He gave a scathing laugh, 'Anyway I thought you might have a room that he could have for tonight. He asked me to organise it as I know everywhere so well and typically he does seem to have left it until the last moment. I thought he'd enjoy meeting you and he wouldn't have to go far to do the piece.'

'Piece of what?' asked Jo.

'Oh - he's been working for a newspaper for a while now and they've asked him to come down and find an unusual angle on that ridiculous miracle thing and write a piece about it.'

'Surely it's been done to death?' said Jo. What could he find that's new?' Jo certainly didn't want to have any relative of Arthur's staying at the Lodge.

'Well, I'm inclined to agree,' said Arthur. But do you have a room for him, just a single, one night? Short notice, as I said, but I'm afraid that's newspapers for you.'

After his interrogation of her that morning Jo wondered whether he was going to use his nephew to find out how the Lodge was really going. But money was money she suddenly decided. It was unlikely anyone else was going to book that room at that late stage and the other rooms were filled. What the hell. 'Yes, we do as it happens,' she picked up a pen, 'what's his name?'

'Rudolph, Rudolph Timms, he says he'll arrive just before 5 o'clock.'

Rudolph Timms arrived in Porthcwm at about half past three, rather earlier than he had anticipated. Parking up his little car he found his way to Arthur's estate agency to say hello to his uncle and reintroduce himself. They had last met years ago at the funeral of some aged relative. Rudolf had thought his mother's brother was extremely weird and had noticed how much time he spent ogling some young woman who sat down next to him in the crematorium. His mother, it appeared, hadn't got much time for her brother either. 'Poor Linda, I don't know how she puts up with him.' was the only comment he seemed to remember her making. Still, he thought it was good of his Uncle to put him up for a few days whilst he contemplated his future at the newspaper office.

Rhonwen looked up as he came through the door. 'Good afternoon,' she said. 'Can I help you?'

Rudi ran his hand nervously through his hair. 'Yes. Hello, my name's Rudolph, is Arthur Trinder in please?'

'I'm afraid not, he's away at the moment, and won't be in until late tomorrow.'

'Oh, I thought I might catch him before he went off,' Rudi said. 'It doesn't matter though really.'

Rhonwen's eyes suddenly lit up and she gave him a warm smile. 'You're his nephew aren't you? He told me you were coming to Porthcwm for a few days. I just wasn't expecting you 'til later. She looked at the man in front of her. He was taller than she was and not so round in shape, smartly dressed and pleasant looking. Not at all as his uncle had described him to her earlier. Handsomely shy, she thought, and a bit anxious in his mannerisms.

'Would you like a coffee Rudolph, or perhaps tea? I was just about to boil the kettle as it's very quiet at the moment.'

'Tea would be great, and please call me Rudi.'

'I've got some biscuits buried somewhere,' said Rhonwen, 'your uncle is always trying to encourage me to diet, so I tend to hide them away.'

'You look perfectly okay as you are,' Rudolph told her, and quite shocked himself with his uncharacteristically brave remark.

Rhonwen blushed at his compliment and rootled around in the bottom drawer of her desk to retrieve her hidden biscuits. Rudolph relaxed, pulled up a spare chair next to her desk and helped himself to her Hobnobs. 'Great,' he said. 'My favourite.'

'Would you like to know some good places to eat out?' Jo asked Rudolph after they had showed him to his room.at the Lodge.

He looked a little embarrassed. 'I'm already organised thank you very much.' he replied, running his hand through his hair, 'I'm meeting a… a friend…um… for a drink a little later.'

Jo thought he seemed a very pleasant but shy young man and not at all like his Uncle, thank heavens. 'Come and have a glass of wine with us while we wait for the other guests to arrive, Rudolph and tell us what you are up to with the miracle ice cream piece. At least you only have to go out of the drive and turn right down the track to get there tomorrow.'

'Thank you, that would be lovely,' he said, as they led him through to the kitchen.

'Please do call me Rudi… I so hate Rudolph. I expect my uncle told you I work for a newspaper. I hate it to be honest and it's obvious that they are just getting me out of the office to do something that doesn't need doing. I'm assuming they hope that I'll screw it up so much that they can fire me. Of course, there's nothing original I *can* do with the story, so I've just accepted that in a few days I shall be out of a job.'

'Perhaps your Uncle could find you something if that does happen? And it's coming up to the summer season down here so there're lots of part-time holiday jobs that could tide you over for a while,' suggested Cass.

'Mm, I wouldn't want to work for Uncle Arthur. Do you know him well?'

Each twin looked sheepishly at the other. It was obvious to Rudolph that their discomfort was due to a dislike for Arthur Trinder.

'That's a great idea about holiday jobs though,' he added quickly. 'I'll bear it in mind.'

In the morning Rudi set off on foot in the direction of Rosa's farm. It was very early, and no one else was up. He had enjoyed a really good evening with Rhonwen but after he arrived back at the Lodge he spent a lot of the night awake, racking his brains to come up with something new on the Holy Cow story. Eventually he decided that a dawn start would help him get the feeling of the area as part of the background to his interpretation. God only knows if that was actually going be of any help to him because pretty much everything that could be written about the miracle had already been written. He was resigned to losing his job at the newspaper. Maybe that wouldn't be such a bad thing after all, he thought

It was a peculiarly misty morning. The sun was definitely up there somewhere but was not at all prepared to burn down on Porthcwm yet. The eerie light, fine dampness and salty perfume from the sea made him smile with pleasure as he set off down the track. It was how he had imagined really good smuggling weather would have been when he used to immerse himself in his favourite books as a child. He had never experienced such a spellbinding atmosphere before.

He gave a long sad sigh which disappeared into the mist and told himself not to get diverted; this may be the last chance to get a good story into the paper before he was fired.

Somehow he'd never quite cut it as a reporter and although he'd been given several opportunities of getting a great story it had never had quite worked out for him yet. He just couldn't keep his mind on the job in hand. Whatever it was he was supposed to be doing, everything else around him seemed much more interesting. Perhaps he *should* write children's books as his editor had told him fiercely on several occasions…it was apparently all he was good for with the attention span of a five-year old.

The hedges either side of the track were mostly of gorse, its yellow flowers shining out brightly from the hedge. Untamed and untrimmed the sharp branches encroached into his space as he wandered slowly down the unkempt roadway. He paused to look at the spiders' webs clinging haphazardly to the bluey-green gorse spikes, glistening with tiny droplets of condensed mist. He racked his brains about how he could even start the article off.

Concentrate, Rudi scolded himself. *Concentrate…*

He rummaged in his bag and took out his camera to record the hazy scene around him. He thought the eerie light would allow him some original ghostly images of the subject of his undoubtedly doomed article. He snapped a few general shots. Well at least no-one had done that angle before, though he wondered how he would write about it. How could he incorporate them in the body of his article?

I could make the introduction quite atmospheric, he thought, but then what? Perhaps when I reach the shrine I can keep taking photos until the mist lifts to reveal the miracle shit. Oh… I don't know, he thought, this is hopeless… *I'm hopeless.* He returned his camera to his bag and pulled out a tape recorder instead to make some verbal notes. They always laughed at him in the office for using this little machine…Rudi and his recorder…and admittedly he had yet to find it indispensable, but at least he could capture the beauty of the morning in words before it became erased from his memory.

'The morning sun is still in hiding,' he started, 'as I make my way down the track towards the farm. The air is damp and the hedges hang with cobwebs…and the usual wonderful view towards the sea is veiled in mist…' This really wasn't going well. 'Gentle wafts of coconut scent drift across the lane from the gorse bushes…' Oh bugger it, he thought, I'll take pics, it's more fun… perhaps I should become a photographer when they fire me.

Out came the camera again and he wandered on towards Rosa's farm.

Reaching a fork in the track he caught sight of some buildings to his right. He could just make out the outline of a low building, the farm he guessed, because of the bulky looking barns standing near it. He leant on a damp broken gate. It gave him a good view across an overgrown meadow to the group of buildings. Assuming that this was the Holy Cow farm he steadied himself on the damp gate and took a few shots through the mist towards them. Just as he was about to stop he saw through his lens a figure, encircled by a bright shining light.

He clicked away non-stop, then grabbed his recorder again and spoke into it. 'A shaft of light is still piercing through the grey mist hanging over the Holy Cow Farm. It is unusually bright and I'm wondering whether I might be witness to another miracle. I am looking at a figure with rays of light emanating …nice word Rudi… yes, emanating from it. A holy spectre, perhaps adding to the first miracle of the holy shit…mustn't call it that, think of another name, ummm?… ok , pile, yes Holy Pile, much better. Maybe this is an area of strange goings-on, miracles, ghostly sightings, witchcraft, crop circles…no, no maybe forget that one, can't see any crops. But what the hell.

'This light is amazingly bright, it's…oh, the figure's moving and the rays of light are growing around him, I'm guessing it's a him. Another figure has appeared and is waving his arms above his head. I'm hearing sounds of shouting, that's odd…there's more arm waving and …oh the light's gone. I can still see it in front of my eyes though.' He blinked hard a few times to try and rid himself of the bright outline lodged before his eyes. Get a grip Rudi, there are no such things as miracles or ghosts or spectres of intense light…' He switched off his recorder.

Once the lights in his eyes had properly disappeared he began to walk along the farm track towards the buildings. Arriving at what he assumed was the main yard gate he started to push it open, but a bell attached to it with a length of the farmers' best friend – orange bailer twine – rang loudly. It alerted a dog in the small shed nearby which launched into the loudest barking he had ever heard, which in turn alerted a large hairy man who ran out of the house carrying what appeared to be a long stick. Screaming and yelling at the top of his voice and using words that Rudi had never even heard of, but thought possibly might be Welsh obscenities, the figure hurtled towards him.

It wasn't quite the welcome that Rudi had imagined. He rather thought that a jolly farmer's wife would come out and greet him warmly, offer to make him a coffee and invite him to sample her ice cream. After that she would recount the tale of the marvellous miracle and show him the most famous poo in the British Isles, possibly the whole world.

Only as the man approached more closely through the mist did Rudi recognize that the large stick was in fact a shotgun. Not hanging about to ask about the miracle or tasting the ice cream he headed back as fast as he could. As he ran along the lane he could hear the bell on the gate ringing loudly, the dog's mad barking and the man's footsteps echoing behind him. Reaching the fork in the road once again he turned right hoping that his pursuer would assume his prey had turned back left up the track towards the town. He ran on as fast as he could until he reached another farm gate where he stopped to try and catch his breath. His heart was pounding and he was shaking so much he didn't hear someone approaching him.

'Hello?' said a voice. 'Are you Rudolph?'

Rudi jerked his head up. There was the round figure of his imaginary farmer's wife, smiling at him.

'Yes.' He squeaked.

'I'm Rosa, come inside and have some coffee. You are earlier than I thought, so I am not quite organised. You try some ice cream too while we wait for this mist to rise, no?'

A few calm minutes later Rudi was sitting at her kitchen table drinking coffee and eating the most delicious toffee ice cream.

'This won't be good for your fitness regime, no?' Rosa declared.

114

'I'm sorry?' Rudi queried.

'Well you ran here, you are a keep-fit person, no?'

Rudi laughed 'On the contrary, I'm very unfit and not good at sport… or anything else as it happens. I was in fact running like a maniac from a great angry man at the farm up the lane. I thought it was your farm. He chased after me as if he was going to kill me. He had a gun.'

'Well you are safe now,' she smiled at him warmly.

'Yes I am and quite pleased with myself, too,' Rudi said. 'I think I've had a rather good idea.'

Chapter 13

'Hi Rudi, how did it go?' asked Rhonwen when he appeared in the shop the next day. 'You're looking pleased with yourself.'

'I think I am, you know,' he answered with a big smile. 'But I'm sorry again about not being able to meet up last night; I was obliged to do the nephew bit at Uncle Arthur's. Difficult, because he wasn't there most of the time as he said he had to go out on business, but it was nice spending some time with Aunt Linda.'

'Mm?' said Rhonwen. 'He really does think we can't all see through him doesn't he? Oh I'm sorry, Rudi that was out of turn.'

'That's okay,' he replied. 'I feel sorry for Linda. She does just seem to accept it. Maybe she's made of stronger stuff than we think.'

'And what about the piece you wrote?'

'Like I said on the phone yesterday afternoon, when I'd gone back to the Lodge Jo and Cass were really kind to me and suggested I might like to spend the rest of the day writing in their sitting room. Much better to get it done before going to the Trinders and I didn't want to jinx it by telling you or anyone what I was going to write. I told it exactly as it happened, sent it through to the paper and I had an email last night telling me they were going to print it. No quibbling and no nasty remarks, the Editor just said 'You nailed this one Rudi, good lad...' I can't believe it. You are the first person I've told.'

'I'll take that as a compliment then. Have a biscuit to celebrate? Your uncle is out again until later this afternoon so let's have coffee too and you can tell me *all* about it now.'

Rudi recounted his tale of the mist, shining lights, the large man with the gun and the whole miracle ice cream bit and was even brave enough to let Rhonwen listen to his recordings and see the photographs.

'That's very strange you know,' said Rhonwen. 'The Lloyds *are* a very odd family, but I don't get the significance of the light and the fact that he felt he had to chase you with a gun.'

'I was so relieved to get to the right place and Rosa was lovely,' Rudi said. 'Just like I imagined she'd be, and so welcoming.'

'Listen Rudi,' Rhonwen sounded serious 'don't you think you should tell the police about what happened with the gun and all that?'

'I guess perhaps I should.'

'Did your editor say anything about it?' asked Rhonwen.

'Only that I *should* tell the police, but asked me to wait until after the paper came out, just in case they banned the story. This might be the only thing I ever get published so I agreed of course. I'll tell the police later today. D'you think we can sneak off and have some lunch as Uncle Arthur's away?'

'That's a great idea. I've never dared do that before,' Rhonwen admitted. She put a 'Back later' notice in the window and locked up after them.

When they had finished lunch Rudi called in at the Lodge with Rhonwen. He wanted to thank the twins again for allowing him to do all his writing and emailing there and to give them a link to the newspaper's website so that they could look at his article online.

Rudi had been pondering about whether or not he should mention anything about his set-to with Bert Lloyd to Cass and Jo and decided that because they were friends with Rosa and as the Lloyds were neighbours it was important that they should know. He dropped Rhonwen off a decent distance from the shop just in case his uncle had returned then he made his way to the tiny police station at the top of the town.

'Rudi's such a nice young man,' said Cass later. 'Thank God he's nothing like Arthur. He must've been scared witless by Bert, that man is seriously dangerous, he'll shoot someone one day. I do hope Rudi did go to the police, he still seemed undecided when he left.'

'I'm going to take Phil a coffee out now,' said Jo, 'unless you want to?' She poured out a mug of coffee and called Nosey to follow her.

Phil was busy hacking back some of the shrubbery jungle that afternoon. The twins had decided to clear some of the undergrowth near their gate onto the track. It had grown congested over the years and they wanted to let some light in that area. Phil was quite happy to lend a hand outside as long as he wasn't needed to actually *know* anything about plants.

'Hi Phil, why don't you stop for a mo,' said Jo passing him the drink and dragging two of AB's ancient garden chairs over for them to sit on. No sooner than they had done so, Nosey started growling at something that only his acute hearing could pick up.

'What is it boy?' asked Jo, lifting Nosey up and getting out of her chair to have a look about. She could hear the sound of vehicles approaching sensed there was something happening. A couple of cars slid down the track past their gate as quickly and quietly as possible.

'Those were police cars,' said Jo.

A few minutes later another car shot past, but this time with its lights flashing. Without thinking, she put Nosey down on the grass, then watched helplessly as he shot out underneath the front gate barking enthusiastically, evidently knowing this was going to be the best car-chasing-heaven ever.

'Hey, Nosey…' yelled Jo and Phil at the same time. All in vain of course. No self-respecting dog would give up a good game and a bit of excitement to obey a human.

There was no other choice than to try and get him back. 'Can you tell Cass I'm going to find him?' Jo shouted at Phil as she headed off in the same direction as Nosey and the police cars.

She ran down the lane towards Rosa's farm but didn't get very far before having to clamber up into the hedge to allow a van to get past. She hoped that Nosey wouldn't get run over by it or be responsible for causing an accident. She ran as fast as she could. God, I feel so unfit, she thought.

When she reached the place where the track forked, she stopped to catch her breath and held onto the gate that Rudi had stood at early the previous morning. Nosey is a bloody useless disobedient animal, she moaned to herself, why does he think everything in life is a game specially designed for dogs?

Now she was standing still she could hear a racket coming from the direction of the Lloyd's farm down to her right. She stood on tiptoe and looked across the meadow towards the farm buildings where she could see people running around all over the place. She could hear Nosey's barking coming from the direction of the farm but it appeared to be getting closer and closer. She was concentrating so much on trying to make out what was happening in the farmyard that she didn't see a figure coming stealthily up the inside of the field hedge on the other side of the gate. Too late, she was confronted by Bert Lloyd who viciously shoved her away accompanying the move with unintelligible, angry shouting. He jumped over the gate and landed close to where she had fallen. Just then Nosey appeared from nowhere and shot under the gate, sinking his teeth into Bert's ankle. He succeeded in clinging on despite Bert's attempts to kick him away. Jo, incensed by his treatment of her dog, reached out from where she lay winded on the ground and grabbed his other leg. Between them, and more with good luck rather than any skill, they managed to off balance Bert Lloyd and bring him to his knees.

Above the hullabaloo Jo could hear another vehicle racing down the lane. She daren't let go and look up, but she was aware of it skidding to a stop and a man's voice shouting. Then the bulk of a man's body was suddenly next to hers pinning down Bert. 'You can let him go,' a voice said. 'I have him now.'

Jo released her grip and looked up. It was Simple Simon.

'Thanks…' she gasped, more from surprise than relief at being rescued.

She stood up unsteadily, and absentmindedly brushed herself down. She felt quite dazed suddenly. Bert Lloyd was still yelling at her. His face was puce and sweaty, with streaks of oil on it and there were bits of bracken in his matted hair. He was pointing his filthy hands in the direction of his crap encrusted boots where Nosey was still having a go at his ankle and tearing at his farm overalls. He was having just the best game ever. She thought Bert Lloyd was one of the most disgusting looking people she had ever seen.

She began to feel unsteady and everything seemed to start swimming around her. She felt vaguely detached from the whole scene. Nosey was growling somewhere and there seemed to be people shouting and holding on to her. Everything seemed sort of foggy, everything seemed unreal, and she could hear Cass's voice, where was Cass…where was…

'Oh Jo,' Cass cried, 'I was so worried about you.' She turned away from the settee and called out towards the kitchen, 'Jo's opened her eyes.'

Jo could hear footsteps and managed to turn her aching head around to see Phil Fixit and Simple Simon coming towards her.

'So how are you feeling now?' asked Simon, pulling up a chair for himself and passing her a glass of water.

'I feel…' she thought about it, '…I feel okay, actually.' and gave them all a self-conscious smile. 'How did I get back here?'

'We shoved you in the back of my car,' said Simon unceremoniously. 'I'd better give you the once-over to check you really are alright. Cass, you stay here and give me a hand and Phil can get us all a cuppa.'

'I guess I just fainted,' said Jo. 'How embarrassing.'

'I think you're right,' confirmed Simon 'there doesn't seem to be any damage done, except for a few bruises. I wouldn't have thought you were the fainting type though.'

Examination completed, they drank their tea quietly. Jo was given a clean bill of health but told to take it gently for couple of days. Phil left to get home and was followed fairly swiftly by Simon who seemed keen to leave too. 'I must remind you not to overdo things,' he said to Jo. 'Though I realise it's something *you* particularly, may be incapable of doing.' The girls both looked at each other and laughed, but Simon's face remained like stone. 'I know there's a first time for everything so we'll all live in hope,' he added, standing up.

Cass walked him to the door. 'Thank you for rescuing Jo today.'

'Good bye Cass.' Simon muttered and walked to his car.

'He was verging on rude,' said Jo as soon as Cass walked back into the cottage sitting room. 'I don't get it.'

'Perhaps he doesn't like excitement,' said Cass. 'We obviously stressed him out years ago and now we're back doing it again.'

'Well it's not intentional now. How's Nosey doing, he's very quiet?'

'He is utterly knackered and in his basket for once, not on the armchair. He was such a hero apparently. Brave little dog. The local policeman, Bill Thomas told me how he'd chased the police cars down the track and then disappeared. He obviously flushed Bert out from where he was hiding and chased him up the field as he tried to get away. When Bill came up the lane you had Bert by one leg and Nosey had him by the other ankle. Simple Simon had appeared and was holding him down too so the three of you are heroes. You apparently passed out just as the rest of the police arrived.'

'Bert really is a nasty piece of work. He sent me flying when he appeared from nowhere, I'm amazed Nosey and I managed to hang on to him long enough. Thank goodness Simon turned up, I couldn't have held on any longer. Why was he there, did he say?'

'The police had called him to check over one of the officers who'd been whacked round the head with a piece of wood by Bert before he bolted. I think you're very lucky not to have been injured as well and I'm so relieved that you and Nosey are fine. I expect the police will need to talk to you again though.'

There was a great deal of coming and going along the track the remainder of the afternoon. Holidaymakers and locals had gathered in large numbers behind the fluttering plastic tape that the police had put across the top end of the lane above Seaview Cottage and the Lodge.

The twins, who were as glued to the goings-on as much as everyone else outside, were making use of the large front bedroom window which afforded them a view of everything that was happening. They were so pleased that the couple from London who had booked that room for the weekend hadn't arrived yet.

Blodwyn Harris was there in the small crowd, anxious not to miss anything and hell-bent on being the one who took any news up into the town at the first opportunity. She must have bullied someone into looking after the sales counter in her absence so that she wouldn't lose out on any excitement. Everyone craned their necks each time a van or car was allowed through the barrier, anxious to see what was going on.

Rudi appeared through the throng carrying a bag and marched purposefully towards the Lodge. After a short conversation with the two policemen on duty at the top of the lane he was allowed to pass through. There was a buzz of interest from the crowd as he was permitted to slip under the plastic barrier. 'Look there's Rudi' said Cass as she caught sight of him, 'I'll go and let him in.'

There was muffled barking from the depths of the house when Nosey heard the doorbell. He had recovered sufficiently well enough to want to join in with whatever was going on outside so the twins had shut him in the pantry in case anyone let him out by mistake.

'Hi Rudi, come in,' said Cass, 'Did the police let you through without any questions?'

'Yes, I said I was expected here. Thanks so much for letting me know about all this and I'm so pleased Jo wasn't hurt. She must've been scared witless, that Bert is such an aggressive bloke.'

'Come up and see her. It's a great idea of yours to try and get some pics of what's going on down there. You'll be far ahead of everyone else. I'll show you from the window a way across the fields that'll get you down towards the Lloyds farm without going on the track. You can leave your empty bag here to pick up on the way back.'

After Cass had pointed out the directions to Rudi she watched him set off across their garden and through a break in the hedge in search of another good story and some pictures. Then the guests arrived and the twins reluctantly left their perfect vantage point to greet them.

'Is it always so exciting in Porthcwm?' asked the Robinsons when Jo showed them into their bedroom.

'Of course,' she laughed. 'Actually Porthcwm does seem to be getting its fair share of excitement recently what with the Holy Cow Ice Cream Miracle thing and now whatever this is all about. And oddly it's all along this track so I think people are beginning to think we're somehow responsible for it. Porthcwm was a quiet place till we arrived.'

Chapter 14

It was beginning to get dark when Rudi arrived back at the Lodge. The Robinsons had gone out to supper, rather enjoying running the gauntlet of the Police barriers again. The twins were in the kitchen having a glass of chilled white wine, Jo and Nosey both appearing to have completely recovered from their tussle with Bert Lloyd earlier.

'Did you get what you needed?' Jo asked Rudi.

'Yes thanks. That sneaky way across the field was really useful. I got some great pics. Would you mind if I wrote my piece here, I know it's a complete cheek but I can't do it at Arthur's, I'd just rather he didn't know.'

'That's fine Rudi, don't worry, just help yourself,' said Cass. 'And *how* is everything going with Rhonwen?' she added with a twinkle.

Rudi blushed. 'It's going very well, thank you. We're just trying to keep our friendship from Arthur. He would just interfere. Plus be horrified and I'm certain he'd be jealous. Would you think I was mad if I said that I actually think he fancies Rhonwen? I've seen the way he looks at her.'

'I have to say that I do think your uncle has a reputation that *isn't* too impressive, so I expect keeping your relationship with Rhonwen secret is the most sensible thing,' said Cass. 'Anyway we're very happy if you want to write your article here.'

'Here, take this,' said Jo, handing him a glass. 'Have a drink to oil the wheels of journalism. Did you find out anything new about what's going on down at the Lloyd's?'

'Not a lot actually, but if it's okay, can I interview you both a bit later about what *you* saw? Then I'll nip up to the surgery first thing tomorrow to ask the Doc what he saw too.'

'Good luck with Dr Grumpy then,' said Jo. 'We're not his favourite people. Go and help yourself to the sitting room, you'll get some peace in there. We'll pop in in a while and you can ask us any questions about today.'

A few days later Rudi called round with a copy of the newspaper. He was suddenly the editor's favourite journalist and it seemed to have given him a lot more confidence.

'The local paper's been asking questions around Porthcwm, too,' said Cass. 'The only person who had anything to say was Blodwyn Harris from the Post Office. Here, I'll show you.' She fetched the paper from the kitchen and gave it to Rudi.

'She's priceless,' he laughed. 'And the heading - 'I Saw It All Says Local Postmistress'…how imaginative of them. There's actually nothing in this article, except what she saw standing at the top of the track when she should have been standing behind her counter. I suppose they had to write something as they're the local rag as it wouldn't look good not to report on a bit of local excitement. They really should be turning out better articles, especially with everything that has been going on here.'

The twins read Rudi's piece in his paper. 'That's such a great follow-up to the original one you did. And thanks for getting a mention of the Lodge in too,' said Cass 'I like the way you didn't make us sound like newcomers by mentioning that we practically used to live here. All you need now is to find out exactly *why* Bert was arrested, although it could be for just about anything. No idea how you managed it, but you had some good quotes from Simon too. Why are you grinning like that, Rudi?'

'I was surprised that he even agreed to speak to me to be honest, after what you said about him being unfriendly, but he was great. He did fill me in on how you all first met too,' he said, still grinning.

'Oh God,' said Cass. 'It's about when we used to come down here as kids isn't it, and all that stuff?'

'That's the one,' said Rudi. 'You were apparently the most maddening and annoying children. He used to dread the school holidays because he knew you'd be coming down to stay with your aunt.'

126

'Well I'm very pleased he had so much time to talk to you about us, instead of seeing to his patients,' said Jo tersely. 'He's just as bad as bloody Blodwyn Harris.'

'God help us if we are ever poorly,' said Cass. 'He might decide to try and get his revenge if we were feeling ill.'

All these goings-on had diverted Cass's thoughts away from the possibility, or was it likelihood, that Ricco might be somewhere in the area. She was taken aback when she caught sight of someone who looked like him later that afternoon while she was busy chatting to Rev' n Bev who she had just bumped into near the Black Ship.

'You look as if you've seen a ghost?' said Rev suddenly.

'…I thought so too… just someone from way back,' she said.

'Well, you've got plenty of ghosts to haunt you here.' smiled Rev.

'Huw Evans, that was uncalled for, and you a man of the cloth…' Bev teased.

'Oh it wasn't from then,' said Cass. 'Anyway, I must get on. See you soon.' And she walked off swiftly up the hill in the direction that the Ricco lookalike had taken. She knew she had to find out whether it actually was him. If it was then she wanted to know why he was there, and if not…well, she could just get back to normal life. She peeped into the Post Office but couldn't see him there. The man just seemed to have vanished. She turned for home but kept looking around as she walked just in case he reappeared.

As it was hot and sunny she decided to use the lane above the Church for a change. It was always refreshingly cool walking under the trees planted along the side. Suddenly her heart missed a beat as she caught sight of her quarry a little way below her, sitting on one of the Jubilee benches up against the wall of the church. Cass could see from where she was that he was reading the local newspaper. It was definitely him. She so desperately wanted it not to be. Oh God, she thought, he'll be reading all that stuff about us. She believed her heart had actually stopped beating altogether but suddenly it was back, pounding so loudly she felt he would be able to hear it.

She put down her shopping on the ground and ducked down below the top of the ancient wall that separated the road and the churchyard in case he should look up and see her. She put her hands on the top stones to steady herself as she lifted her head up to snatch another peek at him over the top.

All sorts of thoughts were racing through her mind. Firstly, what was he doing there and how on earth was she going to avoid him? She couldn't possibly do anything around the town until he'd gone, whenever that might be. It could be a couple of weeks though so she'd have to persuade Jo to do all the town type chores and goodness knows *how* she would explain that to her. Had he come to give her a well-deserved bollocking for leaving him in such a cheap way? And how would she know anyway when he had left Porthcwm?

'Reliving some of your old espionage methods to see if they still work?' came Rev's voice from behind her.

'Are you following me now?' Cass asked as she went pink with guilt and tried to rise to an almost standing position so that she still wouldn't be visible from the bench where Ricco was sitting. 'Guilty as charged I'm afraid. Never know when a little undercover work might come in useful in the future.' she knew she sounded ridiculous.

'Very handsome man sitting down there, I see,' the Rev said casually.

'Bye again,' said Cass, as she turned to walk away as inconspicuously as possible.

'Well you two have been busy; it must seem a bit like the old days,' said Megan when the twins called on her the next day. 'I read the paper with unaccustomed interest when I saw the bit about the Lloyds. It's usually full of complete drivel so it's good to read about someone you dislike such as the Lloyds getting into trouble. I hope you've come to tell me all about the bits that aren't in the paper?'

'We still have no idea what was going on down there,' Jo said, 'but we've brought you the piece that Rudi wrote for his paper too.'

'Rudi? I haven't heard that name before.'

'Rudolph. Believe it or not he's Arthur's nephew, but very normal.' Jo went on to explain all about him. 'We'll introduce Rudi to you soon, you'll like him.'

'You must have been surprised to be rescued by Simon, Jo,' said Megan.

'Yes, I was. Though I flaked out when he turned up. Quite pathetic.'

'I'm so pleased he was there for you,' said Megan

Cass and Jo carried on telling Megan about their adventures, 'We'll keep you up to date with any new developments,' Jo promised.

'Well, guess what? I had two visitors yesterday,' said Megan, 'Arthur Trinder and Ms Phipps. They were charming, totally charming, couldn't have been nicer. But I know that it was all an act. They were making enquiries about houses that might be for sale around here, and were trying to tempt me with a carrot.'

'What sort of carrot?' asked Jo.

'To be honest girls, I'm not sure, but it was something to do with buying the house now for a lower price than it was worth and allowing me to live in it until…well, until I pop my clogs I suppose. But I don't quite understand how that works. I suppose they were hoping that when I realised I had all that money then I might decide to opt for a smaller house sooner.'

'That all sounds a bit odd Megan, are you sure that's what they meant?' asked Cass.

'No, I'm not in the slightest bit certain, so I said no anyway, I wouldn't trust them at all.'

'Thank heavens for that then,' said Cass, reassured that Megan appeared to have made the most sensible decision.

They spent some time trying to guess what it was that Bert Lloyd had been doing down at his farm and after Jo had finished showing off her bruises to Megan they got into the old Morris to go home. Jo put the key in the ignition and then hesitated.

'What is it?' asked Cass.

'How did Megan know that Simon had saved me from Bert? It didn't mention anything about it in the local rag and she hadn't read Rudi's bit yet.'

'Odd,' said Cass. 'But then, there seem to be a lot of odd things going on Porthcwm right now.'

Rudi knew he was going to have a full day. He had been doing a lot of thinking during the last forty-eight hours and now he planned to make some decisions. Then, depending on the outcome, he was going to take some significant action. He was meeting Rhonwen after she finished at the office and they were going to drive down the coast to a little pub that sold the most amazing crab sandwiches and locally caught lobster.

But before that, there was all this thinking to be done. His Aunt Linda had already gone out. The school holidays had just started and she now had time on her hands to do what she wanted. Arthur was also out. Where, Rudi frankly neither knew nor cared right at this minute, but despite having the house to himself he thought that a walk along the coast path would help calm his mind.

Off he went dressed in flowery shorts and a striped t-shirt, white socks and trainers. Today he wasn't the slightest bit bothered what he looked like; there were more important things to pay attention to and decide about, although it did cross his mind that he must get some decent clothes soon, before Rhonwen caught sight of him. She would die laughing if she saw him like this.

It was relatively early but there were already a few people on the path. He was overtaken first by a group of seasoned walkers. He could tell from their clothes and rucksacks and the way that they were striding out that their holiday consisted of serious hiking. Rudi wondered whether they ever had time to truly admire the stunning coastal scenery. He passed a family with children who were already bored and whingeing, and a young couple with two dogs that were racing madly all over the place out of control. Then he had half an hour of peace and not a person in his sight before his thoughts were interrupted by other ramblers. At least by now things were beginning to fall into place in his head.

Then the path suddenly seemed busy again. Rudi walked past another, happier family who were sitting down eating a picnic all laid out on the grass, then overtook two blokes wandering along dreamily, holding hands and lastly a smart man in a tweed jacket who he had seen talking to Arthur recently. He looks as if he's boiling, thought Rudi, and I was worrying about how I looked.

He decided all these walkers were now interrupting his deliberations too much so he left the path and picked his way up through some gorse to sit on a large inviting boulder he saw a little way above him and far enough away from the path to get some undisturbed pondering time. The stone was warm from the sun so he scrambled up onto it and found a comfortable spot to rest whilst he continued his deliberations. He had no sooner sat down than he caught sight of Linda walking around the bend on the path below him. His aunt, who was walking quite fast back in the direction that Rudi had come looked lost in thought so he felt waving or calling out to her would be intrusive. It was obviously a day for reflection.

This must be one of the most beautiful places in the world Rudi decided. From his rocky vantage point he could see far out to sea. He felt so fortunate to be enjoying it. He could smell the warm suntan lotion perfume of gorse flowers around him again and he could hear waves washing against the shore below the cliff. It was high tide, the air was still and he knew he would remember this day and this place forever. He absentmindedly ran his hand through his hair, and a big nervous grin spread across his entire face. Rudi knew he had made the right decision.

He clambered down from his rock and set off along the same path back to the Trinder's house. Linda wasn't around when he got back so once he had showered and found some smarter clothes he picked up his brief case, climbed into his car and drove off.

He headed inland to the county town, and made his way to the car park below the castle. Here, he sat for a moment going over some scribbled notes he'd made, then got out his mobile phone and called his editor. A few minutes later, call finished, he popped his phone back in his pocket, glanced at himself in the mirror and ran his hand through his hair. Well, that's the best I can do, he thought and climbed out of the car.

He took a deep breath, 'Okay Rudi' he said to himself out loud 'this is most definitely *it.*'

A couple of girls passing within earshot giggled and yelled 'Yeah, go for it.' Rudi smiled and suddenly relaxed and waved at them. After checking some directions on his notepad he climbed up the steep steps out of the car park, and arrived at the top in a very pretty street.

There were trees running all down one side of it on the pavement edge and half way down there was a café with tables and chairs outside. People were sitting enjoying their lunch shaded from the sun by the leafy branches. Just past the café was a sharp turning. He took it. The street wound sharply up past some smart brightly painted townhouses and when he reached the top and the street widened out, he checked his piece of paper again. He rounded the next corner, and there in front of him was a rather shabby brick building. It was flat-roofed, with peeling white paint on what little woodwork there was. He could tell it had clearly once been a smart modern structure and he was disappointed to see how ramshackle it looked. *Okay, Rudi, too late to change your mind, this is it, no messing, just get on and do it*, he instructed himself. Anxiously running his hand through his hair again, he pulled himself up to his full height and marched in through the door.

Chapter 15

Back at the Lodge after their return from Megan's, Jo and Cass found a phone message from Rosa asking them if they would like to go down to the farm for a drink with them that evening.

'I expect she's going to tell us all about the Lloyds police bust the other night. We haven't seen her for ages,' said Cass.

'And what's happening on the ice cream front too. I hope she's got some new flavour to try, I miss the samples she used to bring us,' said Jo. 'I'll ring her and say we'll walk down after the guests have arrived and settled in.'

Whilst she was on the phone there was a knock on the front door and when Cass opened it she was surprised to find Simon standing on the doorstep. 'I thought as I was close by that I'd take the chance to call in and see how Jo is doing since I saw her last.'

Cass invited him in and led him through to the kitchen where Jo was just finishing speaking to Rosa.

'That's good. Rosa says it's ok to go down when the guests have arrived.' Jo said without turning around. 'Who was at the...'

'It's Simon to see you,' said Cass.

Jo turned round quickly 'Oh?' she said feebly.

'I wanted to see how you are. I was almost passing, so it was a good opportunity. I presume everything is alright? No headaches or...?'

'No, no I'm utterly fine,' answered Jo swiftly. 'Apart from some bruising that has come out now and seems to be all the colours of the rainbow, I really am completely, absolutely, totally ok.'

'Would you like me to take a look?' asked Simon.

'No. No definitely not.' replied Jo 'Thank you. I said I was fine and I am. But thanks again for calling in to check up.'

'Would you like a cup of tea, if you'd trust us not to poison you?' asked Cass suddenly.

Simon seemed to ignore the invitation and walked towards the front door.

Cass repeated her offer of a cup of tea. 'Go on, honestly we really make great cup of tea…or coffee if you'd prefer?'

He turned round. 'No… thankyou, I have other patients to see but maybe one day I may risk a cup with you.' And off he went.

'What on earth did you do that for, Cass? He obviously can't bear us. It was so totally embarrassing for me, and he patently couldn't wait to get away from here.'

'Well actually, I think you're wrong,' said Cass. 'I definitely think you're wrong.'

Jo and Cass welcomed in the party of guests and after they had settled them in they said they were going down the lane to see the couple who had had the miracle poo publicity some weeks before. Their visitors were very impressed and told the twins it was because of all the ice cream promotion that they had decided to come and stay in Porthcwm and that they had made an appointment to meet Rosa the next day.

'You know Jo,' said Cass, as they strolled down the track later, 'this miracle of Rosa's has really been a huge help for our business. We've hardly had to do any promotion at all.'

'Yes,' agreed Jo. 'I think we can safely say we now believe in miracles.'

Rosa greeted them with such affection and apologies. 'I am so sorry. It is so long since we first had the miracle sheet from God, and we have been non-stop busy. No time to see anyone, no? But at last we begin to see the light in the dark tunnel? We have time to see you at last,' she gabbled on excitedly. 'So you come in, come in.' And then across the yard she shouted, 'Benito, Benito, the girls, they are here.'

'Ah!' said Benito when he appeared. 'Our beautiful neighbours. It is always a pleasure to see you.'

Cass and Jo had a glass of chilled Rosé thrust into their hands but were only able to have a couple of gulps before they were hurried away on a grand tour of everything that had anything remotely connected to Holy Cow ice cream.

'We start at the shrine,' explained Benito, pausing for a moment on the track. 'We want you to see what we are doing, because next week we are getting our first large orders out and then we shall be so busy we will have no moment to stop.' They continued to walk up the lane to the gateway into the field where the famous preserved cowpat was found.

'This is where we start our tour for visitors. As you remember, this is where it all happened. It is so important,' he waved his arms around grandly and smiled with such pride. 'You see how we have developed this area even more now? We have upgraded the shrine too, the structure, it is much better, no?' He indicated the new sturdier little building, now looking a little less like a cabin from the Alps.

'It's truly amazing, Benito, you've both worked so hard, and you deserve every bit of your success,' said Jo.

'Thank you, Jo,' he said, closing and locking the field gate behind them. 'Now come down to the yard and look at everything else. I show you where we store the milk when it arrives. We have to buy milk in now as we need so much. Then we go to see where we make the actual ice cream.'

'I suppose everything has to be on a much larger scale now, so that you can keep up with orders for Holy Cow?' asked Cass.

'Yes, of course,' answered Benito. 'It has been a steep curve of learning for us. We have to look after our customers and let them have what they want when they want it. Every day we learn more about the business. It is quite different to when Rosa used to make small amounts of ice cream to sell locally. Being on time, managing supply and demand, it is so different now we are becoming larger and more commercial.'

They followed Benito around, peeping through doors and exclaiming over the gleaming, environmental-health-checked facilities. They discovered the small room where the Bellinis experimented with new flavours and were given two new samples to taste and then they were shown into the room where the ice cream was packed and labelled.

'The packaging is brilliant,' said Cass. 'The label is so apt and attractive too, clever you.'

Benito led them across the yard to another shed with newly painted woodwork around the windows. 'This,' he said, with a flourish of his arms, 'is where all the design is done.'

'How do you get the time, to do it all?' asked Jo as Benito threw open the door into the shed.

'I have my cousin here working with us; he did the website, remember. He is responsible for the label design and so on.' In the corner on a smart desk were a couple of computers set up and running. A figure, who was engrossed on one of them, suddenly stood up and turned around.

'Oh...my God!' gasped Cass, as she found herself staring straight into the face of Ricco. She looked at Benito and then at Jo.

'*This* is the bloke who chatted me up in the town that day, Cass,' said Jo.

Cass just couldn't speak. Somewhere inside her, words were all tangled up. She wanted to say something, or did she want to scream. Whatever it was, no sound came out of her mouth and she just began to shake.

'Are *you* alright Cass?' asked Jo.

'N-no.' she was shaking a lot now. 'What are you *doing* here?' Cass asked Ricco. 'What is he *doing* here?' she turned to Benito. Without waiting for an answer she ran out of the shed and across the yard to the farmhouse.

Rosa looked up as she burst into the kitchen. She filled Cass's glass with more wine and smiled. 'So you have met our computer man then? Ricco is Benito's cousin.'

'Rosa, you *must* have known… he … he must have said something. You never told me he was here, why?'

At that moment Jo and Benito came in from the yard, followed by Ricco.

'I still don't completely understand what's going on. Do you know him?' Jo asked Cass. 'This is the man who chatted me up.' she repeated, 'Remember? I told you he quite unnerved me.'

'Yes, yes, I remember, Jo.'

Ricco turned to Jo 'I thought you were your sister,' he explained, 'I couldn't believe that you weren't as surprised to see me as I was to see you. She did not ever tell me she had a twin.' He looked towards Cass. She had sat down at the kitchen table and refilled her glass again. They all sat down too.

'Why didn't you explain to us, Rosa? He's been here over a week already and no-one said anything or called in. He bumped into Jo in town and when she told me what happened and described him to me, I thought it sounded like Ricco, but it just seemed impossible for him to be here, to find me. I never imagined there could be another explanation.'

'Well, why would we think that you knew our cousin?' asked Rosa. 'We didn't realise *you* knew him and he did not know *you* were here. He just said he had spare time to come and help us with Holy Cow when we need it most. We could not do it all ourselves.'

Jo was still looking puzzled. 'Everyone else seems to know what's going on except me.'

'He is your sister's boyfriend, of course. You will know …' said Rosa.

'WAS, was…' butted in Cass, her voice unduly raised 'he *was* my boyfriend.'

'And no, I don't know. What, where…from Paris?' asked Jo.

Benito opened another bottle of wine. Rosa put some bread and cheese on the table. For a moment or two everyone just sat in silence.

'I do not understand. Why does Jo not know about Ricco?' asked Benito.

Jo opened her mouth to answer, but Cass blurted out 'I never told her. I never tell her about boyfriend stuff. She doesn't understand that I don't want commitment like she does. We're just different like that. And then I behaved badly and ran away from Paris without telling Ricco and then Jo and I ended up here, miles from anywhere. I thought our paths would never cross again...'

'What I don't get is why didn't Ricco try and find you?' asked Jo.

At last Ricco himself said something. 'Because she never told me about family or anything either. I knew little about Cass really, her background, where she came from, I did not know she had a twin. But it did not matter to me because I was just happy to be with her. I did not mind that she would not share information. I trusted her and I respected her decision to keep things to herself.'

'I still don't understand,' Jo turned towards Cass. 'How could you *not* talk about us? Surely it's only natural to talk about family and all that isn't it?'

'I was in another country Jo, I just felt I could manage my life like that, compartmentalise it, I suppose. I felt in control. I know it seems weird...'

'But Rosa *you* must have known tonight that we would all meet and realise everything?' said Cass.

'Was Ricco's idea, no?' said Rosa 'He tell us he meet an old sweetheart when he get off the bus. He describe this girl and I say to Benito how it sound like our friends the twins. When I tell Ricco there are twins and give him your names, he say he had been living with Cass in Paris. He tell me Cass left him without saying where she went. As you live at the top of the lane you would bump into each other sometime soon. So we thought if we ask you down here then you could meet again and maybe...'

'And what?' snapped Cass. '*Maybe* what exactly?'

'Look Cass,' said Ricco. 'I have seen you in the town trailing after me at a distance trying to see if it is truly me. I know you see

138

me near the church reading the paper too, is that when you knew for real it is me?'

'Okay…Yes, you're right; I thought you'd come to find me and I felt nervous, I never for one moment imagined there was any connection with Rosa and Benito.' Cass finally began to look embarrassed.

Back home the twins sat in the kitchen with a mug of hot chocolate each. Cass broke the silence. 'Remember how AB used to give us hot choc when something was wrong? It feels like that now, you know, and it is entirely my fault, I'm sorry Jo. I know you think it's odd that I keep secrets, and I know I play all my cards close to my chest, but I promise I'll try and share stuff with you. So next time I get a boyfriend, if that ever happens again, I'll tell you all about it.'

'Look you don't have to share every last detail with me, in fact I'd really rather you didn't, but just a *bit* of info-sharing would be great. Not that I have anything to share with you in return at the moment. We're both a bit lacking on the romance front. Although I do wonder whether you and Ricco might get things going again…?'

'Enough, enough, definitely not, so forget that. I was responsible for ballsing up that relationship good and proper and now I'm dedicating myself to celibacy and the Bed & Breakfast business.'

'The last few words are best not said in the same sentence, Cass.' declared Jo.

They both laughed and relaxed again. Things were just about back to normal.

Rudi held the pub door open for Rhonwen. 'After you…' he grinned at her. 'Let's sit over there in the corner.'

Once settled with their drinks in front of them Rudi and Rhonwen looked over the menu. 'Well I'm going for the lobster, because that's what this place is famous for, but I'm going to have chips too. What about you Rhon?'

'I'll have the same. No chips though please, just the salad.' When their orders had been taken and the waitress had left them alone Rhonwen could hold back no longer. 'Rudi, you have been grinning from ear to ear since we met up this evening, what's going on?'

'No wonder my uncle employs you, you don't miss a trick.'

'Sarcastic bugger. I'll pretend that's a compliment.' Rhonwen retorted.

'Well since you ask, I have decided to change my life. I've been pondering on it for a few days. I really love it down here and I really... uh, and now I've met you,' his cheeks went all pink and he ran his hand through his hair 'and so . . .'

'So... what *are* you going to do?'

'If you give me half a chance Miss-Hugely-Impatient, I'm trying to tell you. I have, as it so happens already done it.'

'What, done *what*? . . . You're being infuriating, Rudi. Stop doing stuff to your hair and tell me what's going on?'

'I've handed in my notice at the paper. There, now you know. And I feel fantastic.'

'Rudi, how could you? What will you do now? I can't believe you've done that even though you weren't happy there?'

'Hang on a sec and give me a chance to finish. I gave in my notice and immediately got a new job. Though I realise it was a bit of a risk doing it in that order.'

He put his hand up to fiddle with his hair, but Rhonwen leaned forward and grabbed it. 'Stop doing that Rudi, chill out and tell me slowly what you're going to do.'

Rudi looked at her across the table. Rhonwen was still holding his hand and stroking it gently. It was very reassuring and rather arousing at the same time. Nice... he thought.

'Now tell me slowly Rudi,' said Rhonwen encouragingly.

140

'Okay, I told you that I really love being in Porthcwm and I've found a good friend in you,' he smiled at her warmly, 'and Cass and Jo have been so kind me, and helpful when they needn't have been. I hated working for the paper back home and even though the editor seemed to think I was flavour of the moment, I knew it'd only go downhill when I returned back after my break here.

'They'd all start to torment me again, but even more so now I've done two great pieces. They would still find reasons to ridicule me so I just didn't want to go back. I know I've been a wimp about it all but I needed to sort myself out. Anyway yesterday I decided to hand in my notice at the paper and so I did just that. I phoned them and said that I wasn't coming back.

'Then I went to the County Times office and asked if they had a job for a journalist. I showed them the two pieces I'd written about the Porthcwm goings-on and told them I had some inside info on what was happening with the Lloyds. Amazingly, the editor said their main journo, Mags, was going on maternity leave in a fortnight and the guy they'd offered to employ as a fill-in had buggered off up to some popular local paper in Yorkshire. So he offered me a job until Mags comes back to work. I'm so lucky Rhon, aren't I? I simply can't believe it.'

Rhonwen let go of his hand, stood up and walked round the table to give him a big hug. 'You certainly are Rudi.' She leant forward and gave him a big kiss. 'And so am I.'

'Here's our food,' said Rudi 'are you sure you didn't want chips? I could still order you some and you can share mine till they come.'

'No thanks, I've decided I'm off chips from now on. It's not just you who has decided to change their life, I have too. And I am starting with no more chips or hidden biscuits!'

They chatted more about Rudi's big decision whilst they ate. The little bar-cum-restaurant had filled up to bursting point. The window behind their table looked out across the road and then over the pebbly beach towards the sea. The view was perfect. Everything felt perfect to Rudi and he knew that he had made the right decision.

'What is your Uncle going to say?' asked Rhonwen.

'I dread to think. Something truly cutting about me being thoughtless and rash and irresponsible, I guess. I'll deal with it when it happens. Aunt Linda will be pleased I think, so at least I'll have one person on my side.'

'And me too! Will you go on staying with them for a while?' asked Rhonwen. I'm sure Mum would be happy for you to have the spare room, but I think the longer we keep *us* secret the better. What do you think?'

'Well I'm going to stick it out as long as possible at the Trinder's and see what happens. At least I can be out most of the time just like Uncle Arthur seems to be.'

They finished their meal and sat back smiling at each other across the table. Rhonwen held Rudi's hand. 'That was so delicious. Thank you. I'm going to find the Ladies now if I can fight my way through all these people,' she said. 'I won't be a mo.'

Putting her napkin on the table Rhonwen stood up and began to follow the signs to the toilets. It was very difficult to weave her way between the full tables, her bulk made it impossible to slip through comfortably without diners having to stand up and let her squeeze past. She felt quite positive though since she had made the decision to control her eating and lose weight and she knew Rudi would help her. She could tell he liked her even as she was but she was determined to make a change too.

When she got to the little corridor which led to the gents and ladies and the fire exit, she realised she had forgotten her bag. Bugger, she thought. As she turned around to fight her way back to fetch it she caught sight of Arthur Trinder sitting at a table close by. How on earth had she not seen him, or he her, for that matter, as she passed by? She stepped back into the corridor quickly and tried to melt into the shadows, a manoeuvre singularly difficult to achieve. She decided not to risk fetching her bag in case he saw her, and went into the cloakroom anyway.

When she'd fluffed her hair up in front of the mirror and done what she could without her make-up, she peeped round the edge of the cloakroom door to try and see who Arthur was with. She gasped

142

as she saw it was Fishnchips and they were holding hands. *Holding hands...yuk ...* how could she fancy Arthur? In fact how either of them fancy the other? They appeared so lost in each other's company that it was no surprise to Rhonwen that they hadn't spotted her. Between them on their table lay some sheets of paper. Fishnchips picked them up and pointed at something. Rhonwen could see there was a picture of a house on the page she was holding. She craned her neck a little so that she could see more clearly. 'How odd,' she thought 'I don't recognise that house but it seems to be on our headed sale particulars.'

She couldn't risk Arthur catching sight of her so she escaped into the fresh sea air outside through the fire escape door next to the gents. She fished her mobile out of her pocket and turned it on. She dialled Rudi's number. 'Rudi, it's me,' she said when he answered. 'Yes I know, but hang on and let me tell you...no, I haven't run off. Look, your uncle is in the bar next door. He didn't see me because I escaped out of the side door near the loo. Yes, that's the best idea, and can you bring my bag with you please, I left it under the table, and don't let him catch sight of you.' Rhonwen went round to Rudi's car and tried unsuccessfully to hide behind it.

Rudi finished his drink and bent down to pick up Rhonwen's handbag. Bloody hell, what on earth has she got in here, he thought. It weighed a ton and was bright pink and it appeared to him to be the size of an overnight case. How had he not noticed it earlier? There was no way he could disguise it, so clutching it in his arms he started to make his way towards the front door. He tried to squeeze between the chairs as casually as possible, but was immediately observed by a group of lads slightly the worse for drink. 'I like the pink handbag, mate,' one of them bawled at Rudi. 'So what have you got in there? Doesn't match your outfit does it?' Then laughed deafeningly at his own joke.

People at other tables turned around to see what was going on. 'Matches the colour of your face now though,' the first loudmouth continued. Rudi briefly considered turning round and whacking him with Rhonwen's handbag, but thinking that there was a chance that the weight of whatever it contained might possibly kill him, he stopped in time. I can cope with this sort of crap now, he thought, no one is going to get at me like they did at the paper. And after all, he was trying to get out of the pub *without* his uncle noticing him. At any moment Arthur might appear to see what all the hilarity was about. At last he reached the door but just before bursting out through it, he turned, bowed generously to everyone in the bar and held the bag aloft. A loud cheer rang through the pub as he ran off across the car park.

Chapter 16

'Blimey Rudi, what kept you?' asked Rhonwen, when he got to the car.

'Could I persuade you to carry a smaller, dull coloured handbag in future please? It was so embarrassing carrying this through the pub.' He thrust the article in question into her arms. 'Come on, let's go.'

They clambered into Rudi's car and as they set off along the coast road back to Porthcwm Rhonwen described how she had seen his uncle and Fishnchips in the next room at the pub.

'So what d'you think my uncle is up to with *her*?' asked Rudi. 'He seems to go for younger women normally, he's always ogling at them, but not someone like her. She's all cheap blond hair dye and fake tan and big flash jewellery and…and well, well…*old*.'

'Got the message I think. She's not that old though. Maybe just a little more mature than his usual mistresses. You're right though you know Rudi; he does ogle women in the most eerie way and he used to be like that when I first went to work for him. He was always looking out of the corner of his eye at me. It made me feel so uncomfortable. I know I could have left and tried to get another job, but a lot of what's around down here's seasonal and in hotels, and anyway I love the actual job and I meet lots of people. And to be honest I know I'm good at it.

'When I started to put on a bit of weight he dropped hints about it and talked about diet programmes and exercise but I began to notice that he wasn't looking at me in such a lustful way or speaking to me in a lecherous manner,' she continued 'so I didn't bother to try and get slim again because he was leaving me alone. Only problem was that I just kept eating and getting bigger. Anyway, I felt safer that way, but now I'm going to make a supreme effort to lose weight. First thing in the morning when I get to the office I promise I shall bin my secret stocks of biccies.'

'Well done Rhon.' Rudi smiled at her. 'Uncle Arthur has a lot to answer for. I'm proud of you for deciding to stop eating stuff that's bad for you just to keep him from thinking about you as a possible conquest. He's not going to get at you anymore now.

'I wonder whether Aunt Linda knows what goes on. Poor thing, she gets a raw deal doesn't she? I don't know how she's stuck it for so long, maybe she doesn't know about his wretched affairs. I guess she just loses herself in her job. I can't wait to find somewhere of my own to live and move out. I'm sure Uncle Arthur will be on the phone moaning to my mother about her ungrateful son as soon as he finds out about my job change.'

'There was something else odd about this evening though,' said Rhonwen reflectively. 'Apart from them holding hands, which just on its own makes me want to vomit...'

'Yes?'

'Well, Fishnchips was holding some sale particulars in her hand,' said Rhonwen, 'I could see quite clearly the main photograph. It's definitely one of our sales particulars as our logo was at the top of the front page.'

'So, maybe she's looking for a new house then, nothing strange in that.'

'On the surface maybe, but I don't recognise that house at all, it's not on our sales list to sell.'

The twins were thrilled to hear Rudi's news about his new job when he and Rhonwen called in a couple of days later. 'I also plucked up courage to tell Uncle Arthur that I was going to be staying in Porthcwm,' he told them. 'He accused me of acting irresponsibly, leaving my old job for one on a two-bit local rag. He ranted on about frying pan and fire stuff, and when I told him about looking for somewhere to rent, he completely lost the plot. Then he suddenly stopped ranting as if he'd been struck by lightning and got all pally and invited me to continue staying with him and Linda. I can only imagine that he thought that if I stayed I would be company for her.'

146

'Creep. How obvious is that? He must think you can't see through him,' said Jo.

'Oh he definitely thinks I'm too stupid to understand. All he wants is for me to babysit Aunt Linda so that she doesn't have time on her own to think about what he's up to. To be perfectly honest she does seem to keep busy and occupied anyway most of the time. After all, she's got all her homework marking to do and meetings to go to, and when Arthur's not there she just goes out walking or visits friends. He's not bothered what she's doing, so he's not the slightest bit interested where she's been or whether she might even have enjoyed herself.

Rudi and Rhonwen then recounted their avoiding Arthur episode in the pub when Rhonwen had caught sight of him with Fishnchips.

'We always wondered when he was trying to get hold of our house for her with what seemed like a scam whether there was something going on between them,' said Jo.

'It looks as if he is still trying to find her a place because she was looking at some sale particulars when I saw them,' said Rhonwen.

'It's as well he didn't see you two together, can you imagine how tough it would be for you, and Rhonwen in particular?'

'Yes, I think we're going to have to be very careful,' said Rudi.

'We're finding it difficult to see each other now,' said Rhonwen 'and I'm really nervous about him finding out we're…friends… well, who am I kidding? … that we're a *couple* now.' Rhonwen smiled at Rudi and he looked back at her like a happy puppy.

'I have an idea,' proposed Cass. 'Why don't you use our cottage to escape to? You can do what you like there, just make yourself at home.'

Rudi now looked like an embarrassed but even happier puppy. 'Thank you so much. That's so kind,' he said, and in an unusually daring moment gave both Jo and Cass a hurried peck on the cheek as he and Rhonwen got up to leave.

'Cass, that was such a tremendous idea of yours to let them use the cottage. AB would be proud of us. It's exactly what she did with Bev'nRev.'

'Well I think Arthur would go nuts if he found his nephew was going out with his receptionist,' said Cass. 'I'm convinced he'd come up with some fake reason to terminate her employment, which wouldn't be fair.'

'He wouldn't understand the meaning of 'fair',' said Jo.

At last, when Rhonwen was convinced Arthur was out for a whole day, she was able, between dealing with customers and phone calls, to look through all the photographs in his archive of house details. She wanted to find the house on the sales particulars she had seen Fishnchips looking at in the pub. He had left quite early in the morning which should have given her plenty of time, but it was already halfway through the afternoon and she seemed to have made no headway at all. She had looked through his desk drawers, none of which were locked. They were tidy and organised and she went through them quickly, but found nothing of interest. She checked through the bookshelves behind his desk and those in the corridor, but nothing at all looked like the house she had seen in the pub. Surely Fishnchips didn't have the only copy.

It was nearly five o'clock and Rhonwen had decided she should just tidy her desk, lock up the shop and go home. She returned to Arthur's office to check she'd left it just as she'd found it, and for some reason she straightened the long blue curtains behind his chair. Just tucked in behind the left one was Arthur's briefcase. She lifted it onto his desk and was surprised to find it unlocked. She emptied the contents out carefully and started to search through the envelopes and papers. Most of the files contained properties she knew he was currently dealing with. His office diary was in there too and she flicked through the pages to see if anything fell out. When Rhonwen tried to tuck it back into the front pocket of the briefcase where she had found it something prevented it from sliding it in. She removed it again, felt in the pocket and pulled out an envelope. The envelope was lumpy and bendy and when she looked inside she found half a dozen condoms in their little wrappers. Rhonwen instantly felt sick and dropped them on the floor as if she had burnt her hands. How perfectly grim and revolting she thought. She picked them up hurriedly and returned them and the diary to the case. Surely he wasn't actually having sex with Fishnchips. Maybe they were there for any other chance encounter he might have. The very thought of it was repulsively vile. It wasn't that he was having sex with anyone at all that baffled her but more how could anyone in their right mind want to have sex with *him*.

The next envelope contained what she had been looking for all day. There were the sales details and photograph of her mystery house. It was painted white and had obviously once been very smart. It had a short drive and broad stone steps up to an elegant front door. There were only a few interior photos, all of downstairs rooms, but oddly none of the rooms upstairs. It was a house with charm by the bucket load she thought, but it looked slightly faded and past its best. Printed in the details was the clichéd observation that it was in need of sensitive restoration to return it to its 'former glory'. Rhonwen winced, she just hated that expression; it was so overused, particularly by Arthur.

Hearing the shop door open, then close with its familiar squeaky click followed by footsteps approaching Arthur's office she replaced the details quickly and slid the briefcase behind the curtain.

'Ah there you are Rhonwen, just checking everything before you close up? Well done, well done. I came back for this,' he bent down and picked up the briefcase from behind the curtain. 'I completely forgot to take this with me, thank heavens I didn't need anything important out of it today.'

'Yes, thank God for small mercies,' agreed Rhonwen, shivering at the very thought of the condoms.

'I thought we should talk properly,' said Ricco when Cass had answered the cottage door to him.

Bugger, she thought, why did I bother to answer the door, I could do without this.

'I'm busy,' she said.

'Could I come in please?' he asked politely with a smile.

A little butterfly in Cass's stomach began to flutter. 'I … I don't know, I really am busy.'

Ricco's mood appeared to change, 'Look,' he said brusquely. 'I won't take too much of your very precious time then, I just think we need to have a short discussion.'

Cass's butterflies stopped fluttering. 'I suppose you could come in, but I can't talk for long as I'm …'

'Yes Cass, you have made that perfectly clear.'

She led him through to the kitchen, but didn't offer him a coffee or even the opportunity to sit down.

'This is nice,' Ricco said.

'What do you mean?'

'Well, I actually meant this lovely cosy old room, but it's nice to talk to you too.'

'Look Ricco, please can we hurry this up?'

'Okay. I wanted to clear the air. As I said the other evening I was perfectly aware that you have been half stalking me half avoiding me in the town. So obvious. That nosey woman in the post office said you used to do that as kids too.'

'What are you doing talking to her about me?' Cass snapped at him.

'She volunteered it, apparently there are lots of people here who remember you following them around and being annoying.'

'So what, I was a kid having fun, what's wrong with that? So is that all you came to tell me about, bloody Blodwyn?'

'No Cass, I actually wanted to find out why you ran away from me in France. I thought we were very comfortable together. Then I come home one evening and you had vanished. So what do I think? Have you run off with someone else or did you suddenly stop loving me? I want you to tell me.'

'I left you a note,' said Cass, defensively.

'Come on Cass, you just said you had to go because your Aunt had died and you wouldn't be coming back because you wanted to 'move on'.'

'It was true, completely true, I just...well, I just needed to leave.'

'What do you mean, leave? How did you think I would feel when I found your pathetic departure message? I had no idea where you were 'moving on' to. You never told me anything about your family or where you lived in England. I didn't know you had a sister, let alone a twin. And then by some strange coincidence I come to this place in Wales to help my cousin out and I find you live up the lane. I thought that Jo was you when I got off the bus that day, you are so alike. And now I find out you didn't tell her about me either. What is it with you that you keep everything secret? Or do you feel vulnerable when you get too close to someone and they begin to know the real you?'

Cass was beginning to feel her eyes pricking with tears. He was right, he was so right. But he wasn't going to see her get upset.

'Well you're allowed your opinion,' said Cass.

'Thing is Cass, I am *here* in the same town as you and I have got a lot of work to do helping Rosa and Benito. I'm sure we'll bump into each other around the place, especially as they are friends of yours, so can we each just get on with our own life and try and be pleasant to each other?'

'Yes. I'll try. But I don't want us to discuss this anymore.' Cass pushed past him so he couldn't see she was upset and opened the front door. 'Bye Ricco, question time's over...'

Chapter 17

Rudi's new job was going surprisingly well. The editor seemed to like him, and the other people he worked with were friendly. How different it was to his last place. He had written some well received pieces in the last couple of issues and felt that his life changing decisions had been worth every second of deep deliberation.

There had been a lot of speculation in the town since the arrest of Bert Lloyd. Rudi knew that the article he had written about Bert being detained in custody and the one about the police raid on his farm had been instrumental in him getting his new job.

He had struck up a friendship with Bill Thomas, the local policeman in Porthcwm. It was Bill who had taken the details of Rudi's encounter with Bert and the shotgun incident, all those weeks ago and it was he who had subsequently set up the raid on the farm. Bill had been decent enough to slip Rudi a little extra information about that police swoop at the Lloyd's and about Bert's forthcoming trial and Rudi was now building the framework of a piece in advance of the hearing.

The Rudi-Rhonwen relationship was going very well too. The twins' offer of the use of Seaview Cottage as a place that they could meet up had moved their friendship forward. Rudi had blossomed, if that was the right word, under Rhonwen's influence and after one or two false starts he had turned into rather an accomplished lover.

He had found a purpose in life and had matured almost overnight. He was less anxious about all the complicated choices that had always seemed to confront him and he had even stood up to his Uncle Arthur when he grilled him about the reason for his decision to stay in Porthcwm. He was still managing to keep his relationship with Rhonwen from Arthur, but it was proving quite challenging.

'Rudi's got a short piece about Bert Lloyd in the paper this week,' shouted Cass as she dropped the weekly paper on the kitchen table. Jo came through from the yard behind the Lodge with a basket full of dried sheets. 'Tell me what it says while I start to iron these?'

Cass picked up the paper again and began to read the article to Jo.

'*A 50 year old local man will appear in court on Thursday charged with producing and cultivating cannabis and dishonestly using electricity at a farm near Porthcwm.*

A police swoop on the isolated coastal farmhouse has led to the discovery of a cannabis growing operation. The raid on the property, revealed a sophisticated setup in several of the outbuildings.

Inside one building 180 cannabis plants were found with a potential street value of approximately £61,000. In another building 113 more plants, with an estimated value of £40,000, were found. As well as the plants police also recovered several electrical generators and drums of diesel from the yard.

A police spokesperson said, "This has been one of the most significant drugs seizures in Wales and the first in this area. We are very grateful for the tip-off from a sharp-eyed member of the public."

The illegal operation was decommissioned by an expert who said the extraction system had been silenced and filtered to remove the pungent smell of cannabis production. The lighting and watering systems were all automated, and he discovered 88 lighting units, 11 fans and nine silencers.

Police destroyed the cannabis plants on site, by burning them, and crushed all the cultivation equipment. It was also discovered that the electricity meter had been bypassed so the operation could use copious amounts of energy at no cost.'

'And then there is an old picture of Bert looking quite young and oddly handsome sitting on a tractor smoking a roll-up, very appropriate. And another that Rudi took of the police burning all the cannabis plants on the evening he sneaked down the field to see what was going on.'

Mildred had begun to make rather weird clunking sounds recently which seemed to come from underneath her bonnet so the twins had left her at the garage near the top of the town for some investigations. When Jo and Cass heard that she had been given a clean bill of health they decided to walk up to collect her, calling in on Megan on the way. But Rudi realised he and Rhonwen were going in the same direction and he offered to give them a lift

He arrived to pick up the twins later that Saturday morning when their guests had gone and they had left Gloria to do the bed changes and clean around.

'Thanks so much Rudi,' said Cass.

'It's the very least I can do after everything you've done for us,' he said.

'This is the life,' Jo said from the back seat, 'having a chauffeur. We've read your piece in the paper, by the way, it was great. Funny to talk about yourself as 'a sharp-eyed member of the public' though.'

'Only way I could think of putting it,' said Rudi. 'It wouldn't be a good idea to mention that it was just me happening to be there at the right moment, thanks to you.'

'Take a left here, and it's the third drive on the left, where that big fir tree is,' said Cass. Rudi slowed down as if he was going to drop the twins off at the gateway entrance.

'No, no, you must both come in and meet Megan, she's heard so much about you and we'll never hear the end of it if she's missed the opportunity for us to introduce you both.'

So Rudi turned left into the drive and around the sweeping bend which brought the house into view. Suddenly Rhonwen grabbed the back of Rudi's seat. 'Stop ...' she yelled.

Rudi slammed on the brakes. 'What's happened?' he called over his shoulder.

'It's that house, the one on the sale particulars that Fishnchips was looking at in the pub,' she answered.

Rudi switched the engine off and undid his seat belt. He turned around so that he could see Rhonwen properly. 'Are you *absolutely* sure Rhon?'

'Totally, no question about it, but what's interesting is that they're obviously recent photos of the outside. I remember thinking how bright those pink flowers were right by the front steps. They're still blooming so it can't have been taken long ago.

Rudi turned to Jo. 'Has Megan said anything to you about selling it?'

'No, but I never imagined it could be this house when you told us about what you'd seen.'

Rudi sat still for a moment. 'Okay, so we have to ask Megan about it, but we mustn't panic her if she's oblivious to the whole thing.'

'C'mon,' said Jo. 'She's there at the window now, waving at us, so let's go and introduce you.'

By the time they had parked the car Megan was on the doorstep waiting.

'Hi Megan,' called Cass. 'Did you think we'd broken down half way up your drive?'

'Come in my dears, it's lovely to see you,' said Megan.

With the introductions over they sat around her kitchen table. Jo busied herself getting coffee for everyone whilst Rhonwen and Rudi answered all Megan's questions. 'I have been so looking forward to meeting you both,' she said.

'Megan, I don't suppose you've had a call from Arthur Trinder recently have you?' Jo enquired casually as she carried the coffee over.

'Well it's funny you should say that, my dear. He did just appear at the door out of the blue a few days ago. And I foolishly invited him in as he patently wasn't going to shift and I was getting bored standing out there. So I sat him down in the drawing room and made him a coffee. He asked for decaffeinated which rather surprised me. I knew I had some tucked away in one of the cupboards, but I'm really getting forgetful and couldn't find it for ages. Oh dear, do you think I'm getting senile? I seem to mislay things all over the house and it is beginning to bother me. The other day I couldn't find the back door key. And then I bought the same newspaper twice.'

'You aren't going senile, Megan,' said Cass. 'You mustn't get upset and worry about it. Did you manage to find the coffee for Arthur in the end?'

'Yes, eventually, then we had a chat about this and that. He asked me how you were doing at the Lodge and if I saw you often. He asked how I was and whether I was managing to cope with the upkeep of this house. He talked about all sorts of things really. And then he just said goodbye and off he went taking all his clobber with him.'

'What clobber?' asked Rhonwen.

'Oh my dear, I can't remember *exactly*, but he had a briefcase, and his camera and some loose papers I think.'

Rudi really liked Megan and felt they should be direct with her about their discovery of the weird sale particulars that Rhonwen had found. He could tell that there would have been ample time for Arthur to have taken some quick downstairs shots of the interior whilst Megan was searching for the coffee, but he reckoned that there wouldn't have been time to take any of the upstairs and that was probably the reason for there being none in the brochure. 'Rhon,' he said. 'Would you like to explain to Megan about what you've discovered?'

He could see that Megan was in shock after listening to Rhon's explanation and rather sweetly went round and sat on the spare chair next to her and took hold of her hand. 'We'll try and get to the bottom of this Megan, so we don't want you to spend any time worrying yourself about it.'

After they had collected Mildred and arrived back at the Lodge Jo went in search of Gloria who was almost finished in the front bedroom. She was vacuuming under the bed in her usual very short skirt and nothing much was left to the imagination. Jo had noticed Mr Rogers, one of their elderly guests earlier that week watching her with intense concentration as she reversed down the stairs cleaning as she went. His wife suddenly appeared from nowhere and bustled him off, tut-tutting under her breath. Jo couldn't help but think that Gloria had made his day. Maybe even his week?

'Hi Gloria,' she shouted above the vacuum cleaner din. Gloria was obviously deep in thought. 'G-l-o-r-i-a-a-a...' she tried again.

Gloria turned around, saw Jo and turned the machine off. 'I was miles away,' she said trying to produce a smile with her botoxed features.

'That's okay,' said Jo, wondering what anyone would find attractive about all the surgically adjusted parts of her body. Obviously some people did, thinking of old Mr Rogers.

'How's Mrs Hughes?' Gloria enquired.

'We're a bit concerned about Megan really,' said Jo. 'She always puts on a brave act, but I think she worries about her health ever since her fall and being on her own in that large house. She seems to be worried at the moment about her memory, you know, forgetting where she's put things and so on. But I think she'll soon get back to normal. She's amazing for her age and she's so young in her attitude. She's an inspiration really.'

The front doorbell suddenly rang, and Jo ignored it until it rang again. She realised that Cass must be busy somewhere else and couldn't hear it. She ran downstairs to find Ricco standing outside in the porch holding a large bunch of flowers. She noticed his look of disappointment that the wrong twin had opened the door.

'Hi Ricco,' she said.

'These are for Cass,' he said, pushing the flowers into Jo's arms.

'They're beautiful,' said Jo. 'Is there a message to go with them?'

'She will know when she looks at the date today.' he gave her a big smile and walked off up the drive.

'Gosh, who gave you those?' said Cass appearing behind her. 'They're gorgeous.'

'Actually, they're for you,' said Jo passing them across to her twin. 'From Ricco, he just left them and said something about the date today and you'd know why he was giving them to you?'

Cass thought for a moment and then said, 'It's today, today last year. The date we met on the Car Rouge in Paris. He's remembering that. He said he would buy me flowers every year on that date, because it was the most important date in his life.'

'Oh that is *so* romantic Cass,' said Jo.

'No - it's so *not*, is it? I left him months ago and here he is giving me flowers as if we were still together.' Cass headed towards the compost bin. 'I can't keep these, it's too eerie.'

'No,' said Jo, making a dash to rescue them. 'You're not chucking those out. If you don't want them, that's fine, but at least let's put them in the dining room for the guests to enjoy.'

Jo liberated the flowers from her sister's grasp and fetched one of AB's large cut glass vases from the cupboard in the corner of the kitchen. 'How are you going to thank him then?'

'Why should I thank him, Jo? He's doing it to make me feel awkward.'

'Well he obviously succeeded then, but I honestly think he did it because he still feels something for you. He seemed very genuine and I'm sure he'd have preferred to have given them to you personally instead of me.'

Cass stomped out of the kitchen and went upstairs to her bedroom in the attic. She opened the bottom drawer in her cupboard and lifted out a small package. From the middle of the crumpled white tissue paper she took out the little photograph of herself and Ricco that she had slipped into her bag when she left Paris.

Rhonwen planned to bring Megan's name up somehow with Arthur when she went back into work on Monday but knew she needed to find just the right moment.

Her day didn't start well. Fishnchips came marching in almost before she had sat at her desk, and made her way straight towards Arthur's office without offering so much as a 'good morning' in Rhonwen's direction.

'Mrs Phipps, you can't go in without an appointment, and anyway Mr Trinder isn't here.'

'I'll just wait then.' she snapped, disappearing into Arthur's office and slamming the door behind her.

Five minutes later she reappeared 'I thought you *might* have offered me some coffee as I'm waiting for Mr Trinder?' and then disappeared back into Arthur's office.

Rhonwen waited a while, then calmly opened the office door and said, 'Good morning Mrs Phipps isn't it a beautiful day? May I get you something to drink?'

'Don't take that tone with me, young woman,' she responded. 'I've already told you I could do with some coffee.'

'I won't be a moment then,' said Rhonwen, and walked slowly out. She took her time pottering around the tiny kitchen and making the coffee then popped her head round the office door, 'Milk, Mrs Phipps?' she asked. Receiving a grumpy nod, she then enquired, 'Sugar, Mrs Phipps?'

'Yes, milk *and* sugar, for heaven's sake.'

Eventually Rhonwen carried the finished, but somewhat lukewarm drink, through to Fishnchips.

'Just put it there,' she said waving her hand at Arthur's desk. Rhonwen stood for a few moments vainly wondering whether she would get a thank you tossed in her direction, but went back to her desk without one.

Half an hour later she collected the empty coffee cup. She paused at the door on her way out and said, 'Mr Trinder isn't coming in today, he's doing some valuations.'

'What?' shouted Fishnchips. 'Why did you *not* tell me this earlier, I've been wasting my time sitting here all this while. You're a disgrace to your job. I shall make sure Arth…Mr Trinder knows about your impertinent behaviour.'

'Oh I'm so sorry; I thought I *had* told you,' Rhonwen lied. 'Shall I tell Mr Trinder that you would like to make an appointment to see him later?' There was no response from Fishnchips except the sound of the front door slamming shut after her stormy exit.

A short while later Arthur turned up. 'Mrs Phipps has been leaving messages on my mobile phone about you telling her I wasn't coming in today, and how belligerent you were towards her this morning.'

'I'd completely forgotten you weren't out all day.' Rhonwen lied again, thinking what a devilishly insincere and untruthful, and therefore utterly delightful morning she was having, 'I'm sure Mrs Phipps will call in again.' She was definitely not going to apologise for her alleged rudeness to one of Porthcwm's most unpleasant inhabitants.

'I'll bring you a coffee in now Mr Trinder shall I?'

'Yes please, Rhonwen.'

Taking a new jar of coffee out of her favourite pink hand bag she realised that making coffee and lying was all she seemed to be doing so far this morning. God…there are times when I love my job she thought contentedly.

As Rhonwen entered Arthur's office she caught him hurriedly hiding the document he had been studying underneath a pile of other papers.

'I've just spoken to Mrs Phipps,' he said, 'and she is coming in again shortly; please show her straight in here would you?'

'Of course. I've bought some new coffee, Mr Trinder, decaffeinated, much better for us. I've left the jar in the kitchen in case you want to make some more.'

'I never drink the stuff,' he replied, 'I need the boost *real* coffee gives me,' he laughed at his little joke. 'Would you mind getting me a cup of the normal stuff please?'

Rhonwen couldn't help but smile to herself. She made him a fresh cup of coffee and took it through to him. 'I was introduced to the new coffee by Mrs Hughes, Megan Hughes, you know, on Saturday,' she told Arthur, 'it was she that suggested I should be using decaffeinated coffee. Much better for us apparently.'

'Who on earth introduced you to her?' Arthur asked, looking slightly uncomfortable.

Rhonwen ignored the question and just said, 'When she realised where I worked she mentioned that you'd popped in to see her recently. Such a nice lady isn't she?'

Arthur now appeared more than a little concerned. Suddenly he changed tack completely.

'May I say Rhonwen, how very well you are looking these days, and slimmer too. I noticed that you are not eating your biscuits or other naughty bits and pieces. Have you started on a secret diet? I'm well aware that you have been slipping off at lunchtimes so I'm guessing you have been using that new little fitness centre up near the library?'

If only he knew, Rhonwen thought. Still, it's all exercise isn't it…?

She was surprised that giving up her secret stash of biscuits and eating more sensibly, plus becoming a member of said local fitness centre and her private 'exercise' with Rudi could make a difference so quickly. She was losing weight and enjoying the compliments she was receiving. Of course being in love had a lot to do with it, what with the motivation and all that extra exertion.

She had noticed how Arthur had begun to make suggestive remarks again, but she didn't care anymore. Far from stopping him Rhonwen had been egging him on somewhat as she could sense his anticipation growing the more weight she lost. She knew he had expectations that she would never deliver on, despite offering her all kinds of inducement including a slight pay rise. She was very pleased to accept that in the flutter of an eyelash, but kept Arthur at a very cool arm's-length otherwise.

'Or have you got a young man hidden away?' Arthur continued, laughing at the unlikelihood of his suggestion. 'Don't worry, there'll be someone special for you somewhere, just you wait and see.'

Rhonwen smiled, 'I do hope so...' she said and opened the door to leave.

'Rhonwen...' Arthur started.

'Yes, Mr Trinder?'

'I wonder whether you would like to come and do a couple of house valuations tomorrow evening, it would be very good experience for you?'

Yuk, Rhonwen thought, but before she could respond she turned to look into the shop behind her when she heard the front door open and close. Saved by the bell she thought. 'Mr Trinder, here is Mrs Phipps *again*...'

164

Chapter 18

Jo was pleased to see that Megan looked fine when she called in on her the next day. She had been concerned that now she knew about Arthur actually having sales particulars about her house she might become worried about it. She seemed to be her normal jolly self as they chatted about all sorts of things, except Arthur Trinder. But although Megan appeared to be absolutely alright, Jo couldn't work out whether it was an act or not.

It was only when the doorbell rang that Megan's demeanour altered and she suddenly appeared unsure and nervy. 'I wonder who that is,' she said anxiously. 'Would you mind answering it please my dear?'

Jo opened the door to the smiling face of Simple Simon. His pleasant manner disappeared instantly.

'Oh, good morning Doctor,' she said. 'Is Mrs Hughes expecting you?'

'Well, you certainly seem to pop up everywhere. Years of practice I guess,' he added sharply. 'No, she isn't expecting me. As a matter of fact,' he dropped his voice to a whisper, 'I just called to check on her. She rang me yesterday afternoon saying she was feeling a bit frail and wobbly. Most unlike her. She obviously didn't want to go into details on the phone so I thought she might be more relaxed about talking to me if I just called in. I wondered what had brought that on.'

'I was worried too,' confessed Jo in a low voice. 'We called in yesterday to introduce Rudi and his girlfriend to Megan. She's wanted to meet them for ages. We are all concerned that Arthur Trinder is trying to con her into selling this house or frighten her into leaving it. I suspect it's probably to do with that. It's all very peculiar. You should speak to her yourself so you'd better come in.'

Simon followed Jo through the hallway to the sitting room. She could see that Megan relaxed immediately when she saw who it was and was really pleased to see him. 'I'll sort some tea shall I?' Jo suggested and disappeared off into the kitchen to let them chat.

When she carried the tea tray through to the sitting room their conversation had already changed to the weather and barbeques. 'We have a fund raising barbeque in Porthcwm every year my dear' Megan said to her. 'It's a week on Saturday, down on the beach.'

'That sounds fun,' said Jo. 'What's in aid of?'

'We raise funds for the church restoration trust. The conservation work has been going on there for years, there's always something falling off the building or something in need of repair. Your Aunt came up with the beach barbeque idea about ten years ago and never imagined that it would be so successful,' said Megan. 'She loved any excuse for being on the beach. You two took after her in that way.'

'Oh - yes we loved it and...' Jo caught Simon's look of irritation and stopped abruptly. 'Will you be going to it, Megan?' she added quickly. 'I'm sure Cass will be up for a beach barbeque so why don't we go together?'

'That would be lovely my dear. I'll get one or two others to join us as well. You'll come with us too of course, Simon?' Megan requested. 'I know you usually go.' She obviously wasn't going to wait for his answer. 'I'll sort out tickets then,' she added quickly.

Jo was patently aware that Simon hadn't uttered a word and knew that he would think it would be a fate worse than death to go to anything with Cass and herself. Anyway it would spoil the whole evening for them too to have him moping along in their party. 'Well maybe Simon has to be on call, Megan?' she suggested hopefully.

'No, he doesn't,' said Megan with a big smile. 'I'd already asked him that. So that's lovely, all of us together.'

Jo stood up to leave just as Simon said, 'I must get back to the surgery now.'

'Me too... must go, I mean. Lovely to see you, Megan.' gabbled Jo and giving her a hasty kiss rushed down the corridor so she didn't have to leave the house at the same time as the grouchy doctor.

166

Jo hadn't been able to work up any enthusiasm about the barbeque, whether it was for charity or not, because she realised the whole evening was likely to be a disaster. She had no intention of attempting to have polite conversation with Simon and wished she hadn't been persuaded by Megan to join in. She hadn't picked up any gossip or info about it before they'd been invited along, but since being unwittingly enrolled into it she seemed to hear nothing but excited chatter about it around the town. The barbeque was obviously an immensely popular event that had somewhat crept up on her and Cass without warning. Now they were stuck with having to go along.

The evening of the barbeque was sunny and still. It couldn't have been more perfect in that respect. Jo and Cass arranged to meet Megan there and made their way by foot to the beach. At least they could enjoy a drink without worrying about having to drive back. Jo felt that a drink or two too many would more than compensate for the fact they would be forced to tolerate Simple Simon's company for the evening.

'C'mon Jo,' said Cass. 'It's all in a good cause'. There'll be masses of other people there as well and the Doc probably feels the same about being stuck with us too. Perhaps Megan is trying to build bridges with us all?'

'Well it isn't working,' sulked Jo. 'He really seems to particularly hate me and I didn't do anything in the past to him on my own. It was always both of us.'

As they neared the beach they could smell food and hear music and Jo's spirits began to lift and once she had a glass of red wine in her hand she began to feel happier. What could be nicer she thought than being in this idyllic place with Cass and our friends, eating and drinking and listening to a local band playing their hearts out?

She caught sight of Megan and made her way over to join her. 'Gosh Megan this is fantastic,' Jo said. 'the whole town seems to be here.'

'Pretty much my dear, it's one of the best annual events... Ah hello Simon,' she said over Jo's shoulder.

Jo turned to catch Simon's cheery expression for Megan slump into a scowl when he caught her eye.

'Well, you two chat to each other, I'll be back in a moment,' said Megan and off she went across the sand in the direction of the bar.

'Do you always come to this?' asked Jo feebly, hating the strained silence.

Simon chose to ignore her, 'Is your sister here?'

'Yes, she's talking to Rhonwen and Rudi who are trying hard not to look as if they are together.'

'Why?'

'Why what?' Jo responded.

'Why are they pretending?' Simon asked.

'Long story really but it's to do with Arthur not finding out about them,' said Jo.

'Oh good, I'm glad you two are chatting away,' said Megan as she returned, jigging to the band's rather ropey rendition of the beach Boys 'Surfin' USA', a bottle of Sauvignon Blanc clutched in her hand.

'We'll have to drink this fast so that it doesn't get too warm. Cass is bringing the glasses and Rudi and Rhonwen are coming over too.'

When everyone else had joined them Megan pointed to a table and chairs behind her. I asked Phil Fixit to bring all this for us so we've somewhere to perch and watch what's going on.'

'What actually *does* go on, Megan?' asked Cass.

'Now, who's for a glass of New Zealand's finest?' said Megan brandishing the bottle as if she hadn't heard Cass's question.

Suddenly there was an ear-piercing whining sound followed by a voice bursting forth over a loudspeaker across the beach.

'Ladies and gentlemen...' Jo looked around to see where it had come from and saw Rev Huw standing on a bit of staging made up from a pile of precariously positioned wooden pallets seemingly held in place by orange binder twine and a single stake driven in to the sand. She thought how relaxed he looked in his knee-length red and white checked shorts, dark top and the ubiquitous dog collar. His white legs were stuck into even whiter socks and brown sandals. Goodness, thought Jo we used to see an awful lot more of him down on this beach when we used to spy on him and Bev. She turned to say as much to Cass but caught Simon's eye instead. She felt as if he had been reading her thoughts.

'Memories?' he asked, and poured everyone another glass of wine.

Bugger, Jo decided, this *is* going to be a tortuous evening.

'Ahem, Ladies and gentlemen,' Rev continued. 'Now that my wonderful technical team -AKA head choirboy, Oscar, has sorted the sound system problems I shall make one or two general announcements before you continue boosting the restoration coffers by polishing off everything on the bar and scoffing yourselves silly from the Barbeque run by the lovely ladies from the WI.

'Firstly, please support the raffle. There are some magnificent prizes up for grabs. The ticket sellers will be moving amongst you extracting even more money from you as I speak... Mr Trinder..., Mr Trinder? Ah there you are. Mr Arthur Trinder and his little band of helpers are selling the tickets here tonight. Thank you very much Arthur.'

'Now, please can you give an encouraging cheer to our own town band led by Bill, Porthcwm's finest, and of course, *only*, member of the Police Force. Let's hope there are no incidents that require his official attention tonight. They are playing a selection of tunes with a nautical theme, chosen by our hard working church committee. So a big thank you to the baaaaand...'

Everyone cheered as loudly as possible.

'The other announcement concerns the team sandcastle competition which will commence in half an hour. Thank you to all of those who have put their names forward to participate in this and to those who have suggested the names of other victims… or perhaps I should say volunteers. There will be, as is customary, four people to a team and I am pleased to announce that there are enough names for eleven teams. Now, as is usual I shall name the members of each team one by one as we pull them randomly from this hat.' He wobbled unsteadily on his podium as he indicated Bev who was standing below him on the sand. 'Just bear with me as this takes a little while to do but always seems the fairest way of dividing you all into teams.'

Rev began running through names as Bev pulled small pieces of folded paper from an old top hat. Megan's group were on their third bottle of wine and not taking any notice of what was going on anywhere else. Jo was busy filling everyone's glasses once again and beginning to think it was all becoming rather jolly after all. Simon, who had his back to her now so she couldn't see if he was glaring any more, seemed to have relaxed and was chatting to Rudi. She caught the sound of something familiar and looked up from her wine pouring to see Megan's group all looking at her.

'What?' she asked.

'Rev just called your name out so you are in a team,' said Cass laughing.

'Don't be ridiculous,' said Jo 'I haven't given anyone my name.'

'Well then, someone else must have,' said Cass.

Jo felt rooted to the ground. Suddenly the fun had stopped. Now the evening was going wrong again.

Over the next few minutes there were groans from other members of the group who heard their names called out. 'Megan,' asked Rudi, 'can you tell us what's happening please? We weren't listening as we weren't involved; or rather we thought we weren't involved.'

'Well this was an event that Jo and Cass's aunt started years ago. It's all about making money to restore bits of the church, but she thought up the sandcastle part of it a year or two later because

170

she felt people tended to stay in their little cliques and not mix. So everyone who wants to join in sends their name in to the Rev and then their names are randomly drawn out of the hat so that people end up in unplanned teams. Of course sometimes friends end up in teams together but it is pure chance. That way everyone has to muck in together and build the best sandcastle they can. The winners receive £50 which traditionally is handed over to the Church Funds anyway. It's just a bit of fun of course and entertainment for everyone else.'

Jo was feeling irritated that she had been drinking rather too many glasses of wine in an effort to dull the annoyance of being stuck in close proximity to Simon and was now expected to build a sandcastle. It would have been bad enough sober.

'Megan, how would they have got hold of our names?' she asked, but looking directly at Simon.

'Steady on,' he said to her. 'Why would I have done that?'

'Revenge?' she growled in a low voice so that no one else could hear.

Simon's face lit up in a huge smile and then he laughed. In fact he laughed so much that the others all stopped talking and turned to see what was going on.

'Believe me, it never even crossed my mind,' he said, standing so close to her that she could smell his aftershave. 'But I *shall* get a little revenge, as you so neatly put it, by watching you.'

'Sorry to spoil your fun Simon,' said Cass who had overheard their short exchange, 'but your name has also been called out. As has mine,' she added unhappily.

Jo noticed, not without some distinct pleasure, the smile vanish from Simon's face in an instant.

She was now feeling slightly better about not being the only one forced onto one of the teams and celebrated with another glass of wine.

'Jo…Jo, what are you doing?' asked Cass. 'If you really intend having another, I'd turn it into a consolation drink if I were you. I hate to spoil your fun but you and Simon appear to be on the same team.'

'Noooo…' cried Jo and grabbed the large glass of water that Cass was holding out for her.

Megan who had been watching them all said, 'I've heard some of your names called out but we've all been chatting so much that we didn't catch the other team members so let's go and have a look at the list to see who's on which team. There'll also be the plan pinned up of which team has which plot of sand.'

The band had just murdered "Beyond the Sea", Bobby Darin's old hit, and was half way through a grinding rendition of the Beatles' "Octopus's Garden" as they began looking at the list of teams pinned to an old sea worn mooring post. Jo caught sight of Cass's name first.

'See your name got sent in too, I wonder who did this? You seem to be with Rudi, Rosa, and Gloria, well lucky you; at least you know them all. I'm with… God, I thought you were joking, Cass, a fate worse than death…the team mate from hell, Doctor Unfriendly. I'm with that head choirboy too and Arthur Trinder, Arthur TRINDER for goodness sake…well he wouldn't have put his own name down would he, I can't imagine why he's even here. What a crap team. It'll be an hour of hell. Megan…' she called 'Megan… just look who I'm with…'

Jo glanced down the list at the other names, picking out a few familiar ones, but a there were alot which she didn't recognise. She saw Ricco's name but didn't bother to tell Cass. She was feeling so annoyed inside about being stuck with Simon, she wasn't even bothered about Arthur any more. Another glass of wine will help she thought and headed back to Megan's table.

'So have a last drink or two to summon up your strength and design expertise…' as if reading her thoughts Rev's voice came through the sound system and out over the throng of partying people spread across the sands. '…and make your way to your building plots.'

Bugger, thought Jo, let's get this over and done with. Feeling irritated and more than a little inebriated she made her rather wobbly way across to her sandcastle plot.

Each team had a clearly defined area of exactly the same size and the plots were all in a row. She discovered that Rudi, Gloria, Rosa and Cass had the plot on her right. Thank goodness it was people she knew. At least she could talk to them. Gloria was already there waiting. 'Hi Gloria,' said Jo. 'Isn't this jolly?' she added sarcastically.

'I love doing this, I put my name forward every year,' Gloria replied.

No wonder, Jo thought, she must get so much attention. Gloria it seemed didn't have sandcastle building clothes. She was wearing the usual tiny bit of material that masqueraded as a skirt, a very tight, low cut lime green top that showed off her enhanced boobs and her spray tan. She would never go on a suntan bed she had told Jo, far too dangerous, and yet she was having plastic surgery like tomorrow wasn't coming. The only difference from her usual clothes was the fact that she wasn't wearing stilettos for once but high wedge shoes which helped give her a little balance on the sand. Peculiar thought Jo. Very, very peculiar…Oh God I do feel a little squiffy…

Rudi, Rosa and Cass turned up to join Gloria. 'You're lucky to be together,' said Jo. 'Have you seen who I've got? The doctor from hell, a choirboy, and an estate…' Jo could see Rudi pulling meaningful faces at her and looked up. She hadn't noticed Arthur Trinder arriving, his footsteps muffled by the sand. God he must boiling she thought. He had on his usual work clothes and shiny brogues. Arthur appeared to be very pleased to be on the next plot to Gloria.

Oscar the head choirboy turned up next and Jo introduced herself. 'Oh hi,' said Oscar, 'the Rev has told us all loads about you and your sister when you used to stay here.'

'I bet he did,' she replied.

Cass said, 'Look Jo, there are some other unfortunate mixes too, what about poor Rhon? She's with Ricco, Fishnchips and Linda Trinder next but one to you.'

'That's unfair Cass,' said Jo, checking to see who was within earshot. 'Linda's lovely and your ex is fine, it's only you that feels that way about him. However I wouldn't want to be in Rhon's shoes with Fishnchips.'

Oscar offered Jo a little smile, 'You'd better know that Fishnchips is my mother.'

'Oh my God, I'm so sorry, she offered feebly.

'Yes it's a pain, I agree.' Oscar said.

'I meant sorry for being so rude, I had no idea she has any children.'

That's okay,' he said. 'I understand. She doesn't usually mention me. I can't wait to be able to leave home. I spend quite a lot of time at the Rev's.'

Rev Huw's voice came out loud and clear over the beach again. He explained that there were four kid-sized buckets and spades for each plot and that they could build whatever they wanted. One nominated member of the team would be able to race around the beach begging, borrowing or stealing any embellishments to decorate their creation. He would blow the whistle to start the competition and again to let everyone know that their hour was up.

'Okay? Are you all ready?' called out the Rev. He blew his whistle loudly, the teams started filling their buckets with sand and the band lurched awkwardly into the opening of "Sittin' on the Dock of the Bay".

Jo was relieved that she couldn't see Simon anywhere. Perhaps he wouldn't show up. Arthur was busy talking to Gloria but all the other teams seemed to be deciding what they were going to build and organising who was going to wander around finding things.

'Okay,' said Oscar. 'I've done this before so shall I make some suggestions?'

'Sounds good to me. Anyway, there are only three of us,' said Jo.

'No it's fine, the Doc's on his way now,' Oscar pointed out.

Jo looked up and saw Simon coming towards them.

'Bugger it,' she said. 'I thought we'd been spared.' Everyone else around them was digging and building and look generally busy.

Arthur had become engrossed in Gloria the moment she bent down and started filling one of her buckets with sand. He seemed oblivious to all that was going on around him.

'Mr Trinder?' called Oscar. 'Mr Trinder…we need to start. Which of us is going to go and get any shells or seaweed and other bits and pieces from round the beach?'

'Oh I'll do that,' volunteered Jo. Anything to get away from Simon she thought.

'Not a good idea,' said Simon. 'You're not sober enough to find your way back here in one piece. I suggest that Oscar does it when we've nearly finished as he's young and quick?'

Jo glared at him and had the decency to look somewhat ill at ease. Or maybe she was just looking ill?

'Good idea,' said Arthur vaguely. He had suddenly joined the group and stopped ogling Gloria when he caught sight of Fishnchips watching him like a hawk from two building plots along. The other member of Fishnchips' team was watching him being watched too. Linda Trinder didn't miss a trick.

Chapter 19

Cass noticed that Simon seemed to be joining in with surprising enthusiasm on his team's plot next door to her after his sharp comment about Jo being inebriated had hit the spot. Oscar appeared to be doing most of the work which Jo in turn, managed to destroy as she stumbled around getting in their way.

Their other team member, Arthur, was clearly useless at anything practical. Cass could tell his mind was certainly not on the job in hand. How could it be when he was busy trying to keep three women happy? As Gloria had most of her body on show, Arthur was finding it easy to get distracted. She obviously saw the Sandcastle Competition as a perfect opportunity to display herself to a greater audience and most particularly to Arthur on the next plot.

Cass could see Arthur glancing nervously at Fishnchips who was in turn trying to keep him permanently in her sights and she couldn't decide whether he was being fielded smiles or snarls. She noticed him acknowledge Linda's presence occasionally, but he was so preoccupied with the other two that his wife barely got a look in.

Cass felt sorry for Oscar who had been lumbered with a pretty useless team one way or another. They did appear to have built something - of sorts - eventually, yet what it was exactly no one seemed to know.

Cass found she was rather enjoying trying to build a sandcastle after all and was getting quite adventurous with a random turret design that appeared totally isolated from the main structure that Rudi and Rosa were trying to construct.

Rudi had taken charge. He was extremely artistic, a discovery that didn't go entirely unnoticed by his uncle who looked immensely astonished from his position on the adjacent plot. Under his leadership the ragtag group did eventually manage to build something - of sorts – less fairy tale Disney lair, more entrance gate to a long deserted Soviet theme park, but a sandcastle construction all the same.

Cass could just see Rhonwen's team a little further along. They too, were a funny bunch she thought, and couldn't wait to find out how Fishnchips and Linda managed to work together, if at all. She had tried a couple of times to see how Ricco was getting on and was annoyed with herself when he caught her sneaking a look.

When Rev blew the final whistle to let everyone know that the hour was up and they should lay down their buckets and spades, Cass was relieved for her sister that it was over. Jo had looked as miserable as sin the entire time.

As the groups dispersed, the judges began making their way around the sandcastle plots scribbling on notepads and taking photographs.

Cass, like everybody else, made her way back to their table where Megan was waiting for them. She had splashed out on some Prosecco to celebrate their sandcastle building achievements.

'I thought you did splendidly well, my dears,' she said, lifting her glass up towards the group in a toast, 'congratulations to you all and well done. I'm sure that despite your initial reservations you will all find that it was a very worthwhile event to have taken part in.'

'Thanks Megan,' said Cass. 'At least we can relax now and enjoy ourselves.'

Jo's eyes had lit up when she saw the Prosecco. She felt she deserved a drink now having had to put up with being on the same team as Simon. Fortunately he had ignored her most of the time. but in a way that had annoyed her as much as if he had been constantly sniping at her. Not that she *would* have wanted him to talk to her anyway, of course.

Cass watched Rudi sidle up to Rhonwen and drop a gentle kiss on her bare shoulder when he was sure his uncle was miles away, his attention diverted by one of his women elsewhere.

After the band finished performing a strange folk version of the Disney classic Under the Sea, there was a shrill whining sound before the loudspeaker boomed out again.

'Ladies and gentlemen, we have nearly finished the evening but first I have two very important duties to perform. The first is to announce the result of the sandcastle competition...'

Cass could see how all Megan's guests switched off at this point as they were fully aware how wonderful some of the other entries had been. There was a lot of cheering and clapping as the lucky winners went to receive their prize money.

There was more piercing loudspeaker noise and Rudi who could just make out what the Rev was saying turned to the twins and said, 'Shhh, the Rev's talking about your aunt.'

'...tirelessly organised this event almost up to her death last year and we all sadly miss her commitment and energy. It seems only right therefore, that the raffle prizes should be presented by her nieces who are now very much part of our community. Many of us will have memories of them staying here years ago every school holiday. Those of you who were not here then will doubtless have heard about their... what shall I call them...exploits! It is a joy that they are living here in Porthcwm now and putting something back into the community.'

Cass could see Jo's face and the look of horror on it as everyone laughed and clapped their hands.

'Cass and Jo,' continued the Rev, 'please would you be kind enough to come over here and present the raffle prizes?'

'Shit,' said Cass. 'No choice Jo. He's paying us back, you realise, for all that stuff we used to do. It's his revenge. We've got to do it, let's just get it over and done with.' she looked at her twin who appeared glued to the seat she had just lowered herself onto, 'For God's sake put your glass down and try and act slightly soberish at the very least.'

As they walked over the sand towards the Rev, Jo began to look a little green about the gills and finding it almost impossible to travel in a straight line took her sister's arm to steady herself. Cass couldn't remember ever seeing Jo in this state and hoped she wouldn't make a scene in front of everyone. She was relieved when Rudi came up and took Jo's other arm, and between them they managed to get Jo to the foot of the pallet platform in one piece.

Rev carefully bent forward and offered Cass his hand to help her up onto the top. It suddenly dawned on her that the whole structure was about as insecure as their poorly built sandcastle. Much to everyone's amusement Rev and Cass clung together as if trapped in some strange dance as it wobbled to and fro, but once they had got their balance they both very carefully leaned forward to offer a hand each to Jo. This whole exercise would have been difficult for a sober person but Jo was finding it impossible to climb up and join them, even with Rudi's steadying grip on her arm.

'Here, I'll give you a hand,' said Simon from behind Rudi and taking an arm each they managed to manhandle Jo up to join Rev and Cass.

There was a cheer from the crowd who were thoroughly enjoying the extra bit of entertainment, though sadly the band looked slightly dejected that this inebriated twin was receiving the loudest applause of the night so far.

Rudi and Simon stayed, holding on to the shaky pallets whilst the Rev introduced the twins and started to read out the winning raffle ticket numbers. Cass handed out the prizes which were passed to her by Bev who had the good sense to stay at sand level. Jo clung on, in turn, to Cass and to Rev as she swayed and wobbled with every shaky pallet movement. The most amusing part of the prize-giving for the already well entertained onlookers was when a pink ticket belonging to Jo was pulled out and she won a bottle of whiskey. Rudi thought she was going to throw up at the sight of more alcohol and grabbed the bottle as she lurched forward to receive it from Bev. In doing so she completely lost her balance, somewhat stylishly pitched off the pallets into Simon's arms and passed out.

'I've had a really great evening,' said Rhonwen as she helped Megan into the passenger seat of Phil Fixit's van. Rudi and Cass packed her table and chairs and other beach stuff into the back and waved Megan off homewards. Then she joined Cass and Simon who were trying to bundle Jo into the front seat of Simon's car.

'Thank goodness you had your car here,' said Cass gratefully to him. 'I don't know how we'd have managed otherwise. The Lodge isn't locked so you can get in okay and we shan't be far behind you.'

'She's going to be feeling pretty grim tomorrow and embarrassed at her public antics,' said Simon. 'She won't want to be looking at fry-ups so I guess you'll be doing breakfast for the guests on your own.'

'You're right. And thank you so much, Simon, you seem to keep coming to her rescue.'

She turned and joined the others to make their way back up to the town. 'How was your sandcastle team Rhon?' she asked.

'It was pretty dreadful as no one took it seriously, but because we were only a few plots down I had a good view of *you* all,' Rhonwen said, laughing. 'The dynamics of my group would have been interesting for anyone watching us too.'

She explained how Fishnchips decided to be in charge of her team and how no one took any notice, how Linda was the peacemaker when she got too bossy and how Ricco couldn't take his eyes off Cass. Rhonwen could see Cass getting embarrassed but although her observation was acknowledged with a dismissive grunt she rather got the impression that Cass was quite pleased. She continued to tell them how people kept coming along and interrupted them, mostly talking to Linda, 'She's so nice and friendly to everyone. Arthur is mad to mess her about. Douglas Sidebotham came and diverted her for ages. He must have been boiling in his tweed jacket.'

Rhonwen told them how Linda had taken her aside and whispered that she knew that she was 'seeing' Rudi and how pleased she was. She promised not to tell Arthur of course and asked if there was anything she could do to help. Rhonwen could see the look of pleasure on Rudi's face despite the fading light and gave him a big hug. She had nothing good to report back about Fishnchips who she had overheard making it clear to Linda in no uncertain terms how attentive *her* Arthur was in helping to find a place for her dream B&B.

When they arrived back at the Lodge there was no sign of Simon or his car. Rhonwen gave Cass a hug before she and Rudi went off to stay in Seaview Cottage to save them both a long walk back to their respective homes.

Cass went inside as quietly as possible so she wouldn't disturb Jo or the guests. The house was completely silent. Even Nosey was flat out asleep in his basket in the kitchen. A fine guard dog he is, she thought.

She fetched a big jug of water from the kitchen and made her way up to Jo's room. Her twin was tucked up in bed and all the clothes she'd been wearing were neatly folded on the armchair in the far corner of the room. Realising that Jo was out for the count Cass just poured some water into her glass, left it within easy reaching distance on her bedside table and pulled the bed cover up over her shoulders. She was about to go off to her own room but then had an idea and ran back downstairs to the kitchen. She fetched the porridge saucepan and put it next to Jo's bed, just in case, reminding herself to retrieve it in the morning and give it a good scrub before breakfast should it have been put to use during the night

When Cass climbed into bed she lay there thinking about what Rhonwen had told her earlier about Ricco watching her. She wasn't entirely sure how she felt about that. She was just going to have to accept that he would be here in Porthcwm for a while and she would make an effort to be civil to him when they ran into each other from now on. That way everyone would be able to get on with their own business. Well, she thought, that's a sensible decision taken.

Megan was very relieved to get home that night. Phil Fixit had been such a dear to collect her on the way to the barbeque and help her set everything up on the beach, plus take her home afterwards. But she was pleased that he had turned down her offer of a coffee as she felt completely exhausted and just wanted to get off to her bed.

Still, she thought she deserved a little nightcap, or maybe a generous one after her busy and successful event. Although Megan was very happy with how it had all gone, it had been a long evening and she wasn't used to it. She poured out a healthy dose of brandy into one of her favourite glasses and wearily climbed the stairs to her bedroom.

It must have been in the early hours when she was having a dream about an enormous mouse wearing an apron who was trying to grate a huge solid piece of cheese. Megan could hear the rasping noise. Then the mouse dropped the cheese on the floor and it made a loud bang. Megan sat up. It was still very dark. She smiled to herself as she recalled the little dream she'd had. She lay down again and turned onto her side. She very rarely had dreams and wondered whether the Armagnac had been responsible. A few moments later she was aware of the rasping noise once more but knew she wasn't back in dreamland. She sat up again and listened carefully. It appeared to be coming from downstairs.

There was only one thing for it she thought, and reached to her side table for her spectacles, swung her legs out of the bed and stood up. She slipped on her dressing gown, slid her feet into her slippers and walked as quietly as she could to the door. She managed to open it without a sound and made her way along the landing towards the top of the stairs. She knew that in all movies where there appeared to be an intruder downstairs the hero would pick up a baseball bat, or marble bust, or brass candlestick which were conveniently close at hand to clobber the prowler with. She had none of these of course, but looked around to see what she could utilise instead.

The only thing that she could think of was her old Family Bible which she kept in the oak linen press near the top of the stairs along with some other oversized tomes which wouldn't fit into the bookshelves elsewhere. She calmly turned the latch on the cupboard doors. It just clicked a little but they swung open and she reached inside to pull out the Bible. Goodness, she'd quite forgotten it was such a weight. She held it in front of her with both arms and walked to the top of the stairs. Gingerly she started to go downwards, slow step, by slow step.

The rasping noise was still coming from the direction of the kitchen. She wondered now whether it might just be a branch grating against the outside of one of the windows and thought how funny she would appear if anyone were to see her creeping around the house carrying that enormous Bible. Side-tracked by the thoughts of how mad she must look, she missed her footing and fell forwards, the Bible still clasped tightly in her arms.

Chapter 20

Cass knew it wasn't going to be the usual relaxed Sunday morning at the Lodge. She nipped in quickly to check on Jo on her way downstairs and found she was still fast asleep. Thank goodness, she thought. It was probably as well she was out for the count as Cass knew she would have no time to deal with her twin's alcoholic aftermath for a while.

She could really have done with some help this morning as Gloria wasn't coming in either. They'd arranged for her to take the Sunday morning off for once, not realising of course that Jo would be out of action.

Two of the guests had asked for a picnic lunch to take with them along the Coast Path, and the Americans who were staying for the week wanted a really early breakfast. They had spent the Saturday visiting as many castles and historic destinations as is humanly possible to fit into one day, and had come back exhausted. But instead of lingering a little longer in bed on a Sunday morning and having a late breakfast they had an equally punishing itinerary planned for today. She couldn't imagine how they could even begin to remember clearly any one single place they had visited.

The other guests were a really sweet and shy honeymoon couple who Cass guessed wouldn't be down for ages. Although there were fixed breakfast times, she forgave them and knew she would have plenty of time for other chores before they showed their faces later on.

Somehow, with a little juggling she managed to get through all the jobs that she and Jo normally shared and at last had time to go and see her patient. She took her a cup of tea and a thin, dry piece of toast with some Marmite scraped over it and put them down on her bedside table.

Cass heard a grunt of complaint from her sister when she opened the curtains a little to let in a shaft of sunlight.

'Here you are Jo, drink this. I'm not even going to ask how you feel because I can see from the way you look that it's not good.'

Cass helped Jo lean up on her elbow and passed her the mug of tea. Jo sipped at it unsteadily. 'Thanks,' she mumbled, passing it back after a few moments. Cass fetched the old T-shirt Jo used as a nightie, 'Here let's put this on you, then you won't get so many crumbs on your skin,' she said.

She helped her sister on with the t-shirt and then watched as Jo held the toast in her shaky hand. She stared at it a while before taking a bite and chewing laboriously, muttering something under her breath.

'Can't hear,' said Cass.

'I was just saying thank you for putting me to bed last night.'

'Oh it wasn't me. Simon gave you a lift back as we wanted to walk, so you were all tucked up and flat out ages before Rhon and Rudi and I got back.'

'You let *him* bring me home?' Jo sounded shocked.

'Well clearly you were in no fit state to walk back with us and Phil Fixit had his van full with Megan and her stuff. Simon had his car there in case he got called out during the evening, so we had no choice but use his vehicle after you passed out when you won the bottle of Scotch.'

'Scotch?'

'Yes, Scotch. I don't think you remember much from last evening do you, Jo?' asked Cass.

Jo thought for a while. 'I can remember the wretched sandcastle thing and vaguely the Rev saying something about a raffle?'

'Sorry Jo, can we talk about it later? I must dash now if you're okay for the mo. I've loads to do but I'll bring you up some more toast in a while.'

Cass smiled to herself as she walked across the landing. She wondered how long it would take for the penny to drop with her hung-over sister.

'Cass, Cass…' not long then, thought Cass, as Jo's voice called from her bedroom, 'P-LEASE don't tell me that Simple Simon undressed me?'

Cass wasn't really surprised when Simon appeared on the doorstep a little later that morning.

'Come in, Jo's still in bed.'

'I completely forgot to leave this with her last night when I brought her back here. Probably the last thing she needs to see at the moment, but if I take it home I may end up drinking it,' he smiled passing the whisky raffle prize over to Cass.

Good God, thought Cass, he smiled, he actually smiled. Perhaps he's more relaxed now and beginning to forgive us for all that awful stuff we inflicted on him in the past. Shan't hold my breath though, and Jo certainly won't come down off her high horse especially now she realizes that he undressed her before putting her to bed last night.

'How's Jo feeling this morning?' he asked.

'Pretty shitty,' said Cass, 'but that pales into insignificance now she knows how she was brought home and by whom.'

He smiled again.

Then she saw the look on his face change to a more serious one, 'Actually I did also want to let you know that I was called over to Megan's house in the early hours this morning. Her next door neighbour caught the sound of her voice calling out for help, though goodness knows how he heard her at that time. I'm afraid she's had an accident. She's okay though, amazingly. Frank Jones, the neighbour, said he found her lying at the bottom of the stairs embracing an enormous family bible.'

'What on earth…?' started Cass.

'No idea… He said the front door was wide open. Lucky for her it was, otherwise he might not have heard her. And thankfully he didn't have to break in.'

'I'm relieved she's okay,' said Cass, 'but why the Bible?'

'Don't know. She didn't offer me an explanation but I thought she might tell you if you have a chance to go and see her. I'm a little concerned about her state of mind, especially if she doesn't remember anything about why she was clinging to a Bible that size in the middle of the night, or why she was at the bottom of the stairs with the front door wide open.'

'I'll try and pop over to see her later. She wasn't bad enough to take to hospital then?'

'Shaken mostly. Would you like me to look in on *your* patient as well whilst I'm here?'

'I'll go and ask her. Won't be a mo,' said Cass, running off upstairs.

A few minutes later she was back downstairs. 'Predictably, her words were something like 'not over her dead body' but a bit more colourful.'

'I'll be off then,' Simon said. 'Could you let me know what Megan says?'

It's going to be one of those days, Cass thought when the next doorbell chime celebrated the arrival of Rev and Bev.

'We thought we'd pop down and see how Jo is after her descent into Hell last night?' said Bev.

'You might get the same response that Simon got earlier,' answered Cass. She'll probably never forgive either of you for that raffle set-up. Can't say I blame you at all though. I guess we're getting our well-deserved comeuppance.'

The Rev stepped forward and gave her a great bear hug. 'It was all done in the best spirit. You are both so like your aunt I'm enormously relieved to say. I know that by helping Rhonwen and Rudi through an awkward period you are doing something very similar to what your aunt did to help Bev and me.' He put his arm around Bev, 'She was marvellous to us. The only slight fly in the ointment was you two who decided we were fair game for your sleuthing antics.'

'Rev, could you do something for me please?' Cass suddenly asked. 'I just haven't got any spare time at the mo what with Jo in bed and Gloria having the day off. Are you able to call in and see Megan? Simon said she had a nasty fall during the night and was found at the bottom of her stairs hanging on to a huge Bible. He is quite concerned about her, not physically though, as she appears to be unharmed, but more her state of mind. I thought she might feel more comfortable telling you what she was up to with the Bible? It just seems rather odd '

'Consider it done Cass, we'll pop around to see her a little later to chat about the barbeque and we can find out casually then.'

The next to call was Ricco. Cass caught sight of him from the front bedroom window. She was behind with all the chores and now the honeymoon couple had *at last* vacated their bedroom she was rushing round preparing it for the incoming guests. Bugger, she thought to herself, there's no peace for the wicked today. Of all the days for everyone to call, when I'm having to do everything on my own.

She contemplated not answering the doorbell and pretending no one was in, but she could hear him talking to Nosey who had obviously got out through the open back kitchen door and charged around to the front to see who was there. Remembering her promise to herself to try and be as normal as reasonably possible and not to pick fights and niggles with him she put a slightly false smile on her face and answered the door.

'Hello Ricco,' she said rather over cheerily to him. 'What can I do for you?'

Cass could tell he was somewhat surprised to be greeted comparatively cordially by her.

'Rosa asked me to give you a message as I was walking past…'

'Yes?' said Cass, now wanting him to get to the point as fast as possible.

'Well she said they would value your opinions on something to do with the Holy Cow business. And would you both like to come around this evening and have a glass of wine and your favourite pasta dish with us and she'll explain everything then?'

'Couldn't she just have phoned?' asked Cass, impatient to get on with all the B&B tasks. 'But do thank her very much and we'll pop down the lane later when we've settled the new guests in.'

Was she sounding rude to him, she wondered, recalling her resolution to try and be nice-ish? 'And thank you, too, for calling in with the message,' she added hastily in a far too jolly voice as she shut the door rather prematurely on him.

She thought she had behaved rather better than usual. Perhaps it was going to be easier than she imagined. Oh well… what did it matter anyway in the long run, she thought, as she went back upstairs to tell Jo about the invitation and Megan's strange mishap.

Jo was beginning to feel a tad better at last. She had managed to stay in a propped up position on her pillows for a short while when Cass came in. She felt as if she had rounded that corner of feeling so foul that she 'didn't want to live' and had arrived at the 'never wanting to have another drink' stage.

Cass told her about Megan's Bible incident and the invitation to Rosa's whilst she fussed around her, straightening her bedclothes and fluffing up her pillows.

'I don't think I'll be up to being sociable this evening,' Jo confessed to Cass as her twin was leaving the room to get on downstairs. 'The thought of pasta and a glass of wine makes my stomach heave. Why don't you go on your own and give my apologies. I'll be right as rain tomorrow…I hope. Anyway, you can report everything back to me so I won't really miss a thing.'

She was also hugely aware that everyone at Rosa's would have seen her drunken display and witnessed the final humiliation of being carried off by Simon to his car. She winced at the very thought of it. In fact the whole town would have either seen her exhibition or heard about it by now. How mortifying to even imagine what they must all be thinking. And Blodwyn in the Post Office would have a field day when she opened up on Monday.

It didn't bear contemplating. Oh God, she thought, and what about Simon? He must've actually carried me upstairs too…hell's teeth, I can't remember anything… and then did he really undress me? I'm sure I couldn't have done it myself. What was I wearing? I can't even think what underwear I had on.

She tried to prop herself up a little more so that she could see her clothes, but only managed it briefly before her head began spinning again. It was obviously Simon who must have folded them up neatly and put them on the chair. Who'd have thought all those years that little Simple Simon would ever have got his hands on her bra and knickers. She craned her neck again to see which of her motley collection of under garments she had in fact been wearing the previous evening and was relieved to see that they were at least *relatively* presentable. The effort was rather too much and she had to slump back on the pillows again.

When the telephone next to her bed rang shrilly, Jo prayed that Cass would answer it down stairs. Finally the noise ceased, but only to restart after a few seconds. She leant over and picked up the receiver. Talking to someone had to be better than all that racket pounding though her woolly head.

'Hello, this is the Lodge in Porthcwm, can I help you?' she said, feeling that her bright performance was Oscar worthy. 'Oh hello, Megan,' her voice resumed its wretched-feeling-rough level instantly as she knew she didn't have to pretend. 'No, I'm fine Megan, ashamed to say, but hung-over. Yes, not a surprise of course. I hope I didn't embarrass you too much at the barbeque. But more importantly how are you?'

Jo listened as Megan told her about the previous night. She said the Rev who had just called was of the opinion that she might have been imagining the strange noises but she was absolutely adamant that someone had been in her house.

'I just needed somebody to believe that there really *was* someone here, so I thought if I phoned you two, you would understand. I don't want anyone to think I'm just a silly old woman. Why would my front door be wide open otherwise, for heaven's sake?'

'It's okay Megan. Please don't get upset about this. I understand why it's so disturbing but *I* believe you,' said Jo, though she wasn't totally sure she did. Maybe it was because she suddenly felt nauseous again.

Having settled all the newly arrived guests into their rooms and given her recovering twin even more Marmite toast and a mug of tea, Cass showered and dressed up in a favourite long swirly skirt that she hadn't worn for ages, put a little bit of make-up on and some lipstick. 'There,' she said to the mirror, 'I haven't used make-up for weeks and I feel I look quite presentable for a change.

As she put her make-up bag back in her top drawer she pulled out the little framed photograph and took it over to the window. She stared at the image in front of her. Ricco's arms were around her and both of them were laughing. Whenever she looked at this she remembered what fun they'd had, so why, when she knew she was going to see him this evening at Rosa's did she feel anxious again?

Before she left she poked her head around Jo's door but didn't go in. Jo was fast asleep and snoring like a trooper. She went downstairs, clicked Nosey's lead onto his collar and began to walk down the track towards the Holy Cow Farm.

She noticed how damaged and crushed the plants looked as she walked along. The edges of the lane were beginning to look a bit knocked about and the verges were worn and furrowed from all the traffic visiting the Bellinis.

Benito had put up new signs at the top of the lane since they began to get more commercial about the business. Their tours around the miracle poo site and their pint-sized factory in the converted barn were proving extremely popular. The only down side of it was all the increased traffic on the lane past the Lodge. Often one or even two cars at a time would reverse into the twin's drive to let others pass. Jo and Cass had taken to shutting their gate now. Refrigerated vans with amazing Holy Cow logos decorating their sides, whizzed past regularly on their outward journey to deliver selections of Holy Cow Ice Cream to shops and outlets all over Great Britain. Its fame had certainly grown beyond belief. Price of progress she thought, but a little sad to see.

She picked a couple of delicate pink dog roses out of the hedgerow, rubbed off their little thorns and tucked them into her hair behind her right ear. She delved into her shoulder bag and pulled out the tiny mirror she had stuffed into the one of the inside pockets before she left. She waved it around in front of her until she could see the flowers reflected.

She caught sight of her lips too. They'd looked fine when she was indoors but now she was outside in the low evening sun they no longer looked subtle. She had carefully lip lined, lipsticked and lip glossed them and everything looked red. Far too much red, she thought now, too much of a come-on colour, and why, *why* had she suddenly decided to wear make-up tonight of all nights? How Jo would have laughed if she'd been here. She scrabbled around in her bag again, pulled out a tissue and some hand cream and proceeded to rub all traces of the colour from her lips. That looks better she thought, except it now looks a bit pink and sore, like I've just been snogged rather passionately for the first time.

'Come on Nosey,' she said pulling him out of the end of a rabbit hole that he had taken the opportunity to investigate during Cass's de-lipsticking operation. 'Now your face is all covered in soil, never mind, let's get this evening over with.'

It *would* be Ricco who got to the door first, 'Good evening,' he said, looking from Cass to Nosey and back again. He frowned a little then gave Cass one of his beautiful smiles. 'So you have both got funny faces?' he was looking very amused.

Cass could have hit him, but thrusting the dog lead into his hand instead, she pushed her way past him and in through the loo door just behind where he was standing. She looked in the mirror. Now her whole face was red with embarrassment. Well, there was nothing she could do except splash her face with some cold water and then get on with the evening.

No one else seemed to take any notice of her face when she eventually vacated the cloakroom feeling calmer and cooler, and went into the kitchen.

'Have some *chilled* wine,' said Ricco, handing her glass. 'You'll find it cooling.'

'That's a beautiful skirt,' said Rosa, as she gave Cass a welcome kiss. 'It looks lovely on you.'

'It was my favourite when we were in Paris,' said Ricco. 'Do you remember where we bought it?' he added.

Cass absentmindedly glanced down at it. Why, tonight of all nights had she decided to wear it? Although she didn't respond to his comment, her mind was all over the place. Why did she want to be reminded about Paris? It's going badly already she thought, first the lipstick and now this skirt. How could I have forgotten about where I bought it, how could I have made such a bloody stupid decision to wear it tonight?

But I've made that resolution not to get annoyed by Ricco and act normally and I must do it properly. Get a grip, she told herself, rise above it, ignore it, move forward…all those well-worn phrases that AB used to say to the twins when someone had complained about their pranks.

Cass took a deep breath, 'Rosa, Ricco said you had something to ask me, to do with the business wasn't it Ricco?' she turned and smiled at him as she said it. See, she thought to herself, it's easy when I try.

'Easy when you try isn't it?' volunteered Ricco. 'Smiling, that is.'

Bloody hell - has he turned into a mind reader now thought Cass, or am I really so obvious?

'Yes, that's right,' Rosa said, sensibly ignoring Ricco and just as Benito came into the room.

'Let us all sit down,' she continued. 'Anywhere will do.'

Cass just grabbed the nearest chair at the kitchen table and Ricco quickly sat next to her as Rosa served up the pasta and Benito poured the wine, winking at Cass as he filled her glass.

'So what did you want to talk to us about?' she asked, turning away quickly from Benito.

194

'We are excited,' Rosa looked towards Benito. 'We have been approached by a large company who have made the noises about buying our business. It is good, no?'

'That's amazing, but so soon? I thought that these things only happen later on, years even, after a business has been up and running successfully?' asked Cass.

'We have just been lucky, everything has gone well, lots of good publicity and lots of sales. All made possible by the wonderful miracle of course. It has what they call a good 'back-story' too.' she looked at Ricco for confirmation that she had used the correct phrase.

He nodded and said, 'Yes. It's important for them to have a really good story of how the business started up and the miracle cow poo is perfect, unique of course.'

'Our dilemma,' Rosa continued, 'is whether we should accept this offer. We just wanted to tell you about it as you were involved in a way from the start when I was working for you, and we are keen to know your opinion.'

'I'm very flattered and so will Jo be, that you are asking our thoughts. I'll chat to Jo later of course, but you must do whatever you think will make *you* happy. Do you want to go on making ice cream the rest of your lives or would you rather cut and run immediately? Think of what having some money would do for you right now. It could give you all sorts of opportunities and the freedom to do other things. If you turn the offer down you may find that in the future there isn't so much value in the company and you'll have slogged away for ages for hardly any gain. But if you hang on and the order book keeps filling then you could get an even larger amount of money. It's the proverbial swings and roundabouts thing isn't it.'

The evening continued in a happy vein after that and Cass relaxed a bit once she had a couple of glasses of wine. On her left Ricco did his best to catch her attention and talk to her but she managed to keep any conversation that he made to a bare minimum.

When Cass felt it was time to go she stood up and called to Nosey who was crashed out on an old armchair. 'Thank you for supper Rosa, I shan't tell anyone about your offer of course, but Jo and I will have a chat about it. I have to say that even without knowing details and figures that it does sound like an amazing proposition.'

As she moved towards the door Ricco stood up, 'I'll walk you up the lane if you like? It's quite dark now.'

Cass caught sight of her reflection in the huge overmantel mirror. The person that stared back at her had a panicky look on her face. Her heart and stomach were doing little somersaults in unison, but she heard herself tell Ricco, 'I'm fine thanks. I have my faithful hound to protect me. See you soon, night everyone.' And off she rushed as fast as possible.

What was all that about, she quizzed herself as she and Nosey started to walk up the track?

'Hey wait…'

She turned to see Ricco running up behind her, 'Take this torch at least Cass? If you can't bear to be near me, at least be safe.'

Cass gave him a kiss on the cheek, turned on the torch and walked off, 'Now why on earth did I do that?' she asked the dog.

Chapter 21

Whilst they were cooking breakfast the next morning, a very much recovered Jo was keen to know what Rosa had wanted. She listened as Cass told her about the offer and the Bellini's dilemma about whether to sell up or wait longer. She noticed how happy and sparkling Cass was, glowing almost, except for a sore mouth. When she asked about it Cass went a bit pink and told her sister the lipstick story.

'How did you behave with Ricco this time?' Jo asked. 'Did you manage to resist biting his head off?'

'I was fine after a not very good start.'

Jo smiled, 'You sly old twin, you still fancy him. That's why you put your favourite skirt on and all the war paint. That's why you're in this lovely mood, isn't it?'

Cass ignored her and picked up some linen to take upstairs as an excuse to leave the room and avoid further probing from her inquisitive sister. She put the sheets on the table in her room and looked in the mirror; she did look as if she'd been kissed too passionately. She stood at her bedroom window staring down the lane towards Rosa's farm, remembering Ricco kissing her the first time when they had met that day on the tour bus. How extraordinary it was that they had met up again here in Porthcwm.

It had been strange that day in Paris too.

One place Cass had been desperate to visit was Notre Dame. She had always had a fascination with it since seeing a grainy old black and white film starring Charles Lawton as the deformed and persecuted hunchback, Quasimodo. With this image still in her mind she turned up to visit the Cathedral on a dull grey day that would have done justice to the gloominess of the movie. Despite the foul weather, the area outside the Cathedral was heaving with people. Unwilling to be put off, she had ventured inside where she found even more of a throng. People crowded into every space, moving like hordes of ants and seemingly unaware of the service that was taking place. Cameras flashed, mobile phones went off, and everyone seemed to talk to each other at the top of their voices.

It had been a waste of time and she regretted having made the effort. Despite the fact that she wasn't remotely religious Cass had dropped two Euros into a little tin box and lit a candle. She wasn't sure for whom; maybe it had been for herself...

She hurried back outside and walked round the corner away from the masses. The sun was beginning to make an appearance through the mist and when she noticed a 'Car Rouge' tour bus parked beside the pavement she impulsively bought a ticket. She took a set of earphones from the tour guide and climbed up the stairs to the open deck. Choosing a seat furthest from the aisle on the pavement side, she had sat down, plugged the earphones in and turned the little knob beside her ready to receive the English commentary.

The bus filled up quickly and soon she was aware of someone sitting down next to her. 'Excuse me.....please?' an Italian accent said, '...would you mind plugging this in for me?'

Cass plugged in the earphones as requested and settled down as the bus moved off to listen to the description of all the sights along the way.

But nothing happened; no sound came through at all. She wiggled the earpiece but still nothing happened. She wiggled the connection where the wire went into the socket. Nothing.

'Bloody hell' she heard herself complain. 'What a day.' The people sitting in front of Cass turned around and gave her a look.

'Can I help you?' said the same voice as before. She looked at her companion for the first time. 'Can-I-help-you?' repeated the extremely handsome man, pointing at her headphones.

You sure can, she thought. 'Yes please,' she said.

He raised his finger to his lips, 'Shhh! You are shouting,' he said slowly. 'Excuse me, *perhaps* if I do this?' he stretched across her and moved the wires around.

'It's no good,' said Cass. 'It's still not working. Thanks for trying though. Look, please don't worry any more, you're missing it yourself. I'll just watch everything.'

'Of course you can't. I shall change mine to English and we can share. Here, take this,' he passed her one of his earpieces and moved closer to her. 'It's not perfect for you, but better than silence!'

Cass laughed and agreed, and they had listened together until he kissed her quickly before getting off the bus at the Arc de Triomphe.

Now he's just down the lane… goodness, what on earth is the matter with me? She picked up the sheets and took them out of the room and downstairs.

'What have you brought them back down for again?' asked Jo. 'You *are* in a funny mood. It's all to do with seeing Ricco again isn't it?'

Cass wasn't prepared to allow her twin to get too carried away with her mischievous teasing so she said seriously, 'What about asking Simon to supper, Jo, by way of a thank you for him taking care of you after the BBQ?'

Jo's face was a picture, 'I'd rather stick pins in my own eyes,' she snapped back in utter horror. 'I can't think of anything worse than sitting down to supper with a man who has seen me pissed, passed out *and* naked.'

'For goodness sake Jo, he's a doctor.'

'And that's supposed to make it alright?' she wasn't budging.

With magical timing Gloria appeared through the back kitchen door and they all went off to get on with their allocated cleaning chores.

Later, over a quick coffee they chatted about the beach BBQ and told Gloria about Megan's lucky escape. She hadn't heard anything about it and appeared very concerned.

'Sounds as if she's losing it fast, if you ask me,' declared Gloria. 'Do you think she's safe there on her own? Why don't you talk to her about going into a home? She'd be looked after and wouldn't end up in these dangerous situations, poor love.'

Megan sat in her kitchen with Frank. Simon had just left after checking out she was still feeling okay after her tumble. Everybody seemed very concerned about her but did they all think that she had imagined an intruder? Even worse than that, did they believe she'd actually been wandering round randomly with that huge bible for no apparent reason whatsoever? What if they were right? She could be forgiven for imagining someone was in her house with all the night time creaky old floorboard stuff, but what reason would they find for her bible hugging lark?

Funny things happen, though, she thought to herself. Here she was now, having a lovely cup of tea with the next door neighbour she hadn't spoken to for years. How extraordinary it was that he had heard her shouting as she lay at the bottom of the stairs. She couldn't recall why she had called out. After all she was only winded and would have been alright anyway if no-one had come. But Frank had turned up and she was very pleased. He had appeared out of the darkness and here he was again, sitting with her. But she was beginning to feel weary.

'After last night's exercise I'm a bit achy and tired, Frank,' she said. 'I think I may potter around the kitchen and then get an early night.'

'Probably be the best thing you can do,' he agreed. 'Is there anything I can assist with before I go home?'

'No, I'll be fine thank you, Frank. I do really appreciate your help.'

After Frank had gone Megan cleared away their cups and saucers and remnants of some coffee cake they had shared. She poured herself the remaining measure of the brandy and scribbled herself a reminder to buy some more of her favourite tipple. She filled the kettle for a hot water bottle and popped it on the stove. She moved the ironing board out of the way and folded the laundry ready to iron the following day. There, she thought, everything is organised for tomorrow. Suddenly remembering it was the rubbish collection the next morning she got her bin out and left it next to the back door along with an old electric fire, cardboard boxes, jam jars and the empty brandy bottle.

Then, deciding that having a good soak in a hot bath would be the most sensible thing to help her relax, she picked up her glass of brandy and went upstairs.

The bath certainly worked wonders on her aching muscles and the tipple worked wonders on her busy mind. She fell asleep almost the moment she climbed into bed.

Megan woke later feeling fuzzy. Perhaps it was time to give up her late evening tipple if it was making her feel like this? Her room felt strangely stuffy. She shuffled up to a sitting position and took a deep breath. Her lungs filled with smoke and she coughed sharply. Her hand went to cover her mouth and nose and she felt around under her pillow to find her handkerchief. She held it over her face to try and keep the smoke out but her coughing got more and more painful and her eyes began to smart. She struggled out of bed and felt her way towards her window. She seemed to remember something on the TV advising against not letting air into the room which would feed the flames. Bloody ridiculous nonsense, she muttered from underneath her hanky, I've *got* to be able to breathe…

She flung back the long curtains and found the latch that released the sash window. It rose up quickly letting fresh air pour past her face and into the room.

'This must be her ward,' said Jo, as they reached the end of the hospital corridor. She held the door open a little to peep inside. It was definitely the right room, a small single bedded side ward but Megan already had another visitor. Jo couldn't believe her eyes when she realised it was Fishnchips. She could see the woman standing by the bed and leaning over Megan. Neither had noticed the twins in the doorway. Fishnchips was waving her arms around in a threatening manner and Megan was sitting as far back on her bed as she could.

'What on earth's going on?' asked Jo loudly. 'What are *you* doing here? Why's Megan looking so frightened?'

Fishnchips stood up straight and turned around. She looked aggressive and her face was puce. Jo stood still as the loathsome woman walked over and stood within inches of her.

'I might have guessed you two interfering bitches would be hanging round somewhere,' she spat, pointing her finger in the direction of Jo's face. 'Still meddling with people's lives like you used to when you were snotty kids?'

'I think you'd better leave,' said Jo amazingly calmly. 'You are the one who is being interfering and abusive, coming in here uninvited and threatening Mrs Hughes. If we ever find you near her again we'll call the police.'

Fishnchips opened her mouth to say something but thought better of it.

'Just get out,' yelled Cass, and held the door open.

Jo was already at Megan's bedside giving her a cuddle. 'Are you okay?' she asked, as soon as Fishnchips had stormed out. 'Had she been here long? How on earth did she know you were in here?'

'I don't know how she knew,' said Megan, 'but I am so relieved to see you two. Look I've gone quite shaky…' she held her hands out to show them and started to laugh. 'It looks as if I'm in need of a drink, doesn't it?'

'I've no idea how you can retain your sense of humour after a session with that awful cow. Now tell us what happened last night.'

But before Megan could recount what happened to her there was a knock at the door. Jo stood up and opened it. An elderly man was standing in the corridor, smartly dressed and carrying a bunch of pink roses, 'Hello?' she said.

'Good morning. I am Frank Jones, Mrs Hughes' next door neighbour. I thought I would pop in and see how she's feeling now.'

'Megan, it's Frank,' said Jo. 'Here Frank, have my chair, we'll go and get a cup of tea and come back in a while. Anything you need from the hospital shop, Megan?'

'No thank you, my dears,' Megan answered.

Jo led the way along the corridor to the little café run by the Hospital Friends. Nothing looked very appealing but they ordered a couple of rock cakes and a pot of tea and sat at a tiny rickety table near the door.

'It was lucky we turned up when we did you know,' said Jo. 'How on earth did she know about Megan being in hospital?'

'Mmmm…dunno, no idea. Blimey, you could lose your teeth on these,' answered Cass, inspecting the appropriately named rock cake in her hand. 'You need this filthy builder's tea to wash it down. Thank heavens Megan didn't want us to get her anything.'

'Shall we go back and check on her, then go home?'

Jo caught sight of Frank making his way down the corridor ahead of them as they approached Megan's room. 'Hey Frank, how do you think Megan is now?' she called.

He turned round, 'In remarkably good spirits considering the fright she had.'

'Do you know what happened?' asked Jo.

'Well it was much like last time, I heard her calling out through the darkness at about two in the morning.'

'Goodness, don't you get any sleep?'

'Actually I don't really. Since my wife died I have gone out less and less, and slept less and less. But this was lucky for Mrs Hughes as I was quite wide awake on both occasions when I heard her shouting out. This time though, when I went to the window I could see smoke coming from her kitchen area, so I went in through the door which was open again. She was downstairs by then and heading towards the front door thank heavens. It was the smoke that affected her this time and Dr Rees wanted her checked out because of smoke inhalation, so had her admitted to the hospital. I called the fire brigade too and they came and extinguished the fire.'

'What caused the fire? Did they say?' asked Jo.

'I think she should tell you about that,' he said, looking a tad embarrassed.

'Well it's thanks to you she is safe,' said Cass. 'If you ever need us to come over then please, please telephone and we'll come over whatever time, day or night. Here's our number,' she said, handing Frank one of their B&B leaflets.

Megan was still sitting up in bed when they went back into her little side ward but looking much less shaky.

'Frank seems very nice,' said Jo.

'You're right. Frank *is* such a good and kind man you know,' she said. 'That's twice he's saved me now. He became a bit of a recluse when his wife died and I hadn't seen him to talk to for nearly two years. Now I've seen him rather a lot.'

'You're lucky to have such a good neighbour, Megan. I'm sure you'll be seeing a lot more of him now,' said Jo, winking at her sister.

'I saw that,' said Megan. 'I'm not completely senile yet you know. Anyway the man from the Fire Brigade called in when Frank was here and told me that some articles of clothing had been left drying too close to an electric fire and that's what had caused a small blaze and all the smoke. He was so embarrassed when he felt he should explain to me that I shouldn't be drying pairs of knickers in that way. But why on earth *would* I dry anything so close to that rusty electric fire? Besides which, it was only in the kitchen waiting to be thrown out, I wouldn't have even plugged it in - far too dangerous I would have thought.

'I can't wait to go home now and get the mess cleaned up. Frank's already organised Phil Fixit to come around and has invited me to stay for a few days at his house so that I can pop round and keep my eye on the place while Phil's doing the work. And before there is any more winking and innuendo, I shall be sleeping in a guest bedroom and returning to my own house as soon as possible.'

Chapter 22

When the doctors had given Megan the all-clear Frank collected her from the hospital and drove quietly back to Porthcwm. He planned to call in first at her own house so that she could look at the damage in the kitchen properly and talk to Phil Fixit who had already started on the cleaning up process. He also wanted her to collect some of her things before going to stay at his house for a couple of nights.

Her life had certainly livened up since the twins had come to live in Porthcwm. Goodness, she had missed Bea so much when she died. There had always been something going on in Bea's life, some tale to tell, some action to take. Now here were her nieces taking her place twofold. She sat in the passenger seat and looked out of the window. How lucky she was to have such good, generous hearted friends she thought.

Somehow they had made her feel young again. Only at heart of course. The rest of her seemed to be crumbling rather spectacularly at the moment. But nothing that a little rest wouldn't put right. And things did seem to happen in a strange way she decided. Someone had tried to set fire to her house and because of that now she had Frank in her life too. She felt very blessed.

She knew without doubt that there had been someone in her house that night. Just like she knew there had been the first time. She couldn't understand what they were after though. Nothing appeared to be missing. Why would someone want to burn the house down? Maybe that was never their intention. Perhaps they just wanted to frighten her with the smoke. But why on earth would they want to do that? She was comforted in the knowledge that the twins believed her and so did Frank. Thank heavens for them at least.

Megan was rather looking forward to staying at Frank's. It would be lovely to have company again. She hadn't been in his house for many years. Even when his wife Mary, was alive they had kept very much to themselves, so there had been no neighbourly socialising. What a shame she thought, Frank is such a nice, warm, friendly man. Perhaps by the time Mary had died he had forgotten how to cope with meeting people and making friends.

'Phil Fixit is here already, that's good,' said Frank, as he brought the car to a halt near her front door. He walked around and opened the passenger door for Megan, offering his arm to steady her as she climbed out. They went into the house tentatively and looked around the kitchen area. The walls were blackened with smoke and the place smelled like a bonfire, but it didn't look as bad as she had imagined it might. Phil had actually done quite a bit of cleaning already and all the windows were open to let the sea air do its best to freshen the place up.

Whilst Frank talked over details with Phil, Megan went upstairs to gather clothes and a couple of good books to take to Frank's. At least if she forgot anything she only had to walk around from next door.

Arthur Trinder arrived at his office quite late that day. He had a lot on his mind since being engaged in conversation by a nice young man when he was queuing in the post office. He had been thinking it through all afternoon whilst he was trying to concentrate on valuing a perfectly horrible bungalow that he would rather not touch with a barge pole. He sat at his desk trying to decide how to deal with this bit of information. Along with everything else going on in his life at the moment, it certainly added to all his problems.

'Rhonwen…uh, Miss Travers could you lock the front door please and come in here a moment?' asked Arthur, as he popped his head around his office door. He had no appointments for the remainder of the afternoon, and definitely didn't want to be interrupted by someone coming into the shop.

'Good, now close the door and sit down here,' he patted the chair next to him.

'Something has come to my attention that is giving me an enormous amount of concern, and I hope you are going to put my mind at rest and tell me that it isn't true. I have recently been informed that you are spending a great deal of time with my

206

nephew, Rudolph? What are you nodding for? Are you telling me that this indeed true?'

'Yes,' she knew there was no point in denying it. How he hadn't found out about them earlier was amazing. 'It's true Mr Trinder, is there a problem?'

'Well yes, actually I think there is. *He* is my nephew and *you* work for me.'

'I'm sorry, but I can't see why there seems to be a problem with it at all Mr Trinder,' she replied.

'I can't have you here working for me, knowing where I go, what I do, all my business details and customer confidentialities and be carrying on with Rudolph,' he said.

Arthur knew he was beginning to get a trifle irate and was struggling to control it.

'Oh, you're worried about *pillow talk* are you Mr Trinder, giving secrets away in the middle of…'

'Miss Travers, please…PLEASE don't tell me that you are taking advantage of my nephew?'

He could see that Rhonwen was amused by his question. 'Why no Mr Trinder, I think we are taking advantage of each other in roughly the same proportions,' she said. 'It's all very fairly distributed.'

Arthur realised this was getting him nowhere. He wasn't quite sure what he wanted but he did realise that if Rhonwen was to tell Rudolph about any of his indiscretions that he was sure she must have observed, despite him being so very, *very* careful, it could get back to his sister. More importantly it could get back to Linda.

He decided to try and stay cool. He leaned back in his Mastermind type chair and looked at Rhonwen. What had gone wrong with his plans for her? All his training and nurturing in the business and this is how she repaid him. And look at the woman now. A shadow of her former pumpkin self. Slim, smart, glowing with goodness like a rosy apple. Except she had *already* been picked…Good God, this is why he had been saving her all this time…for him, *him*, not that anxious, irritating nephew of his. Then he does a favour for his sister's boy, and the lad marches into Porthcwm and seduces his receptionist. How did he do it? How did that nervous, inadequate, useless boy snatch Rhonwen from under his nose? He felt this woman who he had invested in so heavily really did *owe* him something.

'I think I have no option but to fire you, Miss Travers.'

'*Fire* me? You can't.'

'I think you'll find that I can,' he said.

'You can't sack me for going out with your nephew. I've never done anything wrong, I'm honest and I work hard, so what could you find to dismiss me?'

'You have been extremely insolent to customers and I've had complaints,' he announced.

'Such as?' she snapped.

'You have a very short memory Miss Travers; do you not remember Mrs Phipps complaining about your rudeness recently?'

'For goodness sake Mr Trinder, she is an impossible person to deal with. When Fishnchips came marching in that…'

'What did you just say, Miss Travers? Did I hear you call her Fishnchips?'

'Slip of the tongue Mr Trinder. I apologise,' she said, cursing herself under her breath.

'Well this certainly adds to your list of misdemeanours and I am going to have to think very seriously about letting you go.'

'You'll never get anyone as good as me, Mr Trinder. You wouldn't want to start again with someone new would you?' she said, straw clutching.

'Well, if you really want to continue working for me, we are going to have to reach a compromise,' he rubbed his hands together in his usual oily way. 'A little overtime wouldn't go amiss I think. We shall start after the weekend. In that way you can prove how loyal you really are. Then gradually we might be able to get back to normal. Go and get on and give it some thought. You'll soon realise what an extremely understanding employer I can be.'

Arthur rubbed his hands together again as Rhonwen left his office. He thought he had, after all, dealt with her rather well. Things were looking up at last. Nice of that Italian chap to have let slip about Rhonwen and Rudolph, even if it was just a throwaway line during their chat in the post office queue.

Chapter 23

Jo was in the garden tidying up one of the borders where Nosey had attempted to bury one of his bones when she saw Rosa walking down the lane past the gate.

'Hey Rosa,' she called out. 'It's not often that we see you on Shanks's pony. What are you up to?'

'No. I have no pony. I have walked to the town to get in some time to think,' she answered.

'Well, that makes two of us, so why not come in and sit down.' Jo said and opened the gate for her. 'Let's have a drink; I could do with stopping for a moment.'

Jo dragged the two old deckchairs into some leafy shadows and fetched a jug of elderflower cordial with lots of ice from the house. 'So what is your thinking time about Rosa?' she enquired. 'Is it about the offer from the company that you told Cass about?'

'That is the one. It has been difficult for us to decide, but your sister was right about biting the hand off while it is being offered. So we have decided to do the hand biting, no? We might have had more money if we waited longer but there is no point. They are giving us good money for what was a miracle. They like the story. I don't think God will mind us selling our miracle. We thought we would give some of it to St Dominic's although we don't worship there, but it *is* the centre of the town here and they need much money for the restoration, no? The miracle happened at Porthcwm and some money should stay here.'

'That's very generous of you,' said Jo.

'We will be comfortable anyway,' said Rosa.

'Well you deserve anything good that you can get out of it,' said Jo.

'Look, have you seen the paper?' asked Rosa reaching into her bag. 'Here it is. There is something about my dreadful neighbour.

Just read the first bit, the rest is a repeat of what he's done,' she passed the paper to Jo.

'*A 50-year-old local man has appeared in court charged with producing and cultivating cannabis with an estimated value of £64,000, and dishonestly using electricity at a farm near Porthcwm.*

'*Albert Lloyd, of Porthcwm Farm, who admitted his guilt just before his trial, was handed a 40-week prison term suspended for 18 months and ordered to carry out 200 hours unpaid community work.*'

'But Rosa that means that he's got away with it and will still be around here being an aggressive bloody nuisance to everyone. It'll be interesting to see what jobs he has to do though. The good thing is that whatever they are, he'll loathe them. Maybe that's better than prison?'

'I hope so. But we shall see,' said Rosa, shrugging.

On Monday morning Rhonwen thought seriously about saying she wasn't well enough to go to work. Arthur was being quite unfair and she knew she didn't deserve the sack. She thought of nothing but his creepy offer and what his interpretation of 'overtime' might mean. She couldn't envisage for one moment that he actually meant just working longer hours.

She hadn't told Rudi about it immediately because she assumed he'd be so angry that he'd probably go and knock his uncle senseless. Though the thought was rather appealing, she didn't want Rudi to get into trouble too.

When she did eventually explain the situation to him he held her close in his arms and kissed her tenderly, *then* he had threatened to go and knock his uncle unconscious. She'd been right.

Rhonwen and Rudi discussed it for ages, and got nowhere. The only solution they could come up with apart from Rhonwen handing in her notice and trying to find a job elsewhere was for her to just hang on there a bit longer and see what happened.

So she turned up at work as usual and tried to act normally - whatever that was. Arthur came in and went through to his office as normal and people came to look at property details as normal. It just seemed to be a very normal day. Fishnchips came marching in just after lunch and Rhonwen was instructed not to disturb them.

Now obsessed with what Arthur was up to she did something she had never done before and put her ear close to his office door. She could hear snuffling noises and what sounded like chairs being moved rather a lot. They're having sex, she thought. My God…they are actually having sex in his office. She suddenly wished she hadn't listened, and began to hum out of tune and loudly and move around the shop more noisily than usual to keep busy.

But it was too late…her imagination had already run away with her. She pictured Arthur on his Mastermind lookalike chair, spinning it around with Fishnchips sitting astride him and hanging on for grim death. Or had he swept everything off his desk and laid her on its shiny surface after groping in his briefcase for his condom selection and then trying to clamber up on to the table top to seduce her. She laughed at the pictures she conjured up and only just managed to keep a straight face when Fishnchips left Arthur's office looking rather redder than usual and raced out of the shop without saying a word.

Rhonwen didn't see Arthur for quite some time. She was on the phone to a customer when he eventually appeared. He didn't even have the decency to look embarrassed. 'Mr Trinder has just come in' she said into the phone. 'He can take your call now.' As he was standing right next to her she passed the phone directly to him and went towards his office to collect his coffee cup from earlier.

'NO…' he shrieked at her. 'No, no I don't mean you Mr Trotman; I was just calling, uh, stopping my assistant from, um… doing something. Yes, yes, I am *very* sorry I shouted down the telephone into your ear. Would you excuse me *just* one moment please?' He put his hand over the phone mouthpiece and hissed at Rhonwen to get back to her own desk.

Rhonwen had been almost at his door when Arthur had shouted at her, so he obviously didn't want her to look inside. Perhaps it was in a state. Yuk. It didn't bear contemplating.

She looked on as her employer offered further apologies in his own smarmy way to the irritated caller and eventually replaced the receiver.

Arthur now looked embarrassed and edgy. 'I think under the circumstances, you can go home, but tomorrow I'd like to go through some of our sales particulars with you in the evening.'

Rhonwen wondered under what *exact* circumstances she was being allowed home.

Rudi was pretty horrified to hear about Arthur's antics when he met up with Rhonwen and the twins at the Lodge later. He listened as Rhonwen told them about Arthur's threat to sack her and his suggestion of doing 'overtime'. He was very concerned about what Arthur might try and do when Rhonwen stayed late the next evening, but needed to think through his plan cautiously.

They had actually all met up to discuss Megan's imminent return to her own house. Phil Fixit had done wonders and there was no hint of the damage caused from the night-of-the-smoking-knickers incident. The twins had been told by Frank that he was more than happy for her to stay in his house until she really felt up to returning, but she was adamant that she wanted to get back to normal. Even though she put on a brave face they all knew that she was quite nervous.

'I think we should take it in turns to sleep there and keep her company until she settles in again,' suggested Rudi 'but I know it'll be more difficult for you two because of the B & B.'

'I think it's a great idea,' said Jo. 'I don't mind going there on my own, what d'you think Cass?'

'I think that'll work. Let's just see how it goes. Megan may be okay after a few days anyway, Frank did offer to do the same but she was positive that he shouldn't. If we just make it a fait accompli then she'll probably accept it!'

Rudi suggested that as Frank was helping Megan move back next door on Sunday that maybe he and Rhonwen should perhaps take the first watch that night so that the twins could work out their own rota at the Lodge.

Rudi rang Megan's doorbell when he and Rhonwen arrived on her doorstep early on Sunday evening. She seemed so pleased to see them both there.

'Come in my dears. I'm sure I can guess why you're here. I'm thinking that you and the twins and Frank have cooked up some OAP babysitting service for me?'

'Mmm, sort of right, but you don't mind really, do you? We thought just for a few nights to help you settle back in.'

'Well, you're all too kind. I'll get you some coffee. Or perhaps you would prefer to stay clear of the caffeine and have a glass of wine instead? You are obviously intending to stay the night by the look of the sleeping bags...'

Rudi and Rhonwen sat in her sitting room and were fussed over by Megan with drinks and biscuits and chatter. Rudi was relieved for both of them when she at last gave in to weariness and went off to bed.

'I can't believe she's got so much nervous energy still, I feel quite knackered,' admitted Rudi looking at his watch, 'and it's only ten thirty.'

'I think it's a bit of an act. She should sleep well with any luck, especially with those tablets that Simon gave her,' said Rhonwen.

They watched a couple of DVD's and were soon all filmed-out. Then when they couldn't hear Megan moving around upstairs any more they decided it was ok to go to sleep.

Once they had both settled down in their little nests near the sofa Rudi leaned over and kissed Rhonwen. He ran his hand down the outside of her sleeping bag feeling the contours of her body beneath the quilted material. He wriggled across, caterpillar like, until he could get his arm right round her, 'Rhon...?'

'Don't even think about it, Rudolph Timms,' she growled. 'Go to sleep just this once.'

Rudi slept fitfully and woke about two in the morning. He had been finding it quite uncomfortable on the floor, trapped in a sleeping bag. Despite having got up again and made himself a mattress of settee cushions he still couldn't settle and had been lying there wondering why they were actually going through this discomfort when he was certain nothing was going to happen. But then he became aware of a sound outside the sitting room window. A gravel-crunching sound.

Rudi had improved in self-esteem and confidence, but he knew still had a very long way to go yet in the heroism department. Shit, he thought as his heart pounded loudly, I'm still a wimp, and nudged Rhonwen until she woke up.

'Whossit? Whotchoowant Rudi? Not now, I'm asleep. Lessdoitlater.'

'No Rhon, no I don't want sex, well I do, but there isn't time. Wake up and listen to that noise outside,' Rudi shook her. 'Don't go back to sleep Rhon, listen to that...'

He heard a clunk outside the window and what sounded to him like footsteps going round the side of the house, 'Rhon...Rhon...oh good, you've decided to join in at last. There's someone outside, I'm going to go through to the back of the house and you're coming with me. No, NO choice Rhon, you've got to come.'

He watched her wriggle out of her sleeping bag and then grabbing her hand they walked slowly through the dark house trying not to make a noise. 'Where's the bloody moonlight when you need it,' he said. 'I can't see where we're going Rhon and I daren't put the lights on.'

'Here's the kitchen,' she said, finding the door handle, and pulling Rudi into the room after her. 'Shhh...let's listen.'

'I can hear something,' Rudi whispered, uselessly pointing in the dark towards where he knew the window should be, 'outside there.'

'I've no idea where you mean Rudi and you must have very sensitive hearing,' said Rhonwen, 'because I can't hear a thing. I'm going to open the back door to listen. Okay?'

216

Rudi could hear her as she edged her way around the kitchen using the side of the worktop as a guide. Just as she reached the back door she caught her foot against something on the floor and went flying into Megan's saucepan stand. There was an almighty crash as the pans, lids and metal stand hit the tiled floor.

'For God's sake Rhon...' Rudi said as he fumbled round looking for the light switch.

'I couldn't help it,' Rhonwen whispered as loudly as possible from her position on the floor where she was sitting in a small puddle of water.

Rudi found the light switch and looked down at Rhonwen, 'Are you okay? You're wet. Rhon, you haven't ...'

'NO Rudi. Don't be ridiculous, of course I haven't peed myself. I don't know what it is, except cold.'

He helped her up, 'I've just realised Megan must've slept through all the noise. Thank goodness for those sleeping tablets.'

Rudi bent down and began to pick up the lids and saucepans as quietly as possible. 'This is what you tripped over.' He held up the remains of white bowl with a picture of a cat on it. This must've been full of water.'

Rudi had forgotten for a moment why they were actually in the kitchen. He opened the back door and peered out, 'Nothing there,' he said. 'But you made so much noise that it would have scared anyone away.'

'Well I'm certain it was just her cat or something Rudi; let's go back to our sleeping bags.'

'If it was a cat then he was very heavy footed. Honestly Rhon, there *was* someone out there,' said Rudi as they wriggled back into their sleeping bags in the sitting room.

'I vote we don't mention any of this to Megan tomorrow. She seems to have slept through it all and is none the wiser, and I really *do* think it was your imagination,' said Rhonwen.

'Rhonwen?'

'Yes Rudi?

'I don't feel tired now…'

'No Rudi, absolutely no way.'

Over breakfast Megan seemed greatly refreshed and didn't appear to have been disturbed at all in the night, 'I had a wonderful sleep,' she declared.

How did you two manage on the uncomfortable floor? I wish you had taken my offer of a bed upstairs.'

'Oh we were fine thanks, slept like logs too,' lied Rudi. 'Except when I tried to get to the kitchen in the dark to get some water. I'm really sorry but I'm afraid I broke your cat's bowl.'

'Oh you must be mistaken, I haven't had a cat for years,' she replied.

Rudi caught Rhonwen's look of astonishment.

'Anyway,' Rudi continued, quickly changing the subject,' Jo is coming over this evening to stay but you have all our phone numbers too if you need us.'

'Is she coming on her own?' asked Megan.

'Yes, she and Cass intend to take it in turns.'

'How kind you are all being,' Megan said, smiling to herself and thinking ahead to Jo's visit.

Chapter 24

Rhonwen was not enjoying being at the office and was constantly thinking about the evening and what might be lying in store for her. She had no idea what Arthur had meant by 'overtime' and she tried not to imagine what unpleasant little plans he might have prepared for her.

She kept remembering how angry Rudi had been initially about his uncle's behaviour and how surprised she was when he seemed to calm down after a while. She had been quite convinced that he would rush off to confront Arthur. But he hadn't. He just looked as though he was doing an awful lot of thinking. Oh well, she had decided, still waters and all that. And when they had left Megan's that morning he had just given her a big hug and a bigger kiss and told her to ring him if Arthur started to do anything she was suspicious of.

Well, so far today Arthur looked like a man who had absolutely no plans at all in his head for her 'overtime'. Maybe he'd just been trying to frighten her into cutting off her relationship with Rudi. He wasn't even keeping Rhonwen in the loop with Estate-Agency-stuff as he usually did. In fact he had hardly spoken to her at all.

She didn't know whether he had arranged any valuations or viewings as a result of the phone calls she had put through to him today. She had no idea what he was really up to. So to try and find out what was going on she'd taken up eavesdropping at his door. She wondered why she'd never done this before; imagine what she could have picked up from listening in to his conversations if she had thought of this idea sooner. She decided she'd been far too honest.

At about 4 o'clock Rhonwen noticed that Arthur was beginning to pack up his brief case with documents and papers and doubtless *that* envelope. It wasn't closing time yet, so she crossed her fingers and prayed that he was going off to see Fishnchips. There hadn't even been the customary daily phone call from her which was a great relief to Rhonwen so maybe he was planning to go off and meet up with her.

Rhonwen stood in the tiny kitchen washing up their coffee mugs and watched as Arthur came out of his office carrying his brief case and camera. He looked a bit nervous she thought.

'Miss Travers,' he called. 'I'm just off to get the car.'

'Okay, Mr Trinder,' she said trying to sound calm. 'See you tomorrow.'

'Good heavens, Miss Travers have you forgotten that you are supposed to be doing some extra work this evening?'

'Uh? No, of course I haven't. I thought you might've changed your mind and decided not to go through any property details with me as you hadn't mentioned it again.'

'Well, that's correct as it so happens, but we're going to do something else instead. Get your things ready, I'll be back to pick you up in about three minutes,' he said, going out through the door and heading up the street towards the car park.

She fished her mobile out of her bag and rang Rudi. Bugger him, she thought, why isn't he answering? She left a message letting him know that she was going off somewhere with Arthur in his car. She managed to slip the phone into her pocket just as Arthur came back in. 'Are you ready?' he asked.

Act normal, she told herself, 'I won't be a moment, I was just tidying my desk,' she said, grabbing some random papers and putting them in her top drawer. 'Where are we going?' she enquired as casually as she could.

'34 Glendwr Street,' he said. 'The owners are away but said that it's fine for me to do a valuation in their absence.'

Rhonwen could see he felt he'd said too much, 'I need to go to the cloakroom, I won't be a mo,' she said.

'Hurry up then, I'll wait in the car. Lock the door on your way out.'

She rushed into the loo and tried ringing Rudi again. 'Bloody hell Rudi,' she complained 'why don't you answer your blasted phone?'

Act cool, Rhonwen kept telling herself as she walked out of the shop and climbed into Arthur's car. It suddenly felt very small to her as she sat next to him in the front.

'These are the draft details,' he said, placing a folder on her knees and letting his hand linger there for a few seconds too long.

She picked them up and pretended to be engrossed. She thought the house at 34 Glendwr Street sounded really nice. She said as much to Arthur and he responded with a condescending smile.

He turned into one of the narrower streets on the edge of the town. It was a quiet area with a neat terrace of six cottages and two or three small detached houses. He pulled the car to a halt outside a pretty whitewashed cottage standing on its own towards the end of the street. He gathered his things together and got out. 'Come on, work to do, Miss Travers, work to do,' he said brusquely.

Rhonwen clambered out slowly and watched as he took out a key from his pocket and opened the front door. They entered directly into the living room. Arthur turned and closed the door behind them and Rhonwen heard the catch fall. He put his briefcase and camera down on a table near the fireplace and got some papers out.

'It's very warm in here Mr Trinder and it smells a little stale, I think I'll just prop the door open to let some air in.' She went towards the front door and put her hand on the handle to open it.

'No. *No* Miss Travers, I'd like you to leave it closed. It will after all look better in the photographs, won't it?' he added hastily.

As he started taking some photographs in the sitting room Rhonwen wandered through to the kitchen beyond. It was a lovely little house. She could still hear Arthur click clicking away so went out into the garden and walked down a gravel path to the end. She couldn't understand why he'd brought her along. He was busy taking all the pictures and she was just hanging about. She leaned against the stone boundary wall and pulled herself up on tiptoe. She could just see the sea. The further she was away from Arthur the more comfortable she felt. She gazed at the view for a few moments until she was suddenly aware of Arthur click clicking in the garden now. She ignored him for a while until the clicking got closer and closer. When she turned around there was the frightful man standing right behind her the camera lens aimed at her legs.

'What on *earth* are you doing, Mr Trinder?' she asked.

'Just getting you in the picture to show the scale of the garden. Now…we must go back inside and do the first floor.' he announced, and marched back up the garden path and into the house.

Rhonwen followed him as slowly as possible. Arthur had already disappeared upstairs and she could hear him clicking away. 'Come upstairs,' he called, 'and bring my brief case.'

She picked up the briefcase, then put it down again and slipped quietly across to the front door which she unlocked. She felt happier now she had provided the means of a quick exit should she need one.

'Hurry up, Miss Travers,' shouted Arthur again from upstairs. 'We have things to do.'

'Coming,' she replied, grabbing the briefcase. She snapped it open and removed the little envelope with its secret contents and left it on the kitchen table. Then carrying the briefcase upstairs she found Arthur in the back bedroom looking out of the window at the sea view.

'Look,' he said, 'come and see this magnificent view.' He had pulled a small bedroom chair over to the window. 'Sit here a moment and look out of the window so that I can take a nice artistic photograph of this room.'

Artistic, my arse, Rhonwen thought to herself, but did as she was told. She had no idea why. Arthur stood behind her and ran his hand along the nape of her neck. She shuddered with repulsion and asked herself why she couldn't move, or just shove him away? Why couldn't she make a run for it? Why hadn't she escaped out through the front door when she had the opportunity just now?

Rhonwen shivered, then sat as still as she could. She clung on tightly to Arthur's briefcase, as if it were affording her some protection. She pulled it closer towards her on her lap shocked that she had done as he'd asked and continued to look at the view silently repeating her 'stay cool' mantra over and over.

'I'll just have my briefcase...' Arthur said and bent down to take it away from her. He ran his hand along the back of her wrist as it gripped tightly onto the case and she pulled her hand away quickly.

'What's on earth the matter with you, Rhonwen?' he asked opening his brief case and feeling round inside.

Rhonwen knew what he was searching for and despite being nervous she couldn't help smiling. He threw the case on the floor, 'Wipe that smug grin off your face and tell me where you've put them.'

'Put *what* Mr Trinder?'

'You *have* taken them, I know you have ... how dare you go through my case,' he hissed. 'It won't make any difference because I'm still going to show you what you've been missing.' He was standing very close to her now. He took hold of both her hands and pulled her to her feet. 'I've wanted to do this ever since you came to work for me. I've been saving you until you were ready.'

She could feel his breath on her face and pushed him away.

'Is this how you choose to repay me after everything I've taught you?' he snarled.

'Repay you? For what? What on earth are you talking about?' she asked him.

'You...you have led my innocent nephew astray. Or was that to *torment* me? You don't need some young kid like Rudolph fumbling all over you, you need someone mature and experienced who can show you the ropes, guide you, and make you feel special. A *real* man.' He puffed his chest out and failed feebly in his attempted to stand tall.

Rhonwen tried to supress a grin. Surely he wasn't serious. 'What? You?' she probed. 'I can't believe I'm hearing this, you still think that if I let you have your wicked way with me you'll let me keep my job? Rudi is worth a hundred of you.'

She started to laugh, partly from nerves and partly because his whole ranting behaviour was ridiculous. He looked like a bizarre cartoon of himself, absurd, stressed, pompous but serious, yes, very definitely serious about his plans for her. She laughed and laughed. How could she have been worried about what this ludicrous ineffectual little man would do? Stuff the job she thought; I'm not going to work for him again anyway.

Rhonwen saw the looked of astonishment on Arthur's face. He appeared to be completely shocked that she found him so amusing. His unpleasant demeanour crumbled before her eyes and he scuffled off towards the bed and sat down looking dejected. Suddenly he put his head in his hands, and wept and wailed like a child.

'That won't work for me,' said Rhonwen. 'You can't come on all tough to me one minute and then behave like a complete baby the next.'

But he just kept sobbing and blowing his nose into a great blue and white spotted handkerchief and rocking to and fro like a little boy condemned to sit on the naughty step for bad behaviour.

'Oh for God's sake,' Rhonwen said. 'If you are going to fire me, then just get on and bloody fire me, I've had enough of this. I think you have a real problem Mr Trinder and you need help.'

He looked up and nodded, his whole body was shaking and tears were streaming down his face. She stared at him for a moment then against her very better judgement, Rhonwen walked over and sat down on the bed beside him. She put her arm around his shoulder to comfort him.

'I've been such a fool,' he said, sniffing loudly into his hanky. 'I just don't seem to be able to manage anything anymore, I'm not selling enough houses and I've got myself into a terrible situation with Trisha Phipps. I don't know what to do, I really don't know what to do; I'm on the brink of losing everything.' He put his head on Rhonwen's shoulder and cried uncontrollably.

Rhonwen was amazed by his behaviour; the letch of Porthcwm had lost the plot.

With a resounding crash the door behind the bed suddenly flew open and Fishnchips catapulted into the bedroom, 'So *this* is what you're up to…' she screamed.

The look on Arthur's face said it all, and he just cowered down pathetically. Rhonwen stood up quickly and narrowly escaped Fishnchips' clenched fist which was aimed, she assumed, at Arthur. She heard it make contact with his jaw and then the howl of pain.

He yelled each time Fishnchips' fist reached its intended destination and then whimpered pathetically from his curled up position on the blankets.

There was another loud commotion in the doorway and Rhonwen was startled to see Linda and Rudi burst in. She felt dazed and confused and now it was her turn to begin shaking involuntarily, 'Oh Rudi, you understood my phone message…thank goodness,' she gasped at him.

He put his arms around her and held her close. 'Of course I did. I let Linda know, then came around here ready to sort him out, but I can see that Fishnchips is managing single-handedly.'

She was still laying into Arthur. 'You useless piece of shit Arthur Trinder, you're no good for anything, going behind my back with that receptionist of yours, screwing her here in this little love nest. You're a lousy lover and a second-rate estate agent. You can't even get me the house I want. I've earned that house, EARNED it I tell you. I've let you crawl all over me with your creepy hands because you promised me you'd find me somewhere...'

Arthur now had his arms in front of his face to save himself from more punches and had his body turned towards the wall. Neither he nor Fishnchips had noticed the two extra people in the room but it was she who was the first to sense that they had company. She stopped her assault on Arthur and turned around to see who was there. Everything went quiet for a brief moment.

Arthur took the opportunity to lift his head slowly and look up. He saw his wife and guiltily fidgeted with his jacket. He attempted to struggle up to a sitting position. Taking advantage of this unguarded move Fishnchips lifted her fist up one more time and brought it down heartily in the very area where he would least like to have had that happen, and then she ran down the stairs and out of the house.

None of them tried to stop her. Rhonwen, Rudi and poor Linda Trinder looked on as Arthur clasped himself between his legs and writhed round in agony, his nose bleeding and his cheeks bruised.

'I'll call an ambulance for him,' said Linda calmly. 'Hopefully it'll take a while to get here.'

Across the other side of the town Jo was preparing to take her turn in staying with Megan. She had been told by Rudi about the noises and the bowl of water and the phantom cat incident the previous night and she could tell that he was a bit concerned about her being there on her own. It had obviously unnerved him, but Rhonwen was still adamant that he'd been imagining it all. Nevertheless, none of them could come up with an explanation about why the cat bowl had been put out.

Jo was dropped off by Cass and welcomed by Megan who was as pleased to see her as ever, 'it's very kind of you all to come in turn and settle me back in here again,' she said. 'Rudi and Rhonwen and I had a lovely evening last night.'

Jo put her stuff in the sitting room despite Megan's offer of one of her spare beds upstairs. She thought she would be happier downstairs where she could hear if anything was going on outside.

It was about eight o'clock when the front doorbell went. Jo nearly jumped out of her skin, 'shall I see who's there?' she asked Megan. They had been sitting in front of the TV enjoying a new gardening programme and waiting to watch the murder mystery film which was coming on straight afterwards.

'Yes please dear. I can't imagine who that could be.'

Jo opened the door and to her great surprise found Simon standing on the doorstep, 'hello' he said. 'I didn't know you were her.'

'Obviously. Come in. Megan…' she called, 'it's Simon.'

'Come and sit down Simon,' Megan said when Jo brought him through to the sitting room. 'I'll fetch you a glass of wine. Jo and I are on our second already.' She disappeared off to the kitchen.

'What are you doing here?' Simon asked.

'I am staying the night to keep an eye on Megan so that she settles and isn't disturbed by anything. We didn't want her wandering around the house thinking that someone has broken in again,' she answered. 'What about you?'

'She asked me around for a drink and I accepted because I wanted to see how she was now she's back alone…except she isn't of course, now you're here.'

'There you are Simon,' said Megan passing him a large glass of red wine. 'Thank you for popping around. Those tablets you gave me certainly did the trick last night, I slept right through. Thank goodness I wasn't taking those when those two break-ins occurred. I shudder to think what would have happened.'

They chatted on about all sorts of things until Megan said suddenly 'Well you two, I'm off to bed. Now Simon you mustn't rush off straight away, I've put a few snacks for you both in the kitchen and I'm sure you don't eat well enough. And there is another bottle of wine in there for you. I don't want to find everything untouched when I come down in the morning. Goodnight both,' and off she disappeared.

They looked at each other awkwardly.

'I think I'm speechless,' said Jo.

'I expect that must be a first,' said Simon.

'And I guess I deserved that comment,' Jo answered. 'Look, as we are here under strict orders to eat and drink Megan's food and wine can I suggest that we call a truce. I'll promise not to get completely legless like I was at the barbeque and you must promise

227

to eat up well as she's obviously convinced that you don't eat correctly.'

Simon smiled at her, 'that's the most sensible thing you've ever said to me. Shall we shake on it?' He held out his hand and so did she.

Jeez, Jo thought, something happened just then, as she pulled her hand away quickly. 'Let's see what Megan's left for us in the kitchen,' her mouth had gone so dry she could hardly get the words out.

Standing up she led the way to the kitchen. The table had bread and cheeses, a little smoked salmon, some country-style pate and some fresh fruit all laid out beautifully. There were crisp white linen napkins, a jug of iced water, a bottle of Fleurie, already opened to breath, and two handsome cut-glass wine glasses.

'She's had fun with this hasn't she?' said Jo. 'Fancy pretending to us that she didn't know who was at the front door when she had invited you here. Shall we take some of it through to the sitting room?'

'I expect she thought you'd run a mile,' Simon said, 'and that would have been a great shame.'

Jo shot him a quick look, there must be something wrong with my hearing, she thought...

She followed Simon back through the house and this time sat beside him on the settee. She watched him as he pulled a small coffee table up in front of them both. She couldn't understand how she'd never looked at him properly before. No opportunity, she guessed. He'd always succeeded in making her feel totally inferior the moment they were anywhere near each other and they'd never managed to be in each other's company without insults flying from one to the other. She hadn't ever been comfortable enough with him to actually look at him properly. He'd certainly had time to study her though when she was plastered and he'd taken her home. And when he'd undressed her and she didn't remember anything, well he certainly had the opportunity to have a good look then. She felt embarrassed just thinking about it again.

She liked what she saw. He had a strong kind face that seemed to have become more relaxed looking now that they were actually behaving like level-headed adults. Very nice, she decided, very nice.

'I wonder if you are thinking the same thing that I am?' Simon enquired. 'We seem to have been in each other's company longer than ever before without either of us biting the other's head off yet. Megan has set us up you know. She's trapped us both here and forced us to talk to each other,' he added, pouring wine into their glasses.

'I felt so humiliated when I discovered how I'd got home after the barbeque,' Jo said, blushing again at the memory of it. 'Despite all the stuff that went on when we were kids and how ghastly we were to you, it was the fact that you'd been able to get your own back, however unintentional that was. I was so mortified that you'd undressed me, I didn't think I could look you in the face again. But now I've been able to tell you that, I feel so much better.

'I want to say how sorry I am for us both behaving the way we did,' she continued. 'It appears we were a pain to almost everybody, but you in particular…you were always there when we came to stay with AB, maybe you were just an easy target for our delinquent behaviour.'

'Just stop apologising Jo,' he said. 'We're both over that now.'

She could see he was deep in thought and she sat in silence with him for a few moments.

'I wanted to kiss you when I was carrying you to my car that night,' he said. '… I can't believe I've just confessed that to you. You just looked so beautiful even though you were completely plastered.'

'But you didn't then? It would have been like taking advantage of me whilst I was as drunk as a skunk,' Jo tried to look solemn, but her heart was singing.

'Exactly. But I should like to kiss you now, in case you are about to become drunk as a skunk again as you so charmingly put it.'

Hell, Jo thought, go for it Simon…

Chapter 25

Jo was having the most surprisingly good evening. Simon's first kiss had been long and passionate. It was as if he was making up for lost time. Then, as the hours passed they grew more and more comfortable with each other and everything he did was perfect. Every part of her body felt loved and cherished. They had shared everything that Megan had left for them on the kitchen table, and snuggling underneath the rug that she had given them, they shared each other too.

Jo woke sometime after midnight. Simon had obviously turned the lights off downstairs and left the TV on standby which gave the room a little glow. He was still there curled up on the settee with her. She put her arm around him and held him close. She listened to his breathing. Deep and regular and relaxing. She started to drift off again.

She was almost asleep when she heard a click. The sitting room door was closed and she couldn't make out where the sound had come from. It definitely didn't seem to be from outside though. She sat up. Maybe Megan had been restless and had come downstairs. She crawled out from underneath the rug and tiptoed to the door opening it as quietly as possible. She listened carefully, standing stock still in the doorway. Hearing nothing further after a minute or two she crept back to bed and snuggled up again.

She had no idea how long she had been back to sleep, but suddenly Simon shook her awake and said very quietly. 'listen Jo…'

'I'm listening, okay I'm listening. What am I listening to?' she whispered. 'I can't hear anything over the pouring rain.'

'There's someone moving around the house. It's probably Megan but I'm going to check.'

'I'm coming too,' Jo said.

She stood close behind him as he opened the door into the front hall. The sound of the rain echoed around the house. 'I'll put the light on, and go up to check on Megan,' said Simon.

Jo seemed to wake up properly just as he flicked the switch and her shout of 'Nooo…' was lost in the flash and bang of the fuses blowing. She had realised too late that it wasn't raining outside but inside. Water was pouring through the ceiling in the kitchen, rattling down onto pots and pans and the work surfaces.

'Bloody hell, that frightened me. I suddenly realised where that sound was coming from,' said Jo.

'What's above the kitchen?' Simon asked.

'I think it may be the bathroom, but I'm not certain. I've not been upstairs.'

'We can't go anywhere in the dark, none of the lights are going to work now,' he said.

'Hang on a mo,' said Jo. 'I remember seeing some candlesticks just through the door here on the sideboard.' She felt her way into the dining room and searched with her hands until she had located them. 'I don't suppose you have a light?' she asked.

'No, but I do have a tiny torch.'

'For crying out loud why didn't you say before? Let's use that then. Should have thought that no self-respecting doctor would go around without a torch in his bag'

'Battery's nearly gone,' Simon said.

'Well what good is that for looking down patient's throats? I'll use its feeble glimmer to find some matches then.'

'It's not one of the medical ones, all that stuff's in the car; it's a tiny one on my key ring.'

'Okay then, what about your mobile?' she asked. 'Could we use that?'

'It needs charging, I'm sorry. I'm not very well prepared. What about yours?'

'Hoped you weren't going to ask… mine too. We're bloody useless,' moaned Jo. 'Let me have that tiny torch then.'

She opened the drawers on the sideboard one by one, certain that there must be some matches in there somewhere. The torch was fairly useless but she kept looking. People always keep matches near candles don't they, she thought. The last drawer held the treasure she was searching for and she hurriedly lit two candles.

'Here you are,' she said, passing the torch back to Simon, along with one of the tall elegant silver candlesticks, 'now let's go and sort out this flood.' She grabbed his hand and held it tightly as they climbed up the stairs.

'Have you visited Megan in her bedroom at all when she's been poorly?'

'Yes, it's this second one on the left. Perhaps I'll just peep in and check on her,' he turned the handle gently and crept through the door.

Jo could see Megan by the light of Simon's candle, fast asleep in bed, her chest rising and falling with her breathing.

'She's out for the count, so I'm not going to disturb her,' he closed the door. 'Okay - now let's go to the bathroom. I think this is probably it.'

Jo opened the door and found herself paddling in water. She could hear a tap running and held her candle up high in front of her so she could see better. 'It's the bath,' she said. 'For goodness sake the plug is in and both taps are running.' She turned around to pass Simon her candle so that she could turn the taps off but stopped midway through the manoeuvre. There, behind the door in the wavering shadows caused by the candlelight was a figure.

'Si…Simon,' she tugged at his arm and pointed to the corner. Jo was shaking like a leaf. The figure didn't move. It just stood there with a hood down as far as possible so that whoever it was remained completely unrecognizable.

The three of them stood transfixed for what seemed like minutes.

Keeping the strange figure in her sight Jo slowly put her hand down to turn off the taps and pull up the plug, and in that instant when Simon looked around to see what she was doing the figure ran out of the bathroom.

They followed after the intruder who by now was already at the bottom of the stairs heading for the kitchen and presumably the back door. Suddenly there was a huge clattering sound and shriek followed by a crash. Jo and Simon stopped outside the open kitchen door and went in slowly, moving their candles around so that they could try and locate the person who had been trying to escape.

The tiled floor was very slippery from all the water which had leaked through from the bathroom above. It had become a skating rink and whoever had run away from them was lying in a concertina-folded heap right up against the far wall of the kitchen, their head stuck uncomfortably into the corner of the units.

'Is he dead?' asked Jo. 'I'm hoping so.'

Simon approached the crumpled figure carefully and holding the candle up so that he could see clearly, he carefully turned the head around to see who it was.

'No, not dead, but I think you'll find that Trisha Phipps is well and truly out for the count.'

Jo gasped and moved over beside Simon then watched as he checked Fishnchips over to make sure she hadn't injured herself badly.

'She'll have a hell of a headache, but otherwise seems okay. I'll call the police now,' he said.

A police car seemed to appear outside the house within minutes and Jo assumed it was because there was nothing criminal going on anywhere else in Porthcwm that night. The local police force, namely Bill Thomas, came in quietly through the front door as Simon had requested. He didn't want sirens or door bells waking Megan up. They wanted to keep her oblivious to the whole debacle as long as possible.

Bill shone his efficient police searchlight around the kitchen. He looked at Jo, 'You seem to appear at all these goings-on Miss. Bit like your aunt used to I suppose?'

He looked at Simon. 'A very early good morning, Doc.'

'Good morning Bill,' Simon replied and nodded towards Fishnchips who was just starting to move about in her wet landing

234

position on the floor. 'This is how we found her after she tried to escape through the kitchen. She doesn't seem to have injured herself but she'll feel rough later. We can probably manage to get her up onto one of these chairs if we all help.'

Unceremoniously, Simon and Bill wrestled Fishnchips into an upright position and then lowered her onto the chair that Jo held beneath her. Simon checked her over once again. 'She really does seem fine, Bill, so she's all yours. I'll help you get her into your car.'

Jo watched as the two men half dragged, half carried, the nastiest woman in Porthcwm through the house and outside to Bill's police car.

Jo and Simon did the best they could under the candlelit conditions to clear up as much of the mess as possible before Megan appeared for her breakfast. They mopped around the kitchen as well as they could. The water had run along the joists and exited at any weak point it could find. It had loosened plaster and left stained trail marks down the wall. The kitchen had certainly had its fair share of fire and flood disasters recently.

When dawn broke and they could see better they crept up to check the bathroom. It didn't appear to be too bad; at least it didn't have a carpet which made drying it an easier job.

At around 7 o'clock, Bill turned up again. 'I took the liberty of calling Phil Fixit on my way here,' he explained to Jo and Simon, 'so he'll be around any moment now. Do you think it might be a good idea, Simon, if you nipped around and asked Frank to come over too?'

Jo realised she could hear Megan moving around upstairs and went up to warn her about the mess in the kitchen.

'Good morning Megan,' she said as breezily as possible. Jo could see she was still in a dozy state and hadn't noticed the bathroom was a bit damp around the edges.

'My word dear, you do look as if you've had a bit of a night,' said Megan, smiling sleepily at Jo.

'It's not totally what you might think, Megan, but I *can* confirm that your wicked plan to get me and Simon together worked, and thank you for that.' She gave her a kiss on the cheek. 'However there *is* a problem with the electrics and your kitchen. I'll help you get your dressing gown on and then we can go downstairs.'

'Thank you dear,' said Megan looking worried. 'What silly thing have I done now?'

'It's nothing that you've done, Megan, so don't be upset. Everything's totally under control,' said Jo comfortingly, as she led her into the kitchen.

Jo watched Megan's look of disbelief when she saw the people who were gathered there and could tell she was trying to make sense of the scene. At least it diverted her from immediately seeing the damage around the room. Megan's eyes alighted first on Phil Fixit, then Frank, who was standing there still in his pyjamas and an old check dressing gown, and finally in the corner by the back door she saw Bill Thomas in his very smart Police uniform next to Simon. They had all stood up as she came in and now began shuffling around to find her a comfortable chair and cushions.

'What on earth has happened? Not another fire?' Megan asked as she sat down.

'Completely the opposite,' said Simon. 'A bit of a flood. It'll all be put right as soon as possible. Jo's going to get some of your clothes and things sorted and then you're going over to Frank's again. Phil is going to start work in the kitchen and Marvin the electrician is going to come round to get the power back on.'

'Thank you everybody,' she said. 'I'm such a nuisance again. What did I do this time? I've been very worried about becoming forgetful, what with the Bible business and the Night of the Smoking Knickers and now this. I'm losing my marbles aren't I, Simon? I suppose I left the taps running?'

Bill stepped forward, 'on the contrary Mrs Hughes, the Doc here will confirm that all your marbles are in perfect working order.'

'Oh I see!' Megan smiled at Jo. 'Did you two lovebirds decide to have a bath and forget to turn the taps off then? I suppose it *was* my fault then really for setting this whole thing up!'

236

'No, Megan,' said Bill grinning at the idea. 'It wasn't them either. But you have had an intruder, yet again. Each time you thought you heard someone in the house, you were completely correct. It wasn't your mind playing tricks on you.'

'Yes, you're fine Megan,' agreed Simon. 'I'm telling you as your doctor and your friend. What Bill said is right. Frank and I are going to take you around to his house again. At least you can have a nice hot cup of tea there and something to eat and then Frank will explain a little about what has happened. Jo will bring some of your clothes and bits and pieces round to you in a while and Bill will call in to have chat with you in about an hour or so after he's checked a few things out here. Right Bill?'

Megan thought it was rather nice being back with Frank again. She'd only left his house a few days ago and she'd rather missed being with him. Funny old world.

Frank had given her the bare bones of what had happened. And now here she was in his little sitting room once again drinking a cup of chamomile tea to calm her nerves. She had no idea what time it was, and didn't really care. Having succeeded in getting Jo and Simon together, they in turn had saved her from that dreadful woman. Goodness only knows what she might have gone on to do if they hadn't been there. Everyone in Porthcwm would have been convinced that she had finally lost the plot and she would probably have been bundled off into a care home. How ghastly, she thought.

When Bill turned up a little later, he sat down with Megan and began to explain in more detail what had been going on the previous evening.

'You might be interested to know that I had a call out to Mr Trinder earlier yesterday evening as well,' he said. 'That was about Mrs Phipps' behaviour too. She was hell-bent on having a busy evening it appears. Mr Trinder was hospitalised as a result of a punch Mrs Phipps gave him in his…in his…his *down there*,' he pointed rather vaguely below his tummy button with his finger. 'Anyway, he wanted to make a formal complaint so we were out and about looking for her. Then the next thing we know is that she's showed up at your house.'

Megan listened as Bill went on to explain about information he had received from Arthur during his interview. Apparently Arthur was being blackmailed by Mrs Phipps after she had caught him in bed with Gloria Prothero. Gloria had been doing the cleaning for a while for Mrs Phipps and one day when she arrived home early from a holiday she found them in her bed in her house. She sacked Gloria and told Arthur that she wouldn't publicise what he had done as long as he found her just the right property at a very, very sensible price.

'She had wanted to start a B&B business in Porthcwm for quite some time and now she actually had the estate agent securely in her grasp,' continued Bill. 'She started to have an affair with him too although he tells us he was an unwilling participant. We don't believe him of course, he has a bit of a reputation for being lascivious. Mrs Phipps made full use of Arthur but she didn't care about him really, of course. She just wanted him to come up with the right property. She had her sights set on two, yours Mrs Hughes, and the Lodge which now belongs to Cass and Jo of course. He failed miserably with theirs so he must have been desperate to get his hands on your house.

'He tried to persuade you to sell up but that didn't work so they resorted to breaking in to frighten you. He even came and photographed your house when you allowed him in that day. He stole your key and he and Mrs Phipps used it to get into your house through the kitchen one night to try and scare you. That was the night you fell down the stairs holding that huge old family Bible. You disturbed them and as they ran out past you as you lay at the bottom of the stairs, Arthur was convinced they had caused your death.'

'Are you saying that they really wanted to make people think that I was a danger to myself, so that men in white coats would come and take me away? I bet when they realised I'd be found at the bottom of the stairs, holding onto that Bible like some batty old woman, it would have been exactly what they wanted.'

'As far as Mrs Phipps was concerned, you're correct,' said Bill, 'but it scared Arthur and he didn't want to have any part of the bullying anymore. Of course he was still panicking that she would

238

tell Linda and she was the last person he wanted to find out about his exploits. He must have been in a terrible state. The doctor who treated him in the hospital earlier yesterday evening seemed to think that he is going through some sort of breakdown. Hardly a surprise.'

'So that wretched woman obviously decided to continue trying to frighten me on her own,' said Megan.

'I'm afraid so,' confirmed Bill. 'Who knows what would have happened if Jo and Simon hadn't discovered her in your house.'

He went on to explain how Gloria had also been part of Fishnchips' plot. She had also threatened to make public Gloria's affair with Arthur unless she gathered information on the Lodge and Mrs Hughes. So when Gloria began working at the Lodge she was able to pick up all sorts of interesting facts about both places and their owners. Arthur, who was under such pressure from Fishnchips knew Gloria was saving for some more plastic surgery so *he* was slipping her some not unsubstantial amounts of money and of course, *other* things, to keep her coming up with info on the two properties. He just wanted it all settled as quickly as possible.'

Chapter 26

Everything seemed to be calm again in Porthcwm. There were no more miracle cowpats or drug raids and no more house break-ins by demented fake tanned women.

Jo and Simon's relationship had developed at a pace following the Fishnchips incident at Megan's and they spent as much time together as possible. They were truly made for each other and although it all seemed to have happened very quickly, it was no surprise to anyone when Simon asked Jo to marry him. Life for Jo was perfect.

Cass's life wasn't quite so perfect but it was improving, and she was very happy. Her relationship with Ricco was different to the one they had in Paris, more relaxed and less stressful for her. She was working on her commitment anxiety and getting closer to him each day. She had begun to feel sufficiently comfortable enough to discuss it with Jo too, so that was a very definite improvement all round.

Then everything went pear-shaped for her.

It came as a shock to Cass, and everyone else, when Ricco announced that he was going back to Italy. Cass was distraught and astonished. But she knew that *he* had done it the right way, the way *she* should have done it when she left Paris. He had taken her out for a walk along the coastal path to the girls' favourite place. Amazingly, Ricco too had discovered that little hollow in the ground above the cliffs which made it even more special. He sat her down at one of the little wooden tables and holding both her hands in his he gently explained. Yes, *he* had done it right.

She supposed it wasn't really a surprise. After all, he had come over to help out Benito and Rosa with their business when they most needed it. He hadn't come to look for her. Now Holy Cow didn't need him any longer and he wanted to go back to Italy and do a business studies course. He had become absorbed by the cut and thrust of a small company whilst he was working for the

Bellinis and even in this seemingly low-key industry he was fascinated by the way everything worked. He had tried to get close to Cass since he had bumped into her again, but as she had been so hostile and shown no real interest in rekindling their relationship, he had decided to confirm the place he had been offered at a college in Rome.

He was leaving in three days' time and Cass felt wretched that it was happening so quickly. But at least it was 72 hours more notice that she had given him.

Megan looked along the length of the dining table at Frank who was sitting opposite her at the other end. It was her 80th birthday and he had, at her request, booked the small private dining room at a new restaurant at the top of Porthcwm.

A month had passed since Ricco had said his goodbyes to everyone. Megan knew Cass had been trying very hard to show them that she was coping perfectly well without him. The Lodge had been exceptionally busy and that had kept her aching heart occupied, but as Megan looked at her, sitting at the party table without the one person she loved, her sadness was still apparent.

This evening Megan was planning to tell everyone some of her secrets and explain how she had been instrumental in 'helping' some of them along.

'This is such a treat Megan, thank you for inviting us,' said Jo, interrupting her thoughts.

'You're welcome dear. You're all welcome,' she smiled at her guests.

The twins were sitting either side of Frank, both chatting to him at the same time. Megan wasn't certain whether he had actually been listening to either of them as she saw him blowing a kiss in her direction and then rise to his feet.

'Ladies and gentlemen... ladies and gentlemen *and* friends, I should say. I would like you to raise your glasses in a toast to Megan. Megan, a very Happy Birthday to you,' he said, holding his glass aloft. 'You have brought something very special into my quiet life and I thank you for it.'

Megan watched as everyone got to their feet too and clinked their champagne glasses with each other. When they had all sat down again she thanked everyone for their gifts and kind thoughts and reminded Frank that maybe he had something more to tell them all.

He stood again and said, 'I hope you'll be pleased with the news that I, ahem...*we*... have decided to live together in Megan's house. It seems sensible really, saves all that tiptoeing around and sneaking up each other's drive.'

Megan looked very thrilled and laughed at all the clapping and bawdy comments about pensioners living in sin.

Her gaze rested in turn on each person around the table as they tucked into their main course. Jo was looking very beautiful with her hair caught up at the back of her head, little wispy bits falling around her ears. Next to her was Simon. How contented and in love they were. But what a lot of scheming it had taken to get them together. She thought that she had been on a hiding to nothing at the beginning when they appeared to dislike each other so vehemently.

Megan shuddered when she thought about her stage managed fall in the garden at the Lodge all that time ago. She could have hurt herself really badly. But it had worked...after a fashion anyway, at least she had managed to get them face to face in the surgery. She had always wondered whether Jo had noticed that she wasn't limping when they had bumped into each other in Porthcwm's car park a day or so later.

Rev Huw had been a good ally and her group invitation to the Beach Barbeque had worked very well. She and Rev Huw had fiddled who was in which team too. It hadn't quite gone the way she had planned it though. Jo getting so drunk nearly spoiled the whole thing, but Simon taking her home certainly moved their 'relationship' up a notch, albeit in a strange way.

The most successful plot of all was managing to get them together at her house that evening. But she couldn't have organised the best bit though. That was down to that awful Fishnchips woman breaking into her house and trashing it. That, she thought ... *that* was the thing that really threw them together. She smiled to herself.

Megan recalled the day that she had come across Bea Seymour sitting on the wooden bench opposite the Post Office, and they had moaned about how quiet and uneventful life had become in Porthcwm. She remembered Bea persuading her to help get the twins to meet Simon again, hoping that one of them would fall in love with him.

Megan could only guess that Bea must have felt responsible for Simon, that quiet shy boy that her Goddaughters had clearly intimidated and teased during their early meetings. She had been quite adamant that they would move to Porthcwm after her death and put everything right, although privately Megan thought it was very unlikely that Bea's plan would ever work. But work, it had. How she missed that determination and strength that Bea seemed to have for everything she loved.

She looked at Cass next. Well, she was definitely another kettle of fish, obviously much more a secret keeper like her aunt. She was as beautiful as her sister but looked sad and lost at times now that Ricco had returned to Italy. Maybe it would make her stronger in the end. Maybe it was meant to be. Or maybe in fact, it wasn't...

And her last two guests, Rudi and Rhonwen. Such an unlikely couple they had seemed to her at first. But look at them, Rhonwen now a slim sophisticated young woman and Rudi who had turned into a confident, talented man. They had become close friends of Frank and Megan despite the enormous difference in age. She had a little surprise for them, but was saving it for later in the week when just the four of them were meeting up.

'Megan, Megan...' called Cass. 'You're not eating.'

'I was just thinking how blessed I am to have such wonderful friends.'

What would they all think when she told them all about her plotting. Would they laugh and be happy that she had thought them special enough to care, or would they see her as an interfering old biddy playing with people's lives despite the happy endings. Perhaps she should leave it well alone and allow Simon and Jo to believe they had made all the decisions themselves and fallen in love in their own way.

Yes, that's exactly what she would do; the less said about that the better.

Megan had also intended telling everyone about how much Bea had wanted the girls to come back to Porthcwm. So much so that she had enlisted the help of a great many people. She thought the twins should know how much Bea had loved them and how she had wanted them to live in Porthcwm after she had died, but suddenly she began to feel that it would somehow be inappropriate to tell them that now. It had been *such* fun though. When Bea had hatched her plan she and Megan had enlisted the help of all sorts of Porthcwm inhabitants, including Rev and Bev, Rosa, Robert Sylvester, Phil Fixit's wife, even Ron at the dog kennels. All of them were to let the girls know when they met them that they would now be able to make up for what they had done in the past, 'put things right', 'sort things out'.

Megan sat back in her chair and wondered what Bea Seymour would have done. She looked upwards as if trying to find inspiration from her old friend. She knew Bea was up there somewhere looking down on Porthcwm and watching everyone's lives unfolding below her… She *would* have kept it a secret, she thought.

'Megan, Megan…are you alright?' asked Rhonwen.

'Oh yes dear, just miles away thinking about Bea and imagining how pleased she would be to see us all here together. I think we should drink a toast to her since in a way she was the one who brought all our lives together.'

They all stood and toasted Bea Seymour.

Mr Sylvester welcomed the twins into his office and invited them to sit down. Then he popped his head around the door of the next room and called through to his secretary, 'Mrs Tyler would you mind carrying in that tray for us in about 10 minutes please?'

He closed the office door again and smiled at the twins.

'Well my dears,' he said, looking at Jo and Cass. 'I expect you are wondering why I called you in here to see me again. The thing is I have one more duty to carry out on behalf of my client, your aunt, Bea Seymour.

'I'm unsure where to start really...' he paused for a moment as if trying to work out what to say. 'You will remember how Bea took Rev & Bev, as she referred to them, under her wing when they fell in love and weren't allowed to see each other. She felt that they were being discriminated against because Bev's father was a steadfast Chapel goer and as Rev was obviously not, he would never have allowed her to be entangled romantically with Huw Evans. So Bea allowed them to meet in secret in Seaview Cottage.

'Eventually Beverley's father passed away which I have to say was a blessing for her mother too. But his somewhat early death enabled the young couple to get married. Miss Seymour would be very proud of the way you have followed in her footsteps by doing the same for young Rudolph and Rhonwen. I know that it is particularly difficult for them both with their unfortunate connection with, perhaps I could say, that absolute scoundrel Arthur Trinder.

'The reason I mention this is that your aunt had a very sad time in her life when she could have done with someone to take *her* under their wing and support and protect her. She fell deeply in love when she was very young. However, she became pregnant and her parents forbade her to tell the baby's father. They did however confront his parents who they felt were responsible for the fact that their son had ruined the life and prospects of their only daughter. Both sets of parents felt disgraced by their children. *He* was sent off to the army to forget about her, and his parents moved away up North to be as far away as possible from this shameful girl in Porthcwm.' He paused for some breath at last.

He glanced at the twins. They looked quite stunned and astonished by the revelations about their aunt.

'Mr Sylvester ... what happened about the baby?' asked Jo.

'Well Miss Seymour was sent away immediately to stay with some distant aunt of hers in Oxford so that no one would see what was happening. She gave birth there to a little girl and remained in Oxford for a month. Her parents began looking for a couple to adopt the baby but when the aunt agreed to take on the baby as if it was her own it seemed the perfect solution. She and her husband were childless and had become very fond of the infant. Bea's parents arranged the whole thing and she was powerless to change their minds, so returned to Porthcwm wretched and alone.'

Robert Sylvester stood up and passed Jo an envelope. She opened it and took out a battered faded old photograph of a very young Bea sitting up in bed and holding her tiny newborn baby. 'I don't know who took this but it was her most treasured possession. This, my dears, is a picture of your mother, Frances.'

The girls remained silent for a moment in amazement then Cass burst into tears. 'Sorry, sorry,' she said. 'I'm just so astonished, I can't believe it. So AB is ... was... our Grandmother...?'

'That's correct,' said My Sylvester. 'Bea Seymour was your Grandmother. She kept that precious little photograph with her in the cottage, but once she realised that she was nearing the end she gave it to me to safeguard. She didn't want anyone finding it and putting two and two together until I knew how you felt about staying here. It must be such an enormous shock for you,' said Mr Sylvester gently. 'Now you can understand how you remind people of her. You have inherited her spirit and zest for life.'

'Do you think having to give up her baby changed her from the quiet young girl that her parents expected her to be into the woman that she was later on?' asked Jo.

'Yes indeed, definitely,' said Mr Sylvester. 'She became resolute, outspoken, supporting the underdog, getting involved with all manner of controversial things, and made all her own decisions herself whether for good or bad. She always wished that she had been stronger-willed earlier in her life and refused to do what her parents wanted, but it was totally different then my dears and down here at the end of the tracks very few people rebelled against the wishes of their parents.'

'We always said she would have been a fantastic mother,' said Cass, 'and all the time she was, and our Grandmother too. How sad and difficult it must have been for her.'

But Jo was thinking it through too. 'What happened to Frances's father, did they ever see each other again?'

'As a matter of fact they did meet up again. Very, very much later. He left the army eventually and retrained as a solicitor. He married and settled in the North of England. Then when his wife sadly passed away he thought the time was right to return to Porthcwm.'

The girls looked at each other and Jo squealed, 'it's you, Mr Sylvester, it's you, isn't it?'

He looked slightly abashed, 'Yes, you're right my dear. She never told me about our daughter until she showed me the photograph after I had settled back down here. What a secret to have kept all those years. She thought that it would turn too many lives upside down. Bea found it very hard, keeping it from you two, and she nearly told you on several occasions.

'She never married as you know, so I had hoped that we could have spent the remainder of our lives together, but she didn't want that...too much water under the bridge by then she said. But we have had very happy times together despite that.'

'It has been difficult for me too, especially latterly when I thought you weren't going to stay here. I believed I had lost my chance to get to know you, both as my granddaughters and as beautiful accomplished young women. I wasn't certain whether to blurt it out when you were considering selling up, but that would have been selfish on my part and might have upset you. Anyway, you decided to stay, so all I had to do was to wait for a sensible moment to... um ... well, to come clean as it were. And this appears to have been the moment. The twins stood up and hugged him. He seemed uncomfortable.

'I'll get better at this,' he said. 'I haven't had any experience of being a grandfather, but I promise to try.'

'When did AB... umm... our Grandmother get the Lodge then?' asked Cass. 'And how did she get to know about us?'

'Well, as I mentioned when we had our first meeting, she already had the little cottage, which she had managed to buy a long time earlier when houses down here cost only a few hundred pounds. When her parents passed away she didn't want to move into their bigger house up at the top of the town because she loved being in Seaview Cottage so much. Then the Lodge came up for sale and so she bought that with the proceeds of the sale of her parent's house.

'As for finding out about you... well, that was both good news and bad news,' he said. 'Frances suddenly appeared at her door one day with you two and introduced herself to her mother. She had just been told that she was terminally ill and when she had shared this with her adoptive parents they felt they should tell her the truth at last. Shortly after that you started to come and stay down here in the school holidays.'

'It's a sad *and* happy story really,' said Jo. 'We can't change what's gone on before, but we've discovered all sorts of answers to questions we had and have found a new Grandfather at the same time.'

Mrs Tyler, who had heard the commotion, came through the door on cue and put three glasses and a bottle of champagne on Mr Sylvester's desk. 'Thank you Mrs Tyler' he said as she left the room. He poured it out and held his glass still for a moment staring at the bubbles rising, 'of course ... absolutely no one knows about this at the moment except the three of us.

'Anyway, first things first. I should like to propose a toast,' he said, raising his glass, 'to your grandmother, Bea Seymour. She was a wonderful, beautiful woman and I loved her deeply.'

As they lifted their glasses to toast their grandmother, they could see a tear in Mr Sylvester's eye.

Megan hoped that Rhonwen and Rudolph wouldn't be offended by the surprise she had planned and invited them around to her house for a drink. They were giggling like mad as they arrived and told her that they had seen Bert Lloyd earlier sweeping the pavement outside the Post Office.

'Only thing he's ever done for Porthcwm,' Megan said. 'He'll be plotting his next scam whilst he's sweeping, mark my words. He's got plenty of time to scheme now.'

Megan showed them into her completely revamped kitchen, all modernised and up-to-date. She had decided that maybe it was time to redesign it now that there were two of them living there. She was proud of the way the house looked and she and Frank were so happy sharing it together.

As they carried their drinks into the sitting room, Rhonwen said, 'we have something else to tell you. Go on Rudi, you say…'

He put his arm around her shoulder, 'well, we were having supper with Aunt Linda last night, we've seen quite a bit of her since Arthur went off the rails. She says he's recovering in Cardiff in a sort of psychiatric hospital. Anyway, the first bit of amazing unbelievable news is that Uncle Arthur has asked Rhon and me to take over his estate agency business. I know it seems rather a weird thing to do and Rhon would be quite within her rights to tell him to get stuffed after all he put her through. But it appears to be an apology to Rhon for his appalling attack on her and also to me for treating me like some sort of second class relative. Maybe there was some good in the old bugger after all. Anyway it's all been dealt with legally by Mr Sylvester and we open it as our business next Monday. We're so excited.'

Megan caught Frank's eye, 'we also have something to tell you that you might find attractive. And it appears that it couldn't be at a better time perhaps. We thought you may like to stay in Frank's house. It's yours to use as long as you like. It's a bit sorry for itself, Frank won't mind me saying that, I know. And when you feel you need to move somewhere else, I know a very good estate agency…'

'You've been so kind to us,' said Rudi. 'It's an amazing offer and I only have to look at Rhon's face to know it's a *yes* from both of us.'

'You said that was the first bit of amazing news, so what's the second?' asked Frank.

'Well … Linda told us that she was divorcing Uncle Arthur, which he absolutely deserves. And she's going to live with Douglas Sidebotham. It's extraordinary. None of us saw that coming.'

'…didn't we?' queried Megan.

'Hello, it is me… back again,' said Rosa, as she marched into the kitchen at the Lodge carrying her old wicker basket, the contents covered with a tea towel.

'We're so pleased to have you back, Rosa. I hope you won't be too bored now after your exciting business?'

'It is true, most exciting, but is *still* most exciting. You will have a surprise when I tell to you that we decide not to sell,' she waved her arms around in the air. 'We are so happy. We continue our big adventure, no?'

'Oh my God, that's fantastic,' began Cass, then stopped. 'But that means that you won't be coming back to help us at the Lodge after all.'

'No, you are wrong. I am here am I not? We employ someone to help with Holy Cow and I come back to work here. There is no one as good as me, no?'

'No,' said Jo and Cass in harmony.

'We have missed you,' admitted Jo. 'I'm so pleased you're here. What's in the basket? Please tell me it's ice cream…'

Cass was already getting three spoons and three bowls from the cupboard.

'Oh this is like old times,' said Cass. 'And it'll be lovely to have someone working for us who hasn't got most of her body on show to everyone who's staying here. Gloria did give a good deal of entertainment to the guests.'

'And about that Gloria,' said Rosa. 'I saw her yesterday walking through Porthcwm wearing her new nose. It is not a good one.'

'What do you mean?' asked Jo.

'It is too small for her face. It look like a tiny ski jump. She will buy another one when she save next money, no?'

Chapter 27

Megan looked at Jo and Simon. What a beautiful couple they made. She was wearing such a simple cream silk outfit with a stunning hat that showed off her auburn hair perfectly, and Simon looked so handsome in his morning dress with a muted gold waistcoat and matching cravat. She was immensely proud of them. How glad she was that she had persevered with her plotting to get them together. Bea Seymour would be very impressed with her determination and resolve. Megan had had a good teacher.

She heard the heavy iron latch on the door at the back of St Dominic's Church drop down with a metallic clunk. She turned around and looked down the aisle, across all the hats and happy faces, and smiled the biggest smile. Ricco was walking down the aisle as quickly and quietly as possible. She watched him squeezing into the pew next to Cass and saw with utter delight the look of total surprise and pleasure on her face.

That is absolutely the last bit of secret plotting I'm ever doing, Megan told herself. I want a quiet life now…

'Megan, ahem Megan…' Rev Huw's voice broke into her thoughts. 'Perhaps we can continue now?'

She looked up at him and grinned. 'Oh absolutely, absolutely, now everybody's here.'

Rev Huw looked at the congregation and said 'I shall now attempt to continue with the marriage ceremony of Megan and Frank…'

The End …to be continued.

About the author

Julia was born, bred and mostly educated in Wales, then finished off in London...

She has four grown-up children, and lives in St David's in glorious west Wales. Julia believes that living in the Pembrokeshire Coast National Park and having nothing to the west but the Irish Sea makes it rather special.

She has a passion for supporting local food and drink producers and using wild food. In fact she admits to liking food a great deal, both the cooking and the eating (but mainly the eating). Since 2004 she has organised an annual food festival which enables her to eat food continuously for a whole weekend.

Julia runs a foraging business and spends a lot of time rootling around the hedgerows and on the seashore, cooking what she finds. She eats seaweed nearly every day (even in cakes and biscuits) and bathes in it in an unsuccessful effort to become a mermaid...

You can find her on the Internet at:

www.porthcwm.co.uk
www.facebook.com/porthcwm
www.wildaboutpembrokeshire.co.uk
www.facebook.com/WildAboutPembrokeshire
www.reallywildfestival.co.uk
www.facebook.com/reallywildfestival

Lightning Source UK Ltd.
Milton Keynes UK
UKHW022358030619
343799UK00008B/745/P